The Rebel Christian Publishing

ISBN: 978-1-957290-36-2 (eBook)
Print: 978-1-957290-37-9

This is a work of fiction. Any references to historical events, real people, or
real places are used fictitiously. Names, characters, and places are products
of the author's imagination. Inclusion of or reference to any Christian
elements or themes are used in a fictitious manner and are not meant to be
perceived or interpreted as an act of disrespect against such a wonderful and
beautiful belief system.

Cover designed by Valicity Elaine & A. Bean
Cover image provided by Envato Elements

The Rebel Christian Publishing LLC
350 Northern Blvd STE 324 - 1390
Albany, NY 12204-1000

Visit us: http://www.therebelchristian.com/
Email us: rebel@therebelchristian.com

Other Books by Valicity Elaine

Cross Academy (Christian Fantasy series)

I AM MAN (Christian Science Fiction series)

Withered Rose (Christian Romantic Suspense Trilogy)

Fractured Diamond (Christian Romantic Suspense stand-

alone)

Contents

The Barren Fields

By Valicity Elaine

A Rebel Christian Publishing Book

1

Shon

I hold my breath as the wheels of my plane crash into the ground. Everyone falls forward in their seats. Some people laugh, I hear a baby begin to cry, the man beside me hoots like he's on a roller coaster. I try my hardest not to vomit.

I hate flying.

Not because I'm afraid of being in the air. Not because I'm paranoid of terrorist attacks. I hate flying because it makes me sick.

Nausea hits me like a storm as the plane screams down the runway, tires screeching. This is the worst landing of my life. The man beside me is still cheering like this is *so* much fun, but his shouts are drowned out by the rapid beating of my heart. I want to squeeze my eyes shut and force myself to calm down, but I'm distracted by the sudden flash of neon blue light that sparks outside my window as we make it to the end of the

1

runway.

It's bright enough to make the passengers gasp all at the same time, faces turned toward the outside. Some people start asking questions, some even start panicking as they wonder if the airport has been attacked, but the flight attendants jump into action to reassure us that everything is fine. Though they have no answer for the bright light in the distance.

I don't care about the stupid light.

When the plane stops moving, I can't get my seatbelt off fast enough. Over the bustle of the cabin, I can hear the flight attendants telling everyone to remain in their seats until we're cleared to get off, but I've been strapped to that chair for the last 14 hours. If I stay seated for another second, I'm going to scream.

A perky stewardess tries to block my way as I move toward the restroom, but I muscle past her and shove the door open with a grunt. I've barely made it to the toilet when puke flies from my mouth.

My eyes water. My nose burns. Over my shoulder, I can hear the stewardess frantically asking me if I'm alright. I hadn't had the time or thought to close the door behind me, so she's got a front row seat to all the action as I retch into the silver bowl.

"Ma'am?" the stewardess says in a fragile voice.

I stand and hit the faucet, gulp some tap water down, and then wipe my mouth with the back of my hand. I am well aware of my mascara running down my cheeks, I know my lipstick is smudged across my chin, and I can see a yellow stain on the front of my shirt. Apparently, I missed the toilet a little bit. But none of that stops me from holding my head high and walking out that bathroom like I own the place.

The stewardess tries to offer me seltzer water and aspirin,

but I ignore her and head back to my seat. The process is slow going—for whatever reason, every passenger is out of their seat now. There is a crowd at the front of the plane and a tall woman trying to keep everyone calm. It's not until I inch around a scowling man blocking my chair that I realize she's the pilot of the plane.

"We will let you off the plane in due time!" the lady pilot is shouting.

The man who'd had the window seat beside me isn't cheering anymore. As I sling my purse over my shoulder, I notice the deep creases in his face as he frowns. His forehead is wrinkled, and his jaw is clenched so tightly I see a vein throbbing on the side of his bald head.

"What's going on?" I ask tentatively.

He doesn't take his eyes off the pilot as he grunts, "Something happened. That blue flash earlier? It wasn't a light show."

"What was it?"

A teenager in the seat behind me leans forward with his phone in his hand. His blue eyes scan the screen as he says, "It was an explosion."

"Is that what your buddies on Twitter said?" the man asks in a biting tone.

The kid pays him no mind. "No. It was all over the news as soon as we landed."

"*Was* all over the news?" I say.

He nods. "My phone lost connection shortly after."

Beads of sweat dampen my forehead. I feel my palms go clammy and I subconsciously rub them on my mini skirt.

"What did you read about the explosion?" the man asks the teen.

He's still looking at his phone, helplessly refreshing a page

3

that won't load anymore. "I didn't get to read much. But there were multiple explosions." He looks up for the first time. "Across the country."

"Terrorists," the man grunts out.

The kid shrugs. "Could've been anything. All I know is we're stuck here now." He jerks his chin at the pilot who's still yelling for everyone to remain calm.

"I'm sure we'll be cleared to unload soon!" she shouts.

A woman shouts back, "How will you know? My phone has no signal, I doubt your radios are connected."

"Can't you just let us out?" someone else begs, voice cracking.

The pilot shakes her head. "I have a protocol I'm required to follow in emergencies."

"What sort of emergency is this?" someone cuts in. "We saw a blue light, that doesn't mean anything!"

Obviously, that guy didn't have the chance to check his phone before connection was lost. Either way, I feel the same way he does. I want to know what's going on. I want to get off this plane. If that kid is telling the truth, we could be in danger. We could be sitting ducks.

I did not put myself through 14 hours of torture to be held up by a blue light. In fact, the only reason I'm even here right now is because of God. That's right, it took divine intervention for me to get on a plane and return home. That's how much I hate flying.

But ... air sickness isn't the only reason I stayed away.

I left my hometown in Georgia, USA to live in Barcelona, Spain for too many complicated reasons to name. My family had fallen apart. My parents were getting a divorce, my mother had lost her job, which she needed to help pay for her divorce attorney, my grandmother had just passed, and to top it off, my boyfriend and I split up.

He'd decided to accept a sports scholarship at a university across the state—effectively ending our relationship since he'd made it clear he didn't want to be long distance and I had made it clear I wanted to stay near home. But I couldn't ask him to pass up a scholarship and it wasn't fair to ask me to quit my job and leave my family. So we broke up.

Too bad I ended up quitting my job and leaving my family anyway.

I was offered the chance to study abroad as part of my college's foreign exchange program. With all the drama going on—death, divorce, etc.—I leapt at the opportunity to get away. No one was surprised that I decided to spend a semester in Spain. But they were absolutely shocked when I called home and told them I wasn't coming back.

With the school in Barcelona being part of the foreign exchange program, it was easy to transfer colleges. But deciding to stay meant I wasn't a foreign exchange student anymore, so I had to get a part-time job to take care of myself and I had to find an apartment since I'd switched in the middle of the semester and didn't have a dorm.

I spent the next three years of my life overseas without ever visiting home. And I would have stayed there if God hadn't told me to return home.

I've never considered myself a deeply spiritual person. In fact, when I packed up and left Georgia, it was because I had decided I didn't believe in God anymore. But I know what I heard when I rolled over in bed two nights ago. I know the Voice that told me to return home was not a dream or my own subconscious. With every fiber of my being, I know it was God. Which is why I listened.

So here I am, wondering if maybe I *am* crazy. If maybe I

was dreaming two nights ago because there is no way God would tell me to return to this chaos.

I adjust my purse on my shoulder as I watch the lady pilot raise her hands and try her hardest to keep everyone calm. Every passenger was already standing, but now some have moved into the aisle, inching toward the woman like they could strike at any moment.

Someone in the crowd yells, "You can't keep us here!"

"I have a family!" another passenger screams.

"It isn't safe out there!" a flight attendant screams back. "Didn't you see the explosions?"

My stomach turns inside out at the sound of that word, at the panic that cracks through the attendant's voice like a bolt of lightning. She just made a terrible mistake. Half the people on this plane were already panicking, but now that she's thrown the word *explosion* out there, the fragile threads of calm we'd had left have shredded into nothing.

We are seconds away from a full-blown riot. I can see the chaos unfolding as a man cocks his fist, ready to attack the pilot. A flight attendant throws herself in front of the blow, another man jumps in but it's unclear whose side he's on. People are screaming, jumping, shoving forward. There is a mass of bodies moving toward the locked steel door of the plane, all while I stand in my seat and stare with my mouth open.

This ... This cannot be what God had in store for me when He told me to return home. This cannot be what I left Barcelona for in the middle of my junior year in college.

Someone shoves past me, and I fall sideways into the man who'd been cheering before. He curses as we're both shoved into the window by at least a dozen people trying to rush forward. The passengers have declared war on the flight

6

attendants and the pilot. They're charging the door, banging on it with their fists while others scream at the attendants to help them open it.

One stewardess has passed out in the front, blood trickling from her nose. The pilot is still fighting a shrieking man and woman who have gone from trying to get off the plane to trying to kill the people they think are holding them back.

The man has the pilot in a headlock. The woman is screaming for her to tell them what's going on—as if she could possibly speak with her neck being squeezed by the guy's bicep.

"Get off me!" the cheering man pushes me, but the shove does nothing as people are still screaming and rushing through the little aisle on my other side.

There is a woman crawling over the seats like a monkey, a deranged look on her face as she heads toward the front. A man is using his carry-on to try to bash the windows out. The teen behind me is yelling as he reaches over the seat to help me up. With him grabbing my sleeve, I get my feet under me, grind my teeth, and let out a frustrated cry as I heave upright and ram my shoulder into the woman who's got me shoved against the cheering man.

Momentum sends me tripping into the aisle. I almost go down again but, to my shock, the woman who'd been shoving me aside has stopped moving. As I glance up, I realize *everyone* has stopped moving. Every single person on this plane is staring out the windows now.

I don't want to, but I force myself to look—to find out what's going on. When I look outside, my mouth falls open.

There is a plane falling from the sky, as if it's lost power.

My heart hammers in my chest, tears burn the backs of my eyes. The cheering man beside me mutters, "My God…"

We're all praying now.

7

"We're all going to die!" someone shrieks, and the chaos unfolds all over again.

The crowd shoves at the door to the plane. Together, three men wind the crank and finally manage to disengage the lock. But it's too late. I can hear the plane roaring toward the ground. I can see it spinning nose over tail like the work of some apocalyptic nightmare. There is no point in even trying to run. When that plane touches down, we will be caught up in the explosion it will set off. Maybe some of the people who've made it off the plane will run far enough away, but I'm still stuck in my seat. I won't make it in time.

So I do the only thing I can think of.

I sit down and strap in, then I tuck my head between my knees and pray to God.

"Please, Jesus—"

Everything goes dark before I can say anything more.

2

Shon

SIX YEARS LATER

The back of my shirt sticks to my skin as I stand in the hot hallway of Terminal D. There are just three people in line in front of me, waiting their turn at the Housing Desk set up at the end of the hall. Terminal D looks nothing like what it used to six years ago, back when this airport was just an airport.

After the blue lights flashed, the world changed entirely. The lights were explosions, bombs planted around the nation and set off at the same time. A coordinated attack. Whether it was done by international terrorists or frustrated civilians trying to start an uprising, I'll never know. The blue lights triggered an event that left little time and chance to investigate the initial attack.

The bombs were small, but upon detonation, they destroyed entire neighborhoods, brought down cell towers and powerplants, and vanquished over 60 percent of the USA's military bases. Our nation was left without power, communication, and over half of our armed forces.

But that was the least of our worries.

The bombs also released radioactive toxins into the atmosphere. I don't think I need to explain the impact of that conundrum. Left unchecked, the gases proved to be fatal to anyone who breathed them in for too long. Plants and animals were not exempt. This forced an entire country to live indoors, preferably underground, or risk dying of radiation poisoning.

When I watched that airplane spiral out of the sky, I thought I was done for. I thought I'd heard God wrong and had followed Satan's voice into hell. Then I woke up in a burning lot, still strapped to my chair with a concussion, a dislocated shoulder, and a broken hip.

Unfortunately, this airport happens to be located very close to one of the military bases that was targeted by the bombs. That's why we saw the blue light from our windows. *Fortunately*, however, that base was only partially destroyed. The National Guard was able to deploy soldiers and aid almost immediately after detonation. My life was spared by the grace of God, and I was given a safe place to live in the aftermath of the attack.

With the military base in near shambles, the National Guard used this airport as an extension to their HQ. What began as a small medical camp soon expanded into a shelter and then became a settlement. Over the course of six years, soldiers and civilians worked together to start indoor gardens for food, collect rainwater for drinking, cooking, cleaning, and bathing, they rebuilt part of the inside of the airport to set up small apartments for families, and they fortified their defenses against the Faceless ones … The people who are left outside, but don't die from the radiation.

I have never seen a Faceless before. I haven't been outside since I woke up from the initial explosion. But I have heard stories from survivors. I've heard of the nightmares that wait outside the airport walls.

The world beyond this isolated settlement is nothing like what it used to be. Radiation has killed almost everything. Those who are alive, living in the cloud of toxins, are forever changed. The poison eats your mind and then your body, rotting the flesh from your bones as it turns you mad. At least that's what they say.

It's a dead world out there. The only ones living are the crazies now, everyone else is indoors.

Absently, I gaze out the floor-to-ceiling windows of the airport. There is a giant gate surrounding the building. I can see it if I squint against the burning sunlight piercing through the large windows. Six years ago, that fence didn't exist. Then again, there weren't flesh eating Faceless running around six years ago.

Beyond the gates is nothing but deadland—what used to be fields of grass and shrubbery is now an expanse of rocks and concrete. Everything outside has withered up or mutated into something ungodly, thanks to all the radiation.

The officials here named our settlement, Rebirth Colony. And they call the outside, the Barren Fields. I think it's the perfect name. There is nothing out there. There is no one left but us and those who were fortunate enough to get inside or underground in time. To seal their windows and doors and make sure they were set up with air filters and proper defenses against the rabid Faceless.

I'm guessing there aren't many out there like us. The three thousand people inside this airport are the last of us.

The line moves and I limp forward a few inches. Since the

11

explosion, I've developed a limp in my right leg from my broken hip. While the National Guard saved my life, they were still recovering from the explosions themselves and trying their hardest to maintain peace, set up a medical camp, and find other survivors. Doctors were strapped for supplies and hard pressed to find a properly functioning facility with comms down and the power out.

Long story short, my hip didn't heal right. And it gives me pain when I stand too long or walk too far. But I'm not getting out of this line. I've been here for four hours. I'll wait another four—another *twenty-four*—if I have to.

Someone sneezes in the back of the line, I glance over my shoulder to see dozens of people behind me. We're all waiting for the same thing. A chance to move into the lower levels of the airport.

The further underground, the safer you are from the radiation and the Faceless. You don't have to worry about the windows cracking during a storm, letting in the poisoned air. You don't have to worry about being exposed to any toxic leaks from a faulty seal on the doorways. You don't have to worry about dying first if the fence is breached by the Faceless.

We all want a room downstairs but there's limited space and the rooms available are almost impossible to claim. I would know, I've applied for a lower-level room every week and have been promptly rejected every week. A few years ago, they would give you a can of beans whenever you were rejected, but they stopped the apology gifts once they realized how many rejections they were giving out and, therefore, how many beans.

The line moves forward again, just two left in front of me now. It's a pair of men who stand at the desk together, scowls on their faces. The guy manning the desk today is a familiar face—Everett James, the teenager who sat behind me on the airplane. He survived the crash too, by strapping himself into his chair after he saw me do it. Thank God.

We really got to know each other after waking up side by side in the makeshift hospital. He was seventeen on the day of the explosion, flying home to visit his father for summer break. Back then, when he was helping me learn how to walk again after breaking my hip; he was shy and quiet, grieving over the horrors we'd lived through and the horrors that would come. But it's been six long years now; he's changed as much as the world has.

Everett joined the Rebirth Colony Union [RCU] when he turned eighteen—that's the new armed forces of our military base. After the collapse of communication and power, the people of this airport declared themselves a free nation. No one was here to stop them, so they took advantage of the fact that we no longer had a functioning government and started their own.

I glance at the patch sewn onto Everett's right shoulder. It's a sunrise with the infinity symbol in the middle of the sun. A symbol that this is not our end. We have many days ahead—infinite days ahead—despite our predicament.

Everett had been so happy to join the RCU. He didn't sign up just for the extra food rations, he sincerely believed he could make a difference in this broken world.

It's hard to believe the kid who became my little brother is now a twenty-three-year-old man, working the Housing Desk on his day off for extra rations. He usually passes them to me when we're able to meet up which is rare because he's so busy. Even now, the two men at the desk hold all of his attention. His blue eyes are focused on the one who is speaking, a tall, skinny man with no hair.

13

"We have applied for a lower-level home every week for four months now!" the man complains. "I don't understand why our application keeps getting rejected."

The other man, a plump guy with glasses, nods vigorously. "This is ridiculous."

Everett takes a slow breath and runs a hand through his sandy blonde hair. This is likely the hundredth time he's had this conversation today. "The lower-levels are reserved for married couples, single parents, or families—"

"We *are* family!" The men simultaneously cock their heads to the side, as if this somehow proves they are brothers. They do look alike, but Everett quickly tells them their relation to each other isn't enough.

"You must be able to procreate." He leaves that hanging in the air.

"This is ridiculous," the plump man begins, but Everett cuts him off and starts explaining the purpose of the lower level all over again.

"The Rebirth Colony Council has made repopulation one of their highest priorities. This means children and couples who can have them are valued above all else…"

Everett's voice fades away as I zone out. I've heard this more times than I can count. I'm sure these men have heard it too. But every day they keep coming back. We all do, desperate for a chance at a miracle. That maybe the Rebirth Colony Council [RCC] will make an exception.

There are people who've gotten married and had kids just to move to the lower levels. As a single woman, I've had to protect myself against men who were willing to assault me just to claim paternity and move downstairs if I ended up getting pregnant.

I've also had to protect myself from desperate men who

tried to bribe and blackmail me into marrying them. Even Everett had asked for my hand when he turned twenty. He's strong and handsome now, but he's still four years younger than me so I've never stopped seeing him as that seventeen-year-old kid I called my little brother.

I watch as he very calmly deals with the angry pair of men at the desk. He's an expert at this, never losing his temper, never reacting to their insults. When the tall, skinny one starts ranting again, Everett glances up and subtly rolls his eyes. I chuckle to myself. He winks.

Gosh, it's moments like this that I wish I had said yes when he'd asked for my hand. But it's too late now. He married an eighteen-year-old three months after my rejection. He's got three kids now and another on the way. Six years ago, three kids at age twenty-three would have been my worst nightmare. Today, however, it's a blessing. Children are rare, having four is like owning a goldmine these days.

I'm happy for Everett. But his wonderful kids don't increase my chances of getting a lower-level room. Still... I've got to try.

The two men finally give up and stomp away with their mouths twisted into frowns. I step up to the desk and offer a sheepish smile. Everett beams.

"Back again, Shon?"

"Back again," I say. "Should I even ask or are we going to do the same routine?"

He just laughs.

"I'm guessing that means my application was rejected."

"Unfortunately."

"Well, it's not like that's never happened before."

"Wish I could offer you a can of beans."

His smile almost makes up for the agony that storms

through me. I let go of a sigh as I lean against the desk and lick my dry lips. "Can I apply for a meal ticket, then?"

"Well, technically, you're supposed to apply for that at the Distribution Desk." He winks again. "But I can make an exception for my big sis."

Everett is the best. It melts my heart that he so easily calls me his sister, even though we look nothing alike. He's got sandy blonde hair and oceanic blue eyes, I'm the color of cocoa with my afro hair twisted back into two chunky French braids. We're obviously not related at all, but that doesn't stop us from claiming each other as siblings.

Everett slides an application over to me while he digs for meal tickets. We get a set number every month and turn them in for food at the cafeteria. It helps the RCC keep track of rations and measure their garden harvests.

I'm halfway through the short application when the two men from before storm back to the desk, still scowling.

"I *demand* fair and proper evaluation of our application!" the plump man declares.

"Oh Lord," Everett mumbles. He sets the stack of meal tickets on the desk and steps aside to handle the situation.

It's at that moment that a wild urge latches on to me. I'm frustrated about being rejected again. I'm irritated that these men are giving Everett trouble. I'm tired of the same routine each day. Begging for a room. Begging for a meal ticket. Just trying to survive *indoors*.

The stack of meal tickets is right in front of me, and Everett is completely distracted. It wouldn't take much to just snatch them and go. Everett doesn't need them—I don't exactly need them either. I'm hungry, but I'm not starving. Everett helps a lot by sharing his spare rations with me, but this isn't even about food or hunger or rations. It's about the

16

RCC. About the Council deciding who gets to live where and how much we get to eat. I know there needs to be order for us to survive, but just once, I want to break the rules. I want to frustrate the RCC as much as they've frustrated me.

Before I can change my mind, I reach up and snatch half the stack of meal tickets from the desk. I stuff them under my oversized shirt, and then I turn to walk away.

Everett catches me leaving from the corner of his eye, he's still arguing with those two guys. He gives me a puzzled look, but I just nod and wave and he drops whatever question he'd had on his tongue. Thank God because I have no idea what I would have told him if he had glanced up half a second earlier and caught me stealing tickets.

A jolt of guilt threatens to turn me around and put the tickets back, but I shake my head to clear it and keep walking.

3

Shon

I would be lying if I said the knock at my door surprised me. I stole almost 50 meal tickets earlier today; it was only a matter of time before someone started making the rounds and asking questions.

I'm an absolute idiot.

I should have known I would be caught within a matter of hours. I was in line when Everett set the tickets down and walked away. I am the one and only suspect. And even if no one suspected me, I can't walk into the cafeteria waving around all my meal tickets. If I start flashing tickets around, the cafeteria workers will wonder how I suddenly acquired a month's worth of meals without first getting a new job.

There are only 3000 people in Rebirth Colony, word travels fast. If I had gotten a new job, someone would know by the end of the day. Someone would be able to verify that I bought all these tickets rather than stole them. But we both know that's not the truth.

I do have a job here—everyone does. We've all got to help keep the place afloat, even the children. They help maintain the gardens and then spend their time learning crafts and taking lessons in history. The older members of the RCC also prioritize the preservation of culture and history as much as they prioritize procreation.

The kids take history lessons every day, but *everyone* is required to take at least one lesson a week. They do check-ins to make sure everyone goes, and they give out free vegetables sometimes when the harvest is good. In fact, I'm scheduled for a lesson this evening, and a tiny part of me hopes the person at my door is Mrs. Barnes who teaches the history and culture lessons for adults. She can be finicky about people being on time or skipping lessons. It wouldn't be outlandish for her to notice my absence and come knocking at my door.

I push from my tiny bed which is just a blanket thrown over a stack of cushions taken from old airport chairs, then I cross my little room to the door. I actually have my own room, unlike most people here. It's a remodeled custodian's closet, but it's not as bad as it sounds. The old Pizza Palooza restaurant in the food court was converted into a room that holds 117 people separated by curtains that hang between each 'room.' It's horrible down there.

But I'm a single woman which means I get precedence when it comes to privacy. Assault was a huge problem for a little while when the colony was first getting started. Most of the tiny closets and offices with lockable doors are inhabited by single ladies now.

I crack open the door and let out a sigh. Everett is standing on the other side, looking very serious and sad at the same time. His eyes snap to mine, and he forces a smile that barely

19

turns up the corners of his mouth. He looks more like he's grimacing.

"Can I come in?"

I nod and step aside, holding the door open wide so he can enter. Everett is tall and large enough to fill out the doorway. I don't know how he manages to pack on muscle when we're living off vegetables and whatever canned meat they scavenge on trips outside, but he's a big boy now. A man.

All the gentleness he normally exudes washes away once I close the door and switch on my battery powered lamp. I'm down to my last two batteries so I use it sparingly. Living in a closet means I'm mostly without light once the sun sets and I close the door, but I doubt Everett will feel comfortable having this conversation in pitch darkness.

"Shon..." he sighs.

He doesn't need to say more. I reach into the suitcase by my makeshift bed that I use as a dresser/storage bin and pull out the meal tickets.

A muscle in Everett's jaw tics as he reaches for them. "I've been retracing my steps all day. Trying to find out where I could have misplaced these."

"I'm sorry..."

He shakes his head. "Shon..."

"I know—"

"No, you don't."

Yes, I do. One of the reasons Rebirth Colony has been so prosperous is because they have strict rules and regulations. And even stricter punishments for those who break them. There are trials and a chance to tell your side of the story before the Council. But the result is more or less the same.

Almost everyone accused of anything is found guilty. In a community with barely enough supplies to sustain itself, the

Council is more than willing—if not eager—to toss anyone out.

"You have the meal tickets back," I say to Everett. "You don't have to say anything."

"I've already alerted my bosses that they were missing. If I show up with the tickets, they'll want to know how I got them back."

"Just tell them you found them."

Everett sighs and places his hands on his hips. He hangs his head, muttering something under his breath. It's at this moment that I realize just how mature he's gotten—more mature than me, obviously.

When he lifts his head, his face is a mess of emotion. Anger, fear, disappointment. His eyes are swimming with unshed tears. That's when I know what he's going to say next.

"I've got three kids, Shon. And a fourth on the way."

"Everett…"

"I can't lie to the Council. If they ever learn the truth, and realize that I covered up your crime, I'll lose my job. I might even lose my room in the lower-level."

Silence swells between us until my battery-powered lamp flickers.

I clear my throat. "You're turning me in."

"I don't have a choice."

"Yeah," I whisper, regretting my stupidity for the very first time. How could I have been such an idiot? How could I have put Everett in such a dangerous position? His three kids—kids I've babysat dozens of times, his cute little wife who is incredible at making veggie soup and always smiles when she greets me. She calls me her older sister and gave Everett the most adorable kids I've ever seen. Three chubby little girls with black hair like their Korean mother and pale skin like their

21

American father.

I've put them all at risk.

Without thinking, I turn to my suitcase and start rummaging through it. I find a backpack and cram clothes into it, then I open my meager stash of supplies and start shoving them inside as well. It's not much, a canteen of drinkable water, a box of Band-Aids, a pocketknife which had been a gift from Everett, a package of jerky, and a pocket Bible. I freeze when I hold the Bible, my fingers brushing the leather cover. I haven't read it much since I woke up in the makeshift hospital six years ago, but when I went through the abandoned luggage in the airport and found this gem, I couldn't bring myself to toss it away.

I don't know if I still believe it was God's Voice I heard that night before I packed up and flew back to the United States. I try not to think about it. Some part of me still believes in God, whether I was fooling myself or not six years ago. I can't run from the truth, and maybe it's staring me in the face right now. Maybe this is a clear sign that it's time to get up and go do whatever God sent me home to do.

"Shon," Everett says over my shoulder.

I zip my backpack closed and stand, slinging it over my shoulder. "The punishment for theft is banishment," I say. The punishment for almost every offense is banishment, honestly. "I'd rather avoid the trial and the public humiliation. If I'm getting sent into the barren fields, then I'll go on my own. I'll leave now."

Everett stares at me for a long moment, like he's contemplating something, then he gives me a firm nod. "I'll help you."

I snort. "I don't need help leaving."

Everett knows this is true. Despite all the rules and

regulations, it is shockingly easy to get out of Rebirth Colony. If you want to leave, the Council is more than happy to let you go—getting back inside is the challenge. Unless you're a member of the Union like Everett, you have to be cleared by the Council to enter Rebirth Colony.

I've met a few outsiders who showed up at the front gates over the last six years; apparently, you get stripped, doused in water, searched for contaminated objects, observed by our doctors for contamination, and then remain in the observation rooms for five days before you're released.

There is a rule about the barren fields…

Breathe in the contaminated air, consume contaminated food, or get bitten/scratched by a Faceless and you face the Rule of Five.

Within five minutes of exposure, you are contaminated. But that's not the end of the world, you can survive exposure to radiation if you get out soon enough. Big emphasis on *if*.

Within five hours of being exposed, you will lose a limb or an organ. If you get contaminated by breathing in the air, you'll lose a lung. If you were scratched or bitten, you'll lose the area that was contaminated. We have a lot of handless and legless people here in the Colony.

Within five days of being exposed, you will die if you do not decontaminate. If you somehow don't die despite being bitten, cut, etc., you'll slowly turn into a Faceless.

That's why outsiders are observed for five days. The doctors have to examine you for signs of transitioning. You're stripped to expose any bites or scratches you may be hiding. You're doused in water to see if it gives you the shivers. Those who've been exposed for more than five hours will catch a fever, which is easy to spot when you're doused in water and can't get your body temperature back up. And if you somehow hide all of that from our doctors, they will definitely notice the telltale signs of the Faceless after five days.

Your eyes turn blue.

Not the pretty natural blue of Everett's eyes. I'm talking a bright, neon, glow-in-the-dark blue just like the flashing lights of the explosions from six years ago. Every Faceless has those eyes. It doesn't matter your race or what color your eyes were originally, getting contaminated turns your pupils that creepy blue shade. Once you've reached that point, you're beyond help. You are going to die or transition.

If you get help before your eyes change color, you can survive. And by *help*, I mean, get out of the barren fields. You can survive up to five days of constant exposure to the toxic outdoors. But that's only if you find clean, breathable air, and a washing station to decontaminate properly. That's why outsiders are rare. Anyone more than a five-day trip from this airport will likely never reach us, not unless there are secure rest stops along the way, and judging from the information Everett has shared with me over the years, there aren't any.

It's just us. At least within a five-day radius of travel.

For some reason, I've convinced myself that I can survive out there. That I can make it to some sort of safety before the Rule of Five kills me or alters my brain. Whether I believe that or not is honestly irrelevant. Once Everett turns back in those tickets, my fate is sealed. I'll be banished. So I'm staying ahead of the game. I'm leaving now. Quietly. Quickly.

That way, Everett won't face any shame and I won't have to say a teary goodbye to his kids—my nieces. But I do have to say goodbye to my brother.

Ev is staring at me with wide, unblinking eyes. He opens his mouth to speak but no words come out except a shaky

24

whisper. "*Shon…*"

I step forward and he immediately crushes me in a hug.

"I'm so sorry," I say into his firm chest. "This is all my fault."

He pulls away. "Let me help you."

"How?"

"I'll give you some supplies. And a gasmask."

That makes me pause. With a gasmask, the Rule of Five won't apply to me unless my filter is compromised. I've never worn a gasmask because I've never left the airport, but I know Ev has plenty of times. He goes scouting three times a week, sometimes he stays gone for days. Never more than five, but I'm sure that's just out of fear of his gear malfunctioning, leaving him facing death within days. He could stay out longer if he doesn't remove his mask for long, but he never has. I'm sure it's against some random RCC rule.

If I've got food and water, I could survive out there. I could make it more than five days. And who knows, maybe there is a rest stop somewhere that Everett hasn't discovered. Maybe there is something in the barren fields. There's got to be.

I don't know why God told me to return home, but I won't find the reason holed up here. Not anymore.

"Okay," I tell Everett, adjusting my backpack. "I'm heading out the eastern exit. Can you meet me there in ten minutes?"

He nods. "Don't leave without me."

"I won't."

It takes me three minutes to reach the eastern exit. Exactly six minutes after I arrive, Everett rounds the corner carrying a backpack larger than mine. He kneels before me and motions for me to pass him my smaller bag while he whispers quickly.

"I've got you more supplies," he says, emptying my contents into the larger bag. "A few cans of food, a bottle of water." He holds up a hunting knife, much bigger and sharper than the little pocketknife I'd packed. "Keep this on you at all times. No matter how peaceful your surroundings seem."

I nod and take the knife, tucking it into my waistband. For the first time, I'm thankful the National Guard used this airport as their military base when the explosions first happened. It's thanks to them that Rebirth Colony has so many supplies and tactical survival gear.

Next, Everett passes me a pair of leather gloves and a hoodie that's a size too big. "Cover every inch of your skin. The gloves might be large, just tug your sleeves over them to protect your wrists."

I nod again, following orders, even stooping to tuck my skinny jeans into my boots like he tells me. Everett has been outside plenty of times. He's seen the barren fields up close, he knows what he's talking about.

When he passes me the gasmask, we both pause and exchange a look. This is real. This is happening.

"I'll help you put it on," he mutters, pulling the straps over my head and adjusting them so the mask fits nice and snug. He pulls my hood over my head when he's finished. "I would've gotten you a suit, but I can't explain a missing hazmat as easily as a missing gasmask." He shrugs sheepishly.

"That's okay, I'm thankful for anything," I say. My voice sounds funny coming through the mask.

"Aluminum foil and plastic will be your best friends," Everett says. "Radiation doesn't travel through them very well.

If you find any out there, keep it."

I nod.

"You only need water to wash off radiation. Even contaminated water will work if you've got enough—it can dilute the toxins."

I nod again, watching as Everett digs into the bag once more and pulls out a small roll of duct tape. "This has a million uses. Obviously, you can seal up any cracks in your mask if that happens. But it's also flammable, Shon. You can use this as accelerant if you don't have a way to start a fire."

I nod.

"Faceless are afraid of fire."

My heart nearly stops. In all the time Everett has been my brother, going out on excursions and exploring the world beyond this airport, he has never mentioned a Faceless before. He told me about the neon blue flowers that let you know if an area is contaminated. He told me about the blue-eyed deer that tried to eat his legs one time. He even told me he suspects the Council knows there are more people out there but is too afraid of losing scouts, so they refuse to let Union members venture beyond five days of travel.

But he's never mentioned the Faceless.

How on earth would he know what they fear if he hasn't seen one?

I swallow, trying not to panic. "Ev," I say, reaching for him.

He hugs me, speaking directly into my ear as I wrap my arms around his middle. "Head east. I don't know for certain, but I believe there are others out there, Shon. Settlements like ours. I've heard whispers from survivors who've made it here. We can't be the only ones."

I sure hope not. Or else I'm dead in five days.

When Everett pulls away, I see his conviction in the tears that swell in his eyes. "I'm so sorry, RaShonda."

I know he's serious since he used my full name, but I won't let him blame himself. I shake my head and pray that he can hear the seriousness in my voice since he can't see my expression through the gasmask. "This is all my fault. Don't you dare blame yourself."

He wipes at his nose, looking so much like a boy that it hurts. "Where are you going?" he quizzes me.

"East. To find other settlements."

"And when you find one, find a way to contact Rebirth Colony again." He sighs. "We're not doing as well as the Council wants everyone to believe. Our supplies are low. Our gardens are not pulling a large enough harvest anymore. We need help." He bunches his shoulders. "A trade route, some sort of bartering system. I don't know. But we won't last much longer if we don't get help."

First, we've got to *find* help. I guess that's where I come in. I'm no longer running away from banishment; I'm searching for a way for Rebirth Colony to survive. My eyes go to the patch on Everett's right shoulder. The sun with the infinity loop in the middle. We're supposed to have an infinite number of sunrises ahead of us. From the sound of things, we may not make it through another year or two.

Is this what You wanted? I pray inside. I don't expect an answer at all. I haven't prayed or read my Bible in almost six years. But, like the night I packed up and left Spain, I get that niggling feeling in the back of my head. A sense of urgency that this is important. That there's more to this mission than just getting the heck out of Dodge to avoid punishment for my crimes.

I don't know if God has this big plan in place. I don't know if I can help. But I won't find out anything until I leave, so I pull away from Everett and shrug on my backpack. I turn toward the door and watch him turn the steel crank so I can step into the makeshift deco-unit. It's a small hallway where I'll be locked inside until I can open the second door which leads outside.

I have to wait until Everett has properly secured the first door to prevent contaminated air from flowing in through the hallway. When I hear the lock click into place behind me, I step forward, taking deep, heavy breaths through my mask. I turn the lock on the final door and engage the release. The door opens with a hiss, letting sunlight spill into the little hall. I want to glance back and wave goodbye to my brother. I want to run back inside and hide in my little closet room. But I know that I can't. I've got to keep going.

So I take a deep breath, and for the first time in six years, I step outside.

4

Erik

There is nothing out here. Ahead of me is an expanse of grey so bleak the sight of it makes me want to weep. It is the sort of grey you see on a day overcast with pitiful rainclouds, angry droplets of rain beating down on the top of your head. I'm sure the air smells burnt, but I've got my mask on so whenever I inhale, I get a whiff of the bitter smell of rubber and, oddly, oatmeal. The filter in my mask must be getting old.

I sigh as I trudge through the open Grey, little rocks crack beneath my feet as I grind them with the heel of my boot. The only color around me comes from the poisoned daisies dotting the hard ground. They are not the little white flowers my son used to pick from the backyard for his mother. These daisies are neon blue with bright purple stems. A daisy like I've never seen before.

These flowers are the only things that grow in the Grey. They sprouted almost everywhere after the blue lights flashed.

It's how I know the air is toxic, they seem to flourish off radiation. Sucking life out of death.

Every few feet a neon daisy bursts from the grey earth. A spot of much-needed color in this grim world. They are beautiful but deadly, eating them would kill me within days. But seeing them gives me a small bit of information; their presence lets me know I can't remove my gasmask. The air is contaminated.

I suck in a breath of filtered air and keep walking, crushing a daisy as I move.

There is a dead tree about half a mile ahead of me, it's my three-day landmark, but I've hit it early. I left camp 48 hours ago, which means I need to slow down or else I might overexert myself. Not that it matters if I get tired and pass out. No one will miss me if I never make it back to camp. No one will even notice that I'm gone. Sometimes I wonder why I even bother going out to scavenge. I've got nothing left to live for. I don't fear death anymore. In a twisted way, I think I might find it entertaining.

At this point, anything is better than the Grey.

Something snaps behind me, but I don't look. The Faceless do not sneak up on their prey, they have lost all grace with the rapid decaying of their muscles. It's impossible not to hear them coming. Besides, I didn't set out on this scavenging trip alone.

Ozzy barks as she runs past me. She's a grey mutt that looks like she could have been mixed with Retriever and maybe Collie, but there's no real way to tell with all her scars and deformities.

Ozzy is hairless, for one. She lost it all three years ago when a Faceless bit her. Somehow, she survived the bite, but ended up losing half her tail—it literally just fell off one day—and her left eye rotted away too. She was born in the Grey, so I know she's hardy and has a small resistance to the radiation that should've killed her years ago. I'm not worried about the fact that she doesn't have a mask. She's never worn one, and also… I don't know where I'm supposed to find a doggy gasmask anyway.

My boss found Ozzy as a puppy wandering around an abandoned hockey stadium. She couldn't resist her which I'm thankful for because she's saved me more times than I'm willing to admit, like when she was bitten by the Faceless that'd been coming after me. And when she was stabbed by a wild man in Faceless transition while I was fighting his Faceless wife.

But I didn't bring Ozzy to help me fight this time. In fact, my boss has no idea I snuck her out of our camp. I brought her along because she's not just an excellent guard dog. Ozzy is a heck of a hunter too.

She dashes by me and yelps as she crouches and starts digging furiously. I watch with a grin splitting my face, though it's hidden behind my mask.

What sort of animals can you hunt in a world destroyed by radiation?

Most of the animals look like Ozzy, hairless and deformed from drinking the contaminated water, breathing the contaminated air, or eating what little forestry remains in the Grey. But that's only the animals who are exposed to the toxic atmosphere above ground.

Underground lies an entire collection of healthy, tasty critters.

Snakes and bugs and worms—even some breeds of frog burrow underground. Before the blue lights, these animals only burrowed to nest and sleep, but they've adapted over time, adjusting to life completely indoors. Just like us.

I'm used to digging for snakes and taking home buckets of worms and bugs, but I'm tired of the usual. That's why I brought Ozzy along, she's excellent at finding the good stuff. Animals like chipmunks, moles, and even some ground squirrels. Meat. Nice, hearty, red meat. I'd kill for a non-contaminated cow so I could enjoy a burger or a steak like the old days. But this is as good as it gets.

We have a cook back at camp who's really good at making snake sausage and squirrel stew. But nothing beats a burger. A big fat juicy double cheeseburger with melted cheddar and a dribble of grease running down the side of the one-inch-thick patty.

I sigh, forcing myself to come back from my food fantasy and focus on Ozzy who's still digging like her paws are on fire. It's unhealthy to think about good food. It'll just remind me of how awful the menu is these days. Then the depression will get worse.

After another minute, Ozzy sticks her hairless muzzle into the hole she's dug and comes up with a fat gopher. It squeals as she shakes it around, trying to break its neck. I would feel sorry, but I've got a camp full of people who are protein deprived and sick of eating cockroaches. We need this meat.

Once the gopher is dead, Ozzy obediently sets it down and starts digging in another spot nearby. I take this moment to drop our catch into the sack I brought with me, and then I open another bag and sit down on the rocks with the tiny little gardening shovel I brought along too.

Wherever there are critters, there are bugs that they feed on somewhere nearby. I'm tired of bugs, but they are a healthy source of protein in a world in desperate need of it. I wasn't a vegetarian before the blue lights, and I don't plan on becoming one now. So even though the thought of more sauteed worms

33

makes my skin prickle with goosebumps, I sit down and start digging anyway.

For whatever reason, there are tons of bugs available. Because cockroaches can survive anything—even a nuclear explosion that leaves radiation leaking into the atmosphere. After almost an hour of digging, I stick my arm into my hole—all the way up to my shoulder—and retrieve a handful of sowbugs. They look like big roly polies you used to play with as kids. They're crawling all over my gloved hands, I can't help but shiver, thinking of how much I hate eating these things.

Bugs are awful.

Technically, sowbugs are isopods—not insects. That means they're more closely related to lobsters than spiders and cockroaches. That's what our camp cook says, anyway.

Whenever I complain about eating them, he tells me, "They're like the shrimp of the underground!"

Except they taste nothing like shrimp. And this is coming from someone who hates shellfish—though I'd give two of my fingers for a pound of shrimp right now.

Ozzy drops a second gopher on the ground beside me as I'm shoving my third handful of isopods into my bug bag. She sits and yelps at me, the stump of her short tail wags back and forth excitedly. I'm as happy as she is, we're eating meat tonight! Well, we're eating meat when we get back to camp. That's almost a two-day trip. Until then, it's bugs. Excuse me—*isopods*.

I glance at the gophers. Two days is far too long for them to keep, but I can make great time heading back if I pack up now and keep them cool at night. I start packing up to head out. No matter how fast I travel, I'm stopping as soon as the sun sets. You can bump into Faceless at any time of the day, but I've noticed they're stronger at night. And bolder too.

"Come on." I whistle at Ozzy, and she dashes away, already knowing where to go. She's taken scavenging trips with me dozens of times, so I don't need to guide her back toward the path we always take. We walk side by side in complete silence for the next few hours, only coming alive when Ozzy spots the abandoned elementary school we use as our campsite on scavenging trips.

The school is dilapidated; it was caught up in the aftermath of the initial blue light explosions. The entire west side of the building is missing its roof, and the walls that remain are charred black from the fire that broke out when the flames of the explosions expanded into the area.

There used to be small houses surrounding the school, it was tucked away in a nice little neighborhood where parents walked their kids to school and children trotted home alone afterward, unaccompanied by an adult because the neighborhood had been that safe.

And then everything was blown away, and whatever wasn't destroyed was burned. Whatever didn't burn was looted by desperate survivors. Whatever wasn't looted was soon contaminated by the toxic winds blowing in debris containing radioactive particles.

Still … the school is a symbol of hope for drifters like me.

We are the ones who have eked out a living in the Grey. We have found a way to survive the wilds. We have found life in the barren fields.

Drifters are nomadic people who go from place to place, scavenging whatever we can, setting up camp for months at a time before we decide there is nothing more to be collected or hunted, and then we move on. I've been a drifter since my first settlement was overrun by the early looters five years ago. This life works for me. It keeps me sane in the midst of all the chaos.

My camp has been set up a few days from this school for the last two months. We cleared out the basement when we first found it, taped off the windows and covered any cracks in the ceiling. It took all month for the place to decontaminate, we were thankful it hadn't been exposed to much of the toxic air since the basement had been relatively untouched. Regardless, I keep my mask on as I head downstairs, reaching into my sack to retrieve a neon daisy.

I hold it out in front of me as I walk through the dark halls, a solar powered flashlight in my free hand. Ozzy stalks beside me, walking slow, her head down as she sniffs the floor. The flower just sags in my hand, that means there isn't any radiation inside. I walk a few more feet just to be sure, and then I see it.

The daisy slowly leans toward my left, the same way a plant moves toward the sun. Except this happens much faster, and it feels unnatural. Like the plant is reaching out for help. Searching for poison to feed on.

Beside me, Ozzy lets out a low growl.

That's odd. There might be radiation present, but that shouldn't make my dog upset. She was born in the Grey, she's used to the toxic air now. But that isn't why she's growling, and I know it.

If there is radiation present, it's because there's a leak or a broken seal somewhere inside, letting in toxic air. Or because someone came in and didn't properly seal the door or window after they climbed through. The only ones who would do that is a lazy drifter who's likely dead by now. Or a Faceless.

I put my daisy back into the little glass jar I'd kept it in and shove that into my backpack. Then I pull out my hunting knife and twirl it in my free hand before grasping it by the hilt. I have a pistol, but firing a gun indoors isn't wise. I could pierce the wall or ceiling, setting off another toxic leak I'd have to seal up later on. I have a much better chance of not causing accidental damage if I use a knife.

Better yet… I have a better chance of staying alive if I don't creep further into the dark hallway of the school basement altogether. It's getting late. But I'd rather take my chances and try to make it to another landmark than stay locked underground with a Faceless. Or whatever's down here.

I turn toward the exit. "Come on, Ozzy," I say, retracing my steps.

She doesn't move.

"Ozzy!" I snap my fingers at her, and she shocks me by taking a step toward the shadowy hallway.

I swallow beneath my mask. "Ozzy, we don't have time for—"

A low growl cuts me off … a growl that didn't come from my dog.

I raise my knife, standing perfectly still. I can feel the hairs on the back of my neck lift one by one as the sound of footsteps echoes down the hall. They are heavy and uneven, like someone walking with a limp. A growl fills the shadowy hall, dancing into my ears and sending a shiver over my spine.

That's when I realize how foolish I'm being. There is no reason for me to stand and face this enemy. There is no reason for me to put my life, or Ozzy's life, at risk. I've already messed up by taking the dog without my boss's permission. If anything happens to Ozzy, she'll never forgive me. She might even ban me from the camp.

I grit my teeth as I pivot on my heel, my words come out as a snarl, anger and fear cracking my voice. "Let's *go*, Ozzy!"

Obedient dog that she is, Ozzy turns and bolts down the hall with me, but we never get more than a few steps before a man leaps from the shadows like a wild animal. He bursts through the darkness on all fours, running at a speed that shouldn't be possible for a human. Then again, he's barely human anymore.

I run like mad. Light bounces wildly off the walls and floor as I sprint with the flashlight in one hand and my knife in the other. I can see the shadow of the wild man on the wall when I glance to my left. It's a haunting image, like watching a demon sprint up from Hell.

I manage to grab the wall as I round the corner, so I don't lose momentum. Ozzy is at my side, sliding on the stone floor but she regains her balance before the wild man rounds the corner behind us and slides across the floor to crash into the wall.

The sound behind me tears a scream from my lips and I look back to see the monster that's chasing us. His jaw hangs at an awkward angle, making his shriek sound wild and animalistic. His hair is all gone, and his face holds bruises so terrible he looks almost disfigured, but it's his eyes that make me gasp.

They're neon blue, just like the contaminated daisies. But even though he's running mad and chasing us like an animal, he's still got all his flesh. No part of him is rotted or falling off like most Faceless. That means he was recently infected. He's still in transition.

Some part of him may still be there in his head, a human voice drowning in the murky waters of the Faceless void. I try to appeal to that side of him, the part that's nearly gone.

"You don't have to do this!" I shout, panting hard. We're almost to the exit, but I'm not sure that'll make a difference. He'll just chase us up the stairs. We don't have enough space between us to run out the door and close it behind us. If I don't turn around and fight, he will catch us.

I scream as I take two big strides and then turn on my heel, knife up and ready. The plan is to stab the Faceless man as he runs into me, but as I turn, I realize the horrible truth.

He's not chasing me.

He's chasing Ozzy.

Ozzy, who obediently followed me into this dark basement. Ozzy, who turned and ran with me when I decided to sprint away. Ozzy, who isn't running as fast as me because she can't get much traction with her claws on the slippery stone floor.

I watch with wide eyes as she turns, and I see the moment she realizes following me was a mistake. The Faceless man crashes into her and they both tumble a few feet into the wall. Ozzy lets out a yelp and then a snarl as she immediately attacks. But he fights like the wild man he is, grabbing her by the face and shoving her muzzle away, exposing her throat.

He's trying to eat her.

At this point, I don't care about causing a toxic leak. I drop the flashlight and pull out my pistol—but I don't fire. The Faceless is holding Ozzy in the air and she's writhing in his grasp. I could shoot her by accident.

I hiss out a curse as I grip my hunting knife. Before I can talk myself out of it, I lunge forward with the blade, stabbing the Faceless in the side. The man screams and shoves me so hard I trip backwards and hit the wall with a teeth-chattering thud. Ozzy is still in his grasp, but she manages to twist herself around and snap her jaws at his face. She clips his nose, blood spurts into the air as he howls and hurls her down the hall.

Ozzy lands with a pitiful cry, but she's back on her feet the next moment, growling as she takes a step closer. The man yanks the knife free from his ribcage and eyes us both.

Now, I raise the pistol. I've only got three shots—we're six

39

years into an apocalypse, ammo is rare these days. But I don't hesitate to use what I've got.

The Faceless takes two shots to his abdomen and one to his collarbone. But he still stalks toward me.

I drop the gun. This is what madness looks like. This is what evil does when it stands up and takes the form of flesh and bone.

I'm going to die here. I realize this as the Faceless looks down at his gunshot wounds and then growls in anger. All I've done is made him angry. Fear opens a black pit in my chest, releasing a flood of panic that flows into my mind. I want to curl up and let this wild man finish me off—I almost do just that as he takes another step—but the sound of Ozzy's brave barking snaps me back into focus.

I've got a smaller knife in my boot. I yank it out and grab the wall as I struggle to my feet. I am not a spring chicken. I was almost forty when the lights flashed, and that was six years ago. When I get to my feet, I feel every ache, bump, and bruise. But I don't have any time to fuss over my injuries. One of us is walking out of this basement alive and I fully intend for it to be me.

We got meat today. I'm not dying before I get to eat some.

The wild man throws himself at me, clumsy from loss of blood and the insanity taking over his mind. He fights like a true Faceless, swinging wildly and crying out like a banshee. My back hits the wall and we tumble to the floor. I manage to get on top of him, stabbing with my knife but it's much smaller than his and not as effective since he is mindless and deranged, fighting through his injuries like he's perfectly healthy.

He knocks me backwards and then stabs at me, but I roll out the way and his knife slices into the stone floor. I see the very human gleam in his eye when he smiles and swings his blade in an upward arc. *He's going to cut my face off!* But Ozzy latches onto his wrist and snarls as she shakes his arm around, just like she did with the gopher.

He drops my hunting knife and raises his arm. Ozzy still hasn't let go, she's dangling in the air as she tries her hardest to rip his hand off. Any other man would be rolling on the floor in pain. But this man is Faceless. His brain isn't responding to half the pain he should feel right now. So instead of howling and falling to the floor, he lifts Ozzy into the air and punches her in the ribs.

We scream together. Ozzy in pain, and me in absolute shock as the wild man hurls her down the hall once again. This time, she doesn't get back up.

Without thinking, I grab the hunting knife and charge.

5

Shon

The last time I was outside was right before I got on a plane to fly from Barcelona to Georgia. I had forgotten how different the sun looks in person versus through a window. I had forgotten how the wind feels brushing against my skin. I had forgotten the smells and sounds of the earth.

I see none of that here in the barren fields.

I cannot expose my skin for long for fear of contamination. So I do not feel the breeze that pushes one of my thick braids over my shoulder. My face is crammed into a filtered gasmask, so I cannot smell the air around me or else I could contaminate my lungs. And I do not hear anything but my pounding heart.

There are no birds. No squirrels skittering by. No dogs barking in someone's yard. There is nothing out here. Not even any grass to cover the grey earth, no trees except stumps and rotted trunks, fallen over and hollowed out like gaping coffins. I am tempted to lie down in one, curl up in fetal position and never get up again. But I can't stop.

If I stop walking, I will turn around and try to go back to Rebirth Colony. They will not welcome me home.

By now, the Council is aware I am the one who stole the meal tickets. And they are probably aware that I 'escaped' yesterday afternoon. If things go my way, they will leave it at that. They won't send anyone out to retrieve me since the punishment would have been banishment anyway. And they will never suspect that Everett helped me get away.

The reason I left was so that he didn't have to suffer the shame of turning me in. So that he wouldn't have to lie and cover up my theft. But I have to imagine the Council might be suspicious as to how I got out with a sack full of supplies. I'm holding on to the hope that they will believe I'm a dirty thief who stole canned goods and a gasmask before taking off, instead of suspecting Everett of helping me.

Hopefully, they will be satisfied with my absence and leave it at that.

Even if they aren't satisfied. I'm already gone. It won't be worth the effort and supplies to send a team out to retrieve me, just so I can stand trial and be sentenced to banishment all over again.

I walk until my hip aches, and I can't feel my feet. I take small sips from my canteen. I hold my breath when I remove my mask to quickly stuff strips of salty jerky into my mouth. Last night, I slept in one of those hollow tree trunks. It had fallen over, half decayed and splintered, shaped like a gothic manger. I got no sleep. Just stared up at the dark sky through my gasmask, wondering if this would be the rest of my life.

Everett had told me to head east, but he didn't leave me a compass and I have no sense of direction. I'm only 27 years

43

old; part of the last generation of Girl Scouts. The ones who actually went camping and fishing and wore skirts because it was still okay to be feminine. Unfortunately, the extent of my time in the Scouts did not include any of those awesome survival lessons that would be a great benefit to me now.

I quit before I turned seven, only learning how to tie something called a monkey knot—which I have now forgotten—and selling exactly two boxes of cookies before I burst into tears when a lady told me she didn't want any cookies. My mother took me home and I sobbed until she said I didn't have to go back.

I wish she would've made me stay.

I feel like I've been wandering in circles. Like I've ventured into a forgotten world that should only exist in fantasy novels. The air is slightly tainted, like I'm walking through a smokescreen after a fire has been put out. The sun is high in the sky, but I can barely see the light punching through the heavy overcast.

This is not the Georgia I remember.

Street signs have been knocked over or destroyed in God knows what. The explosions, the frightening aftermath, random fires, community gunfights, turf wars amongst survivors. I can only imagine. It's been six long years ... Nothing is the same.

I have no real sense of direction except the beginning of the expressway that used to exit at the airport. I found an entrance this morning and walked until the afternoon, weaving through cars that have been sitting in place for half a decade. Normally, they would have been covered in moss as nature reclaimed the land. But since there is no grass or living plant life in sight, the roads are dusty, and the cars have begun to rust.

I've lied to you … There *are* plants around. Hundreds of little daisies that look like they've been mutated. At first glance, they're pretty little flowers. Neon blue with bright purple stems. But then I remember what the Rebirth Colony Union scouts used to say about them. That they're toxic plants. Flowers that only grow in areas heavy with radiation. So long as I see those flowers, I cannot remove my mask. I cannot drink any water I find. I cannot eat any of the animals—unless I dig them up from underground.

I don't know how deep I'd have to dig. I don't know if they're immune or if they're safe to eat after cooking them at a certain temperature. Unlike Everett, I never left the airport. I didn't get to learn all the amazing things he did about the outside world. And now I'm expected to survive in it.

I'm down to one canteen of water, a pack of jerky, and three cans of beef stew. I don't even know if the stew is safe to eat. How long do canned goods last? These would be six years old now, but I've heard stories of people finding canned food and MREs from the Civil War and giving it a taste. Some said the food had miraculously kept. Some claimed you could die from eating it. Either way, the Civil War is a lot further into the past than the blue lights, so I'm willing to take my chances with the cans of beef stew.

But three cans are not enough to survive on for long. And I need more water.

Where on earth do I find drinkable water in a radioactive wasteland?

Tears burn the backs of my eyes and I almost sob behind my gasmask. "God…" my voice cracks. I haven't prayed in years. I haven't even thought about praying. It's something I try not to think about because then I'll be forced to take a long, hard look at myself. I'll have to decide what I believe. If I'm

45

willing to go down the crazy path of faith, or just keep trudging along like I always do.

I'm afraid to believe. Hope is dangerous in this world. Sometimes it's easier to accept that this is all you've got. This is as good as it gets. Because if you convince yourself otherwise, you may not be able to handle the disappointment that follows.

But I know what I felt. And I know what I heard.

God is real. And He wants me here in Georgia for some reason. I have to trust that He'll keep me alive to accomplish His will.

For now, that's the hope that I'll live for. That God will have my back, at least until I finish this secret mission of His. But in order to do that, I've got to find more water.

After a few more hours of weaving my way through dead cars on the highway, I walk down a ramp that leads to an exit which should take me toward the east side of the city. I don't recognize the area with most of the buildings destroyed or blown away entirely. Landmarks that I would normally be able to point out are gone. Small businesses and corner stores are no longer standing. Streets are destroyed, the pavement cracked, sidewalks totally crumbled. This place is unrecognizable.

Even if I did know where I was going, the airport is still miles from my old neighborhood. In fact, I hadn't reached my final destination that day six years ago. I'd actually had a connecting flight to catch. I'm on the other side of Georgia, another two hours of flying or half a day of driving. Unimaginable time walking.

Now that I've been forced to finally leave the airport, the

only place I can think of going is my old home. Try to find my family. Try to find *something*. But I've no idea how to get there.

Water… the thought pops into my head followed by a sudden urge to gulp down the canteen I've got left. First, I need to find water. Then I can worry about how to cross the State of Georgia on my own with no map or landmarks to follow.

I spend the night in an abandoned car. It isn't fun, but I do manage to get a little more sleep than the night before. I even have a dream about food, and then I'm woken up by the sound of howling. But it doesn't sound like the howls of an animal. It sounds like a person pretending to be an animal.

Slowly, I sit up in the backseat of the vehicle and peer through the dirt-stained window. It's totally dark out. I can't see anything. But I can hear that howling, and I can hear something moving outside the car. I gulp down a breath of air, wheezing through my gasmask. That's when I think I see something. Movement right outside my window.

I lean forward, squinting through the eyeholes of my mask. It looks like a man… A man walking on all fours.

I gasp.

It *is* a man. A Faceless man. And he's joined by three others who sniff at the ground, walking between the rows of abandoned cars. I'm on a dirt road that's packed with vehicles; they're all burned and scorched, the ones in the front are partially crushed, like a cluster of cars that'd been trying to outrun the explosions.

It looks like they all failed.

The Faceless men are hairless and entirely naked, so I can see the scars on their lumpy backs, pocked with overgrowths of flesh, like they're all developing humped backs. Their mouths hang open with thick globs of drool spilling from their sagging lips. Their nostrils flare as they sniff the ground, neon eyes blinking rapidly.

When one of them limps toward a car just two vehicles from my own, my heart stops. They're looking for me... sniffing the ground, everywhere I'd walked earlier as I'd searched the cars for supplies, trying to pick one to sleep in.

The Faceless nearest me grunts and the others limp over to it. They all walk like dogs, or limp forward the way Tarzan does, like he's a gorilla. It's the scariest thing I've ever seen. Nothing Everett could have told me would have prepared me enough to face these creatures. These monsters that used to be men.

I hold my breath as they make their way through the cars. They sniff, peer into the windows, and then move on. There are only three cars ahead of mine now.

Their footsteps are heavy and uneven, limping, dragging deteriorated feet behind, walking on all fours. Each step makes my heart jump, each grunt makes it harder to hold my bowels. I'm shaking like a leaf when they reach the car right in front of mine.

Slowly, I back away from the window. There is no escape for me. If I open my door to slip away, they will hear me and come running. But if I stay here, they'll find me and kill me. Worse ... they'll eat me alive.

I don't know why the Faceless enjoy human flesh. I don't know why the ones who still have some semblance of humanity want to hunt and hurt humans, as if they aren't one themselves. But that's the way it is. Six years ago, the blue lights changed everything. Our environment, our way of life, even our biology.

There is a new apex predator. And it is worse than we've ever imagined.

A wordless cry cuts into my thoughts and I gasp as I

fumble to tug my hunting knife loose. A scream rips from my lips when I glance out the backseat window and come face to face with a wild man. His eyes are bright enough to see through the grimy, stained glass, though each breath he takes fogs the window a little. His nostrils are flared like an animal's, his mouth is sagging open, drool spilling from the corners of his mouth. He is barely human. But he's human enough to feel the biting pain of my knife when he opens my door and I lunge like I've lost my mind.

My blade goes into his left eye, and he shrieks as he stumbles back. I yank the blade loose and try to kick him out the way so I can run, but one of the other Faceless grabs me by the hood of my sweatshirt. He's climbed into the car from the other door, dragging me back across the seats.

Pain shoots through my butt as the wild man pulls me from the car and I plop onto the ground. I struggle as he drags me across the concrete, screaming and slashing wildly with my knife. The Faceless grunts when I cut him—I have no idea where the blade gets him, but I feel his warm blood splatter across my face, and the next second his grip goes slack.

When I twist around to look at him, I almost fall over dead. Somehow, I managed to slice his throat with my wild swings. I praise Jesus… I thank God that I've just killed a man. There is no time to dwell on how twisted that prayer is, but I'm thankful to be alive and no one will ever make me feel guilty for it. There is no time for guilt.

There are two Faceless left, but they don't try to attack me right away. I stabbed one of them in the eye and slit the other's throat. The ones left are human enough to know a threat when they see one.

Thank God they can't tell how badly I'm shaking. Thank God they're too distracted to smell the urine running down my legs as I lose control of my bladder. I've never been so afraid in my life.

I was just a college student trying to make it in the world when I got a stupid message from a voice in my head. Then I got caught up in a plane crash, spent six years living in an airport, and now I'm fighting for my life against mindless, flesh-eating humans whose brains have rotted due to radiation.

How on earth is any of this possible?

Someone sets loose a bloodcurdling scream. It takes me a moment to realize it's coming from me... I have lost my own mind. And I haven't even been infected.

My mask grips my face as I stretch my mouth open and scream, losing whatever vestiges of sanity I'd had left. The shrieking startles the Faceless for a moment. They blink at me like they have no idea how to approach this situation. Then one of them snaps from his momentary shock and dashes right at me.

I know I should turn and run. I know I should raise my knife to protect myself. But I can't get myself to move. My mind and my body are no longer functioning as one. So even though I'm internally screaming for my legs to move, my only physical response is to stumble sideways and sag against the car as the Faceless closes the space between us.

He runs on all four, and as he nears me, I realize this one is actually a woman. The male Faceless is running too, but he's weaving through the cars, probably to approach from the other side so I can't run away. But I can barely get myself to breathe, let alone escape.

There are less than twenty feet between me and the Faceless woman now.

Ten feet.

Five feet.

She leaps into the air—and is caught in a net.

As if someone shot the net from a gun, she flies backwards and crashes into a car so hard, the metal of the hood bends inwards. The windows splinter with cracks as she thrashes in the net, tangled in rope and what I'm assuming is military-grade nylon. The other Faceless blinks back and forth, a flicker of humanity dashing across his face as he looks hopeless for just a moment. Then his mindlessness takes over and he howls before turning and running at me again.

He never takes more than two steps before a bright light illuminates the area. I can see everything clearly in a red, effervescent glow as a flare is hurled past me and lands at the feet of the Faceless man. I hear whistles and yelps behind me, but they are not the mindless calls of the Faceless. These sounds are organized, meaningful. They are calls and responses from a coordinated group that emerges through the shadows between the surrounding cars.

I see two men in gear, a woman wielding a rifle as she holds point, and what looks like a child in a gasmask and black tactical armor aiming a crossbow at the Faceless before me. I am surrounded by mysterious wanderers, but I don't feel afraid anymore. They're clearly human. And the Faceless is their prey.

The wild man cowers at the bright flare, so close its undoubtedly burning his neon eyes. He covers his face and stumbles back, falling into a car. The female Faceless shrieks in her net; I can't tell if she's angry she's been subdued, afraid of the flare, or afraid for the Faceless male.

The team of organized strangers moves in, a man with a riot shield goes first, inching closer as another man with what looks like a makeshift spear moves in. He jabs his weapon at the Faceless male, forcing him to back away from me.

The woman holding the rifle whistles and the man with the

51

riot shield shoves his barrier forward while the spearman thrusts. The Faceless male gets angry and roars at them, but the sound is cut off when an arrow splits his skull.

The Faceless woman shrieks again, thrashing in the net.

The child behind me cheers.

"Good shot, Penn," says the woman. She slings her rifle over her shoulder and whistles loudly. At her cue, the rest of her team steps from the shadows. In the glow of the flare, they look ominous, like they could kill me as easily as they could rescue me, but I don't let my fears surface as I stand tall and hold out my knife.

I feel pathetic, trying to put up a brave front right now. I'm five feet tall and covered in my own urine. There is nothing threatening about me at all. But I don't let that stop me from gripping my knife as I shout, "Don't come any closer!"

The kid with the crossbow laughs, and I realize it's a girl. "We just saved you. You should want us to come closer."

"Where you from, stranger?" asks the woman with the rifle. "How'd you get here?"

"I-I walked."

"Walked from where?" she asks.

"Um…"

"Where you headed?"

"Um…" I clear my dry throat.

"Pretty dangerous to be travelling alone. Especially as a lady," the man with the riot shield says. He's tall and his voice is deep; I imagine an older man behind the gasmask he's wearing.

"I'm not alone," I say without thinking. These people might have caught one Faceless and killed the other, but I don't know them. I don't have a reason to trust them. They could kill me and take my supplies. Or they could track down Rebirth

Colony and take their supplies. It's best to err on the side of caution. Make them think there are as many people with me as there are of them.

The woman steps forward, her hand moving to her side. I realize there's a pistol holstered at her hip, but she doesn't pull it out. She just pats it, and that's all she needs to do. I feel like I can't breathe as she comes closer.

"That's the first one," she says in a flat tone.

I blink behind my mask. "The first one?"

"The first lie you've told." She taps her pistol again. "Trust is worth more than gold out here, honey. You don't know us, so I understand your reservations. But you need to understand that I don't like liars."

I swallow.

She steps closer, close enough for me to see the coldness in her dark brown eyes. When she speaks, her Georgian accent is low and firm, leaving absolutely no doubt that if I don't respond honestly, she will kill me. Or maybe she'll let that killer kid put a crossbolt in me like she did with the Faceless male.

"You've lied to me once," the woman says. "You won't get away with lying again. So I'll ask once more: Where you from, stranger? And how'd you get here?"

6

Shon

Georgia is unnecessarily hot. I feel the heat against my back as I march behind the tall woman who basically held me at gunpoint last night. When she caught me lying, I had no choice but to 'fess up. Only problem with that is my story isn't exactly simple and there wasn't much time to tell it—not out in the open in the middle of the night. We could hear Faceless closing in on us with all the noise we'd been making. So the woman ordered me to walk and talk, and we haven't stopped since.

I'm sure it's just before afternoon now. The sun is high but not quite at its peak—not that it matters. It's still sinfully hot out, and I doubt the heat will let up anytime soon. The gasmask around my face feels like it's sticking to my cheeks, intensifying the heat tenfold. I'm sweating beneath my hoodie, but I don't dare take it off. It isn't much protection against the radiation in the air, but it's better than nothing.

I fight the urge to lift my mask and scratch my face as the

tall woman in charge glances over her shoulder and says, "So, why didn't you just marry the friend?"

She's talking about Everett. I told her absolutely everything about me, even the fact that I believe God sent me here for a reason. I couldn't really read her expression behind her mask when I said that, but her buddies with the spear and shield outright laughed at me. The killer child had just stared, unblinking.

"Everett is like my brother," I huff, tripping over a rock. "I can't marry him."

She snorts. "You ain't built for this world, sweetheart. Not if you get the frilly willies over marrying your best friend."

Pardon me, but I don't think anyone is *built* for a world ruined by radiation and terrorism.

I don't say that, of course. The killer kid—whose name is Penelope, Penn for short—is walking beside me with her crossbow while the two men with the shield and spear carry the rear. Their names are Mike and Taylor and they're dragging the writhing Faceless woman they captured in a net behind them. The sight is intimidating enough, but it's topped off by the tall woman—named Minty—who's holding point with her very large hunting rifle.

I'm literally surrounded by enemies. If I do anything they don't like, they could kill me. Or strip me of my supplies and leave me for dead. Or set loose the Faceless woman they've got and laugh as they watch her chase me down and eat my face.

"I didn't get the *frilly willies*," I mumble. "I just wasn't in love with Everett. Or anyone else who asked for my hand."

Minty glances back again; I can't see her eyes because the sun is glinting off the glass of the eyeholes in her mask. But I can hear the disbelief in her voice as she says incredulously,

"Even though it would've given you a safer place to live? And better food rations?"

I glance away. I'm a Christian. Marriage is different for me. I can't form an eternal covenant with someone for an extra can of beans. But I know from the sound of Minty's voice that this is something she will never understand, so I just shrug and keep walking.

Minty doesn't question me again, but I don't know if it's because she's lost interest or because we've finally arrived at their camp.

Ahead of us is an abandoned factory. It's large and surrounded by a parking lot full of plastic tarp set up like tents and makeshift rooms. As I walk through the area, I see people inside the plastic rooms, lying on cots or sleeping on the ground. The only ones standing are dressed in what look like homemade hazmat suits and they're all accompanied by a Faceless.

There is a Faceless man weighed down by chains who stands growling in the corner of a plastic room while a hazmat man pokes at him with a long skinny pole. Another hazmat man is in the room scribbling on a clipboard.

The sight is enough to make me stop in my tracks and stare openmouthed, though no one can tell from behind my mask.

"You're studying them," I say. That's when it hits me, the people lying down alone are infected. Slowly transitioning.

Penn steps beside me, looking into the tent. "Minty says we can find a cure by learning more about them."

"It's radiation. There is no cure."

"You sure about that?" Minty's voice fills the space, and I suddenly realize there are people staring at us. Hazmat men glancing up in their bulky helmets, resting infected people slowly sitting up to get a better look. Their eyes are slightly

56

blue, sparkling in their faces.

I swallow as Minty crosses her arms over her chest as she waits for an answer.

"I've never heard of a cure for the symptoms of radiation."

"I wasn't talking about the cure." She laughs. "I meant, are you sure the poison in the air is radiation?"

Now I'm left speechless. What am I supposed to say to that? Of course, it's radiation. I lived in an airport for six years that was run by US military personnel, and they all said it was radiation. We had no reason to doubt them. But even if we did, the barren fields proved them right. No one can go outside for long without developing symptoms, plus all those freaky blue and purple daisies that sprout in contaminated areas. What else could it be?

As if Minty can read my mind, she steps forward and pats my shoulder. "Come inside, we'll worry about conspiracy theories later."

When we get inside, I'm still left speechless. I couldn't tell from outside because the front of the building looked so bad, but it's clear from the letters painted on the walls indoors that this factory was not some place producing car parts or building computers. It's an old Amazon shipping facility.

I can't imagine the sort of looting that must have gone on here after the explosions went off and it became clear the government was falling apart. At one point, this place would have been filled with electronics, furniture, cookware, clothing, and even packaged foods—all the things I've ordered on Amazon before.

Now, nothing is left. The place looks like a metal tomb, hollowed and picked clean. Except Minty's friends have set up more tarp and plastic rooms with duct tape sealing them shut to give themselves some privacy. I suppose the looters had no interest in all the packaging supplies of the factory. Even six years after the lights, there's plenty of tape, cardboard, and plastic wrap left. Unless Minty's folks brought the supplies from other places. She mentioned they were drifters and had traveled together over four different states since the explosions first set off.

Minty guides me to the back corner of the factory. By this time, Penn is the only one still with us. Mike, the spearman, stayed in the parking lot to pass off the Faceless woman to one of the hazmat men, and Taylor slipped away as soon as we entered the factory.

Minty passes through a plastic curtain and Penn shoves me inside when I hesitate. It's surprisingly homey in here, a makeshift bed which is just a pile of blankets on a conveyor belt, a round table for two, a crate with an unlit candle on it, and dusty cardboard boxes used for storage.

I don't speak as Minty drops her rifle on her bed and removes her jacket. She tosses it in one of the cardboard boxes and then clears all the papers from her table before motioning for me to sit. While she lights the candle on her crate, I crane my neck to get a peek at the papers she tossed on her bed with her rifle. They're all maps which I guess isn't weird for a group of drifters, but I have to wonder how long Minty's group has been set up here. And when they plan to leave.

Minty catches my attention when she sits across from me and peels off her gasmask. I am shocked to see a pretty Black American woman with high cheekbones and a puff of afro hair tied into one thick French braid down her back, just like mine. Except I have two chunky braids, and they're much longer than hers, just past my ribcage.

"Is the air okay?" I ask.

Minty laughs, the sound is much less intimidating when her

58

voice isn't altered by her mask. "No air is completely safe. But this place has been sealed off for months now. It's safe for at least four or five hours without a mask."

I reach up to remove mine, wrinkling my nose at the bitter smell that hits me. "How do you sleep if you can only go maskless for a few hours?"

Now Penelope laughs and I glance over my shoulder to find a girl with the same brown skin as me and Minty with a smile on her face. Her head is shaved down to half an inch of black coiled hair, and she's got round brown eyes that remind me of my mother's. I would say she's a cute girl except she's still holding that crossbow, so right now there's nothing cute about her.

Penn tosses her gasmask into one of Minty's bins as she says, "We sleep with the masks on. Duh."

I feel my ears burn.

"Now," Minty says in a serious voice. "You said you're from a campsite at an old airport?"

"Rebirth Colony," I say.

"How long were you there?"

"Six years."

"All six?" Her eyes bulge a little.

I guess it's difficult for a drifter to wrap their head around someone staying put for that long.

"All six," I say. "The lights flashed while I was at the airport. My plane had just touched down. The National Guard came in almost immediately, so they sealed the doors, windows, and vents before any radiation could get in."

Minty makes a face when I say that dangerous 'R' word, but she doesn't bring up her theory again, so I keep talking.

"They had tons of supplies and weapons, and the airport was full of clothes and food already. We thrived for a while.

59

Even started indoor gardens and whatnot."

"Sounds cozy," Minty deadpans.

"It wasn't. We weren't allowed to leave because of the..."
I pause. "*Poison* in the air."

"I spent six years looting, stealing, and duct taping every place I slept in." Minty's sharp eyes narrow. "I would've preferred being holed up with the US Army any day."

"I would've preferred to be a drifter," I say firmly. "We had food, but it was severely monitored and strictly rationed. We had weapons, but only the military could use them, and once the government broke down, they formed Rebirth Colony and made their own rules. Rules that said only members of the RC Union could leave."

"Which you weren't part of," Minty surmises.

I nod.

"And now you're free."

"I'm not exactly free."

She raises a heavy eyebrow, it's thick and full and completely black, unlike the hair on her head which is streaked with silver. I can't exactly place her age but there are lines in her face and as she raises her other eyebrow, a row of wrinkles bunches together on her forehead.

Minty might be old enough to be my mother. But she's tough enough to beat up someone half her age. That's why I take a breath and answer her honestly, casting a quick glance at her rifle on the bed. It's out of reach, but I haven't forgotten the pistol at her side. And I remind myself that she never took it off as I say, "I think it's my responsibility to help Rebirth Colony."

A smile stretches over Minty's aged face. "Oh, right. God's got a mission for you." I don't miss the sarcasm in her voice, though Penn doesn't laugh or chortle behind me.

60

"I know you don't believe me."

"You're right."

"That doesn't change what *I* believe." I raise my chin, waiting for her to criticize me further, but she doesn't.

Instead, Minty looks over at Penn and says, "Grab us some lunch."

Penn glances at me, clutching her crossbow. For a moment, I wonder if she's going to argue, but she gives a firm nod and leaves the plastic room without a word.

"Your daughter?" I ask once she's gone.

"Not any more than that airport boy was your brother."

"Right."

"Picked her up three years ago. Don't know where she's really from, or where her folks are. But I suppose that doesn't matter, does it?"

"No. I suppose not."

Minty sighs.

"Do you pick up a lot of strays?"

"Not many people out here are strays, to be honest. But I found a dog four years back. Real cute mutt named Ozzy. You'd love her."

"Is she dead now?"

She chuckles. "No. A friend took her out scavenging." Minty glowers. "Without my permission."

"Maybe your friend didn't want to be in the barren fields alone."

"Like you were?"

"Not by choice."

"Apparently, that was God's choice," she says mockingly. When I don't respond, she asks, "You really think God told you to come home to this mess?"

"Who says this mess only exists here?"

61

Minty presses her lips together like the thought has never crossed her mind before. It's definitely crossed mine. The United States is not the most loved country on earth. My time in Spain taught me that very well. People were shocked by my manners, shocked by my interest in their culture, and shocked that I wasn't some self-entitled brat ranting about my rights. The world outside our borders pretty much hates us. That isn't news to me. But no matter what anyone thinks, the world can't hate us enough to sit back and watch an entire country rot, can they?

Hated or not, no aid has come. Not from Canada, which is so close to us, not from Israel whom we've been allied with since the recognition of their nation. There's been nothing but silence. Which can only mean one thing.

The world hasn't helped because it *can't* help. The barren fields aren't limited to the United States, they stretch across the globe, touching every continent, withering every country. We are all in this together.

Still, that doesn't explain why God told me to come home.

"I don't know why He told me to return to Georgia," I admit. "But I'm here, and if there's a way I can help Rebirth Colony, then I will."

"You would've died if we hadn't showed up. You ain't got much help to offer no one."

Her comment stings. Made worse by the southern drawl that drags out each word, but I don't throw myself a pity party.

"I'm still here. So there's still a chance to help."

To my shock, Minty smiles. "You might be right about that."

I raise my eyebrows.

"We've been here for two months now. In a few weeks, we'll be moving out." She glances back at the maps on her bed.

"But I have no idea where to go next. Perhaps we'll head to a certain airport."

Panic shoots through me. "If you think you can take over—"

"Relax, honey. I have no interest in foul play. Besides, if your little colony is doing as bad as you say, then there won't be many supplies worth attacking them for anyway." Minty pauses. "I'm more interested in setting up some sort of arrangement. A trade system."

"For supplies?"

She shrugs. "We could gather supplies for them, in exchange for access to their military equipment."

"You want weapons."

"No." Her eyes seem to pierce me. "I want a lab to work in."

Now it clicks. "You want to do more experiments on the Faceless to find your cure."

"Bingo, darling."

"What makes you so sure the poisoned air isn't radiation?"

"I don't look like much now, but before the blue lights flashed, I was a scientist. I worked in facilities that produced radioactive waste. I understand enough about radiation to know that duct taping a doorway doesn't clear it out."

There's a weighty pause.

"Why would the National Guard lie to us? Why would they lie to *everyone*?" I ask.

"To keep down panic, probably. And to make sure people took the blue lights seriously. America isn't a country keen on rules. If the government had told us to stay inside, there would have been riots in the streets. If they had told us to seal our windows and doors for our safety, people would have purposely left them open simply because it was their *right* to."

She laughs bitterly. "Radiation was the only thing powerful enough to get people to do the right thing."

I love my country, warts and all, but I can't deny the truth in Minty's words. We're a bunch of rebels, and sometimes that bites us in the butt.

"So, you think you can find a cure?" I say. "You think you're going to be the one to stop people from turning into the Faceless and make the air breathable again?"

Minty blinks. "I think I have a real shot at finding out what the toxins in the air truly are. Then I'll go from there."

"I suppose that's a start."

"There may not be a cure at all." She waves her hands around. "This might be as good as it gets. But we'll never know until we try."

"So, what will you do with me?"

"You're welcome to come along. We'll take you home in exchange for the information you've given us."

I shake my head. "I can't go home. I'm a wanted thief."

"Right." She laughs. "Well, you can join our little group. We ain't much, but we've survived this long."

I shake my head again, earning myself a queer look from Minty.

"Well, what is it you want then?" she asks.

"I want to go home."

"I told you—"

"Rebirth Colony isn't my home." I look her right in the eye. "I want to go back to my *hometown*. I want to find my family."

For a moment, Minty just stares at me. Then she bursts out laughing, muscular shoulders bopping up and down in her black tank top. "What makes you think you can find your family?" She waves a hand, cutting off my answer before I can even give it. "And what makes you think we can help you find them?"

"You're drifters," I say. "You told me you've traveled across four different states so far. You know how to find supplies. You know how to live out here. You can help me if you really wanted to."

"But we don't want to. My camp doesn't owe anyone a trip across the state—"

"The entire camp doesn't have to come. I only need one good drifter."

Minty eyes me like she's seriously considering it. "We're grateful for the information you've shared about Rebirth Colony, but I don't think anyone is grateful enough to voluntarily leave the group just to help you." She shrugs. "You're still a stranger to us."

"And you're a stranger to me. But I've helped you by sharing my information. I've trusted that you're good, honest people just looking for a way to survive, not a band of looters who'll tear Rebirth Colony down." I fold my arms. "Now you owe me."

A bolt of terror shoots through me at the look that crosses Minty's face. She starts to rise to her feet, splaying her large hands on the table before me. Her arms are lined with muscles she's gained from hauling a rifle and survival pack across four states and fighting for her life. They twitch as she leans toward me, and I get a good look at the hardness in her eyes. At the way she can look so dead yet alive with rage at the same time.

"Listen, missy," she hisses, "I saved your life out there."

"And captured a Faceless for your troubles."

"Which means we're even."

I shake my head. "I gave you information. By telling you about Rebirth Colony, I may have just handed you everything you need to save the world. I'd say that's worth more than a Faceless. Even worth more than my own life." I lean over the table too, so we're basically nose to nose. "So you still owe me."

Minty's lips pull back into a snarl. "Who do you think will honestly want to do this?"

I shrug and lean back in my chair. "Aren't you the one in charge? That's for you to decide."

I think I'm *this* close to getting slapped when the plastic tarp is pulled back and Penn walks in with a tall man following behind her. His heavy combat boots hit the floor with a thud on each step, the zippers on his backpack jingle as he walks to the middle of the room. He's not wearing a mask so I can see his salt and pepper hair, the scruff of a beard covering his square jaw. He's squeezing a leather pair of gloves in his large, calloused hands, I notice a scar over the backside of his left hand, like he's been stabbed before.

The man doesn't pay me any attention, neither does Penn. Both of them walk inside and stare at Minty in a sort of silence so awkward and heavy, I shift in my chair, wishing I could disappear.

"What's going on, Erik?" Minty asks. "You're back early."

The man—Erik—takes a heavy breath, his meaty shoulders rise and fall almost slowly. I watch his jacket crinkle with the movement, and then I notice the blood *on* his jacket.

Minty notices too. Her brown eyes stay locked on the stains as she asks again, "What's going on, Erik?"

"M-Minnesota," he murmurs shakily, "I took Ozzy with me."

"Erik…"

"And—"

She takes a step back, shaking her head. "Don't say it."

66

Erik obliges. He just stands there in the middle of the room, squeezing those gloves like he could wring them out. He hangs his head and sees the blood on his chest, it makes him shiver.

Ozzy... That's the name of the dog Minty mentioned earlier. The stray she took in four years ago. A cute mutt I would love.

He's the friend who took Ozzy without permission, I realize suddenly. And judging from the blood on his clothes and the look of remorse on his face, I don't think Ozzy made it back from this scavenging trip alive.

7

Erik

I owe Minnesota more than I can pay. But I don't deserve this.

After a minute of silent glaring, she puts the girl out of her office and sends Penn off in search of lunch, apparently for a second time. We glare at each other again—well, Minty glares, I just stand there, ready to accept judgment. But when she lays it on me, I immediately get angry.

"You took my dog," Minty says in a low voice, it doesn't waver like it did in front of the others. No, that had been a show. The Minnesota I know isn't a woman who would cry over a lost pup, despite being the sort of woman who would take one in. She loved Ozzy, there's no doubt about that, but she didn't love her for the reasons you might think.

"I needed a scouting partner," I begin, but Minty shakes her head and cuts me off.

"You had no permission to take Ozzy."

"I know. I didn't come here to make excuses for what

happened. I'm here to make amends."

Minty crosses her toned arms, they're as scarred and hard as her heart. Minnesota is an excellent leader of this camp; she's kept us all alive and fed and given us hope for the future. But she's not a gentle woman, not in the least.

She sleeps with her rifle. When someone gets infected beyond saving, she handles the execution herself. I've never seen her smile, not unless it's sarcastic.

She isn't smiling now. She isn't even frowning, just staring at me like I should expect her next words. But I don't. They take me by complete surprise.

"As punishment for causing the loss of Ozzy's life, you will escort that girl to her home in Toccoa."

What?

I blink at her. If Minty's maps are accurate, we're in the State of Georgia now, somewhere near a city called Bainbridge, to be specific. I'm not from this area, but I was a trucker before all this chaos broke out, I traveled across the country for a living. I'm familiar enough with Georgia to know that Toccoa isn't close to Bainbridge at all. In fact, it's all the way across the state. Hours away in a car. *Days* of travel on foot—and that's if we walk nonstop.

"You want me to walk across the state for a girl?"

"Her name is RaShonda Banks, and she's looking for a way home."

"Sounds like a problem for RaShonda Banks," I say through gritted teeth.

"Erik." Minty narrows her gaze.

"Sending me off is the same as exiling me, Minty, and you know it."

"You deserve exile for what you've done."

I step closer to her. "You would take my life over a dog's?"

"Ozzy wasn't just any dog!" Minnesota holds my gaze for a moment, daring me to argue with her. She knows I can't. Ozzy was special, even a trucker like me understood that.

It wasn't because she was so well trained or because we liked her so much. Ozzy was special because she had survived. She was born in the Grey, somehow immune to all the radiation in the air. She hadn't gone mad like the Faceless and she hadn't rotted away like most animals exposed for too long. She had somehow thrived.

Minnesota was a fancy scientist before the lights. She has this big theory about the air being poisoned by something other than radiation, and she thinks she can find a cure if she gets into a functioning facility. That's why she's a drifter. Her maps are marked up with all the known laboratories she could find, she's been leading our group from lab to lab, trying to collect tools and information and equipment.

The camp doesn't know. They think this is simply our way of life, a bunch of nomads trying to make the most of the barren fields. But this is bigger than survival. This is the difference between living indoors forever or somehow returning to normal. Sooner than we think.

I don't know if I believe in Minty's theory. I'm not one of them smart science folks. But I know if she's right, she really can change the world. And she was counting on Ozzy to help her.

I didn't just get her best buddy killed, I snatched away living proof that life can exist in the Grey.

This is all my fault.

But I'm not about to pay for my mistakes by dragging a little girl across the state as penance.

My thoughts must be written all over my face because Minnesota lifts her chin and says, "She wants to see her family."

"This is a fool's errand," I hiss. "Her family is probably dead, like the rest of ours."

"It doesn't matter. We owe her."

"*Owe* her?"

Minty nods, one forward jerk of her head like she hates to admit it. "We owe her. She gave us information, Erik. Told us about a colony that's been set up at an old airport."

I shrug. "Okay."

"This airport functioned as a military base before the government completely collapsed. I'm willing to bet they've got equipment and data I could use. This could be exactly what I've been looking for."

Minus the miracle pup.

I bunch my shoulders; they suddenly feel heavy—from exhaustion and from the weight of this conversation. Minty really believes she's got a chance to fix things. She believes it enough that she's willing to send me into the Grey to repay a debt for the information she's gained from this mystery girl.

"What if she's making all this up?" I ask.

"She ain't." That's all Minty gives me. A grunt of an answer that sounds so sure and confident, I have no choice but to trust her judgment and accept my fate. But my pride won't let me go down so easily.

"Toccoa is nearly a week of travel on foot," I say, "that's if I walk without ever stopping. We're talking two weeks with rests—even longer if you consider I'll be travelling with a little girl, and avoiding Faceless, and scavenging for food."

Minty just blinks.

"I'll be gone for weeks!" I nearly shout. "We're supposed to be leaving soon. By the time I get back, you'll be gone."

"You're the best tracker in our camp," she says. "You

know how to find us if we get separated."

"Oh, come on, Minnesota!" My voice is a snarl. "This ain't right, and you know it."

"Ozzy's death wasn't right. You wanted to make amends; this is how."

We glare at each other in silence until she sighs and looks away. "Spend the day packing whatever you need. I expect you to be gone by the morning."

"The morning?" I blink. "Minty, I just got back."

She makes a face that's almost a smile, the right corner of her lips pulling up just a tick. "Then you'd better get out of my office if you want some proper rest."

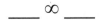

I head straight to my room and sleep for the next few hours. When I wake, my throat is burning, and I know I've left my mask off for too long. As I sit up in bed, I reach for the canteen of water I keep on the stack of crates beside me and chug down half the bottle before I pull my mask on. It zips up the back of my head, completely covering my face. In the dirty mirror on my wall, I can see my greying hair on top of my head, poking out like I'm feral, I can see the scars on my shoulders, going down my arms, and I can see the bruises of my most recent encounter fading on my chest and abdomen.

I sigh and reach for a shirt, placing a jacket over that as I step into my boots. Ozzy died from a punctured lung. The blood stains on my jacket aren't hers, they belong to the dead man who hurt her.

He punched her and threw her down the hall—twice. The second time is what caused irreparable damage. She broke a rib which punctured a lung and caused internal bleeding. So, after I stabbed that wild man to death, I held Ozzy in my arms as she wheezed for breaths that wouldn't come.

I carried her body back myself. It took me two more days of travel, but I did it because Ozzy deserved to be buried with her family. And Minty deserved to have her body back. She might have viewed the dog as an asset, but she still cared for her on some level. At least that's what I tell myself.

Once I'm dressed, I grab a sack and start loading it with supplies. I've got a few bottles I can fill with water, three old MREs, a map I took from Minty's office, my hunting knife, a hatchet...

I stare at the rest of my things in this small space. My room doesn't have much besides survival gear and trinkets I've collected over the years. There had been photos of my son on fishing trips, and a necklace my wife used to wear at one point. But I've thrown them out. My family is dead. No point in holding on to their old junk. It doesn't remind me of *them*, it reminds me that they're gone.

When I finish packing, I sling my bag over my shoulder and step out into the foyer of our little camp. I immediately realize how long I've slept because it's clearly dinner time. The grill is outside but there are plenty of people sitting around inside with plates, eating with their hands and licking their fingers. The food is never all that great, but I brought meat home, so this is basically a feast for everyone.

I weave through the munching nomads and walk outside so I can cross the parking lot to the medical tents. I'll need whatever supplies they can spare; bandages, alcohol, I'll take anything. The doctor with us is actually a former school nurse who is 67 years old and makes me feel young every time I see her wrinkled face through her gasmask. She smiles and says I can take what I need so long as I promise to come back from my trip in one piece.

That lets me know word has spread about Ozzy and the punishment I've received for my irresponsibility. I'm not surprised, word travels fast in our little camp.

From there, I move to our armory and try to convince Mike and Taylor to hand over a few bullets for my pistol but neither of them will budge.

"Minty makes us use a spear and a shield," Mike grumbles. "And we're on her good side. You think she's going to spare ammo for *you*?"

I don't even respond to that, but I do stand there an extra second, wondering if I could take a jab at Mike's fat mouth. He talks too much. And he's ugly enough that losing his two front teeth won't make a difference in his appearance at all. But I decide against it and just walk away without saying goodbye.

By the time I make it out to the grill, our chef is packing up the last of the food, but he still greets me with a smile. "Erik! I saved you a plate," he says, offering me some roasted gopher and what looks like dumplings in some sort of meat gravy. Probably gopher gravy.

I take the plate and hope he can tell I'm smiling behind my gasmask. "Thanks, Thomas."

He nods. "I know you'll need a big meal before you head out."

Sheesh, privacy does not exist here. But at least no one is scolding me for what happened to Ozzy. I think they're all too afraid to mention it.

I nod. "Yeah. Thanks."

Thomas passes me another plate. "Can you take this one to your friend? I don't think she's eaten either."

"My friend?"

"The one you're escorting."

"She's not my friend," I say more harshly than I need to.

Thomas's face sinks, but he continues holding out the plate, so I snatch it from him and stomp away, grumbling complaints under my breath. It isn't until I've left the grill that I realize I have no idea where my *friend* is right now, so I stand in the middle of the parking lot, letting her food get exposed to the poisoned air, while I try to figure out where I should search first.

"Her room is right across from yours," says a voice over my shoulder.

I turn around to find Penn standing in the entrance to the factory with a hand on her cocked hip. "She hasn't left since I took her there, so you can go give her the food before it's too contaminated to eat."

"Why don't you take it?" I shove the plate toward the girl.

She frowns. "I'm not her babysitter." Then she tugs on her gasmask and steps into the parking lot, sauntering past me as she heads toward the grill.

I sigh. "Great."

The plastic room across from mine is dark as I approach. I don't really know what I was expecting. I don't even know what to do now that I'm standing here in front of it.

I can't really knock because the room is made of tarp duct taped together. But I can't just invite myself inside either. She's a girl. All kinds of accusations could be hurled my way if I just barged in.

I set the plate on the floor and turn to walk away but my conscience eats at me, so I turn back and clear my throat. "Girl, there's food out here. If you're hungry."

Girl? I mentally shake my head, not at all surprised when there's no answer.

What was her name?

"Rasheeda," I say. "I've brought you food. So come on out and get it."

Still no answer.

I ball my free hand into a fist. "Whatever, starve then, Rhonda."

"Excuse me?"

I turn around to find the girl from Minty's office staring at me with a bewildered look on her face. My first thought is to go find Penn and drag her around by the hood of her jacket for lying to me. She said the girl hadn't left her room at all.

My second thought is complete embarrassment. First of all, she just caught me talking to no one outside her room. Second of all, this little girl isn't a *girl* at all. I quickly try to find the part of my mind that told me she *was* a girl when I first saw her.

She's younger than me, but she isn't a child. I'd pegged her somewhere around Penn's age when I first saw her. Then again, I hadn't looked at her for more than a few seconds. Now, I can tell she's small and probably still under thirty. But she isn't a little girl at all.

She looks underfed, like most of us, but she also looks afraid. Not of me. Just scared in general.

I'm scared too, but my fear is different. I'm afraid because I know what's out there, and it frightens me. This girl looks like she has no clue what to expect on the journey we're being forced to take together. And she's scared out of her mind because of it.

She's afraid of the unknown. That sort of fear is dangerous. That sort of fear could get us killed. Somehow, I'm positive that's exactly what Minnesota wants.

"Can I help you?" the young lady says. She's not wearing a

gasmask so I can see the way her eyebrows rise slightly when I don't answer right away.

I clear my throat again. "I left you some food."

Her eyes drop to the plate on the floor outside her room. "You brought that for me?"

"Who else?"

She folds her arms. "I don't know, maybe Rasheeda or Rhonda."

I feel a headache coming on. "Look, woman—"

"RaShonda."

That's it…

"*RaShonda*, I brought you food, okay? Eat up and rest up. We're heading out at sunrise."

"What time is that?"

I freeze, blinking behind my mask. What time is sunrise? Is she serious?

"Sunrise is the time the sun rises, cupcake."

She huffs. "I mean… Never mind."

"Eat. Sleep. And meet me outside in the morning. Can you do that?"

"Yes."

I ignore her tight tone and turn away. "Good."

"Where are you going?" she asks behind me.

"To do the same."

I've already packed enough for both of us, and I have no one to say goodbye to. There's honestly nothing left to do except eat and sleep. Even though I just woke up, I feel like I need to lie down again. Something about meeting that girl makes me feel like surviving this trip is going to take everything I've got.

8

Shon

I have the distinct impression that this man hates me. He has spoken exactly eight words to me since we left two days ago.

Miraculously, I did manage to wake up and find my way to the front entrance at sunrise. When Erik glanced up and saw me walking toward him, he nodded and said, "Got everything?" I nodded back, and he passed me a sack of supplies which I crammed into my bag from Rebirth Colony. Then he grunted in his raspy voice, "Well, let's get on it then."

Eight words in the two days we've been walking. And he hasn't spoken to me since.

I wouldn't even know his name if I hadn't been right there when Minty said it in her office. He never introduced himself—he never even told me he would be the one escorting me. I was expected to figure that out by his strange request to meet at sunrise.

Initially, I welcomed the silence. It was early in the

morning, I wasn't in a talking mood anyway, so Erik's broody tension hadn't bothered me. Then the silence shifted into something a bit more sullen, like he wasn't quiet because he was tired and it was early, he was quiet because he didn't want to speak to me.

I was the problem.

Erik marched ahead of me without ever looking back, without ever offering a word or question as to how I was holding up. He never inquired when or if I ever needed a break. He just walked. And walked. And walked. When he was ready, we stopped. When he got hungry, we ate. And when he felt he needed to, he spoke to me. Which, apparently, was never.

Two days into this journey now, I stare at the cracked leather of his black jacket as he walks in front of me. That's all I've been doing. I have memorized the rise and fall of his gait; I have seared the image of the back of his head into my brain. I would recognize his jacket in a mall full of them. It's so old the form of his figure is practically molded into the material.

When he swings his bag around to get his water bottle, I make out the shape of his broad shoulders and how they frame his back. I can see the pokes of his shoulder blades and how the leather crinkles as he stretches and adjusts the straps of his bag before replacing his bottle and shrugging the bag on again.

He's a tall man who takes up more space than he needs, fills out every inch of his clothes, and seems to clear more distance than usual with his long strides. I am speed-walking just to keep up with him, which tires me out faster than normal. But I can't say anything, of course. Because we're still swimming in this dense silent river, drowning in whatever misery Erik is carrying around with him.

Maybe he's really messed up over the dog that died. That's what I've told myself for the last two days, but as time drags on and his mood only darkens, I feel like the dog is the last thing on his mind.

Stupidly, I decide to ask him about it.

"How are you holding up?" I say, almost panting as I try to match his steps. We're walking along a highway, right up the middle of the road. The concrete beneath our feet is cracked, neon daisies poke through the lines in the pavement.

Every car we pass is rusted and covered in a thick layer of dust. Some cars have messages written in the dust on the windows. The driver's window of the pickup beside me says, **GO BACK. KAPPA AHEAD**. I have no idea what that means but Erik doesn't seem bothered, so I tear my eyes away from the eerie warning and jog to walk side by side with him so I can ask again, "How are you holding up?"

Erik casts me a sideways glance, which is difficult to see in his gasmask, but I catch the irritation that flashes in his eyes when he looks at me. "I'm fine," he grunts.

Ten words now. Awesome.

"I'm sorry about Ozzy."

"No, you're not."

I frown. "How do you know what I feel?"

"You didn't know Ozzy. How could you be sorry?"

"A life was taken. That's sad whether you know the victim or not."

Erik keeps walking like I didn't speak at all.

"I had a dog when I was a kid," I tell him. "Her name was Sesame, a little beagle we got as a puppy. I raised her myself."

Erik still doesn't speak.

I sigh. "Have I done something wrong?"

"No."

"Did I say something wrong?"

"No."

I stop walking and grab his shoulder, forcing him to stop too. "Then what's your problem?"

Erik stares at my hand on his arm and then snaps his hard gaze up to meet mine. Even behind the glass eyeholes of his gasmask, I can see his fury. But I still don't understand it.

"What have I done to you?"

He takes a step closer, making me feel shorter than I already am.

"You showed up. I've got to march a child across the state while the only family I've had for the last five years packs up and moves on without me. That's what you've done to me." He yanks his arm from my grasp. "We're wasting time. We're not supposed to break for another hour."

"I'm not a child," I say as boldly as I can.

Erik tilts his head toward me. "No, but you're as burdensome as a child."

"If traveling with me is such a problem for you, then give me the map and I'll make the journey myself."

He laughs. "You wouldn't last a week, cupcake."

Cupcake? That little nickname makes my blood boil. I'm sick of people telling me how useless I am. I'm sick of *feeling* useless. Because I know Erik is right, just like Minty was right. I'm not built for the barren fields. But that doesn't mean I deserve to be treated this way. I was alone before I bumped into Minty, and I managed to survive then. I can do it again now if I have to. God's still on my side, being alone doesn't scare me.

"I can last longer than you think, *old* man." I say that last bit with a little attitude. If he wants to call me a child, then I get to pick at him too. I can tell from the moment of stunned silence that my insult rubbed him a little and it almost makes me smile until he growls out his response.

81

"You wouldn't last a week," he repeats in his southern drawl. His voice is low and almost gravelly, making his accent sound slightly different from Minty's and definitely different from my own. I grew up in Georgia but spending years overseas speaking Spanish and then living in an international airport with people from all over the world for six years has neutralized whatever accent I had before.

But Erik sounds like your everyday cowboy, which is confusing because he has none of that southern charm or hospitality you would expect. He's prickly and irritable and makes it obvious that he doesn't like being around people very much.

I have to fight a very strong urge to kick dust into his face as I say, "I can last longer than you think."

"You ever been in the Grey?"

"Not until recently," I admit.

"You ever had to find your own food or water?"

"No."

"You ever gone *without* food or water?"

"No."

Erik harrumphs like he's just proved some point. "I didn't think so."

As he walks away, I fold my arms and yell, "I've killed a Faceless!"

He stops. Turns slowly. I can't see his eyes very well with the sunlight glaring off his mask, but I can tell from his silence that I've caught him by surprise.

"I've killed two," I say, trying not to shiver as the memory replays in my head. "I got attacked by four of them. They were in a group. I was alone. But I got two."

"How'd you kill 'em?"

"I stabbed one in the eye. And slit the other's throat."

82

Erik doesn't speak for a moment that seems to go on longer than it should. I just stand there, wishing I could sit down because my hip is killing me, but also too proud to take a knee in front of him. He already thinks I'm weak, if I can't walk as long as he can then he'll use that against me. Call me useless and pathetic first chance he gets.

Finally, Erik takes a breath and starts to say something, but he's cut off by the sound of a howl.

Both of us whip around to stare into the distance behind us. The heat shimmers off the metal hoods of the cars abandoned on the road, but beyond the wavy blur, I can see a man-shaped figure standing on top of a truck. It's joined by at least six others who climb onto the vehicles too. They don't howl or screech or roar. They just stand there, watching us.

"Faceless," Erik says behind his mask. "They've been tracking us."

"But…" I step closer to him, as if he can somehow make this situation better. "I thought Faceless were wild and deranged."

"Only once their brain begins to rot." Erik nods at the unmoving bodies that are still standing on the vehicles behind us, perfectly calm and still. "They're still clothed."

Most Faceless abandon their attire in their spiral into madness. Like a child kicking off a diaper and running naked through the house. They strip off their clothes and walk like animals, beating their chests and hunting for human flesh as if they are more beast than man.

But these Faceless are still wearing jeans and shirts, some of them are even wearing shoes. And the one in front has a crowbar in his hand.

"They're recently infected," Erik says, walking backwards through the cars. He has his hands out on either side, feeling his way so he doesn't trip into a vehicle. I start to walk backwards beside him, never moving my gaze from the Faceless. They don't move their gaze either.

"What do they want?"

"What do you think?"

I want to sob, but I take a deep breath instead. If there was ever a time to prove to Erik that I'm not useless, it's now.

"Should we turn and run?" I ask in as calm a voice as I can produce.

"No," Erik says. "Just act normally. After a minute, we'll slowly turn around and face forward. Understand?"

I lick my lips. "What if they chase us down?"

"They won't. Not right away, at least."

"How do you know?"

Erik looks down at me, and even though his face is covered with a mask, I can tell he's frowning. "Because I've been chased by them before."

We turn together and walk side by side through the rows of dead cars. I can feel the hairs on the back of my neck rising with every step I take. Those Faceless are not going to let us get away. They may not be running behind us now, but I won't let myself believe we're in the clear.

When I can't take the crushing anxiety anymore, I turn to glance over my shoulder, but Erik grabs me roughly by my upper arm and keeps me facing forward.

"*Don't* turn around," he orders harshly.

"Are they still behind us?"

"Of course they are."

"Why can't I look?"

"Because I said so."

I yank my arm free and keep marching. We've picked up the pace, taking strides so large and fast I'm a step away from

84

running. "I need to see how close they are," I say quickly.

Erik curses behind his mask and stops dead in his tracks. I almost yell at him to keep moving when I glance over and realize he's staring at something.

Ahead of us, the highway splits into two exits while the main interstate continues forward. The first exit is completely blocked by a bus, the other is blocked by eight Faceless. They stand in a group, huddled like fleshy monsters with scowls on their faces. The pigment has drained from their skin, so they all appear grey with bald heads. The neon blue of their eyes is the only color on them.

The sight of eight Faceless is enough to make me wet my pants, but what truly makes it hard to hold my bladder is the way they're grouped up. The two in front are shirtless men in jeans, glaring at us as they hold crooked weapons—a rusted pole and a thick dead branch. There are four standing behind them, relatively clothed but not holding any weapons.

The last two...

They're completely naked, crouched on all fours like they're animals. And they're wearing chains around their necks. The two in front with the weapons hold the chains, like they've tamed some wild dogs. It's a sight that is so ungodly I have to pinch myself to make sure this is real.

Erik curses again. "They're herding us," he says. "They want us to continue down the interstate."

"What's down the interstate?"

He pauses. "A nest, probably."

"A nest?"

"Where do you think Faceless go when they're not hunting and eating unsuspecting humans?"

I honestly hadn't thought about it before. I didn't need to think about it. Right now, I wish I had.

I look over at the bus blocking the interstate exit. It's not an option for us, we'd have to find a way to climb over it while the eight Faceless just ten yards away chase us down—not to mention the ones who were behind us from the start.

With Erik preoccupied with the Faceless in front of us, I sneak a look over my shoulder and gasp. The wild men we'd first spotted have caught up, walking slowly through the cars. Their heads appear in the distance before the rest of their bodies, popping up over the horizon like well-groomed zombies.

I gulp for air behind my mask, wanting to rip it off so I can have a full-blown panic attack. I feel like I can't breathe. I feel like I'm trapped.

"Erik—"

His big hand clamps down on my shoulder and he makes me face him. "Calm down," he says sternly. "We're going to be okay."

"How can you say that?"

He doesn't respond, instead, he drops to his knees and starts digging through his backpack. A second later, he passes me a signal flare and Everett's words ring through my ears.

Faceless are afraid of fire.

Even the ones Minty saved me from backed away when they threw a flare right in front of me. It didn't send them packing, but it was enough to scare them. At least momentarily.

I take the flare with trembling hands. "What now?"

"Can you run?"

My hip is killing me, but I'm not about to get eaten by Faceless over a sore hip. "Yes," I squeak out. My voice is high and cracks on every word. I sound like a panicked teenager and I hate it. I'm supposed to be proving that I'm not useless. That I can handle myself. But all I've managed to do is panic and ask Erik for directions. Oh well, at least I haven't fainted.

Erik rises slowly, keeping his eyes trained on the Faceless blocking the exit. The ones behind us are still closing the gap, marching through the dead traffic.

"That flare will burn for twenty minutes. That'll give you enough time to find a way over that bus. The Faceless won't chase you because of the flare, so move quickly."

"Why does it sound like you won't be running with me?"

He looks over at me, and for the first time, I don't see any anger in his eyes. All I see is concentration. I have no idea how things will turn out, but it's clear Erik believes everything will be okay. He believes he can get us out of this. I have to trust that he knows what he's doing. After all, Minty chose him for this mission for a reason. She believes he's capable of getting us across the barren fields alive. For some wild, inexplicable reason, I believe that too.

I swallow the lump in my throat. "What will you do?"

"Lead them away."

"Erik—"

"I'll be fine," he grunts in a tone I can't place. Somewhere near anger, teetering on worry.

"Where am I supposed to go?"

"Away from here. I'll find you. Just keep moving. Understand?"

I nod, gripping the flare like it's my lifeline. Technically, it is.

"On three, you run for the bus, I'll run the other way."

"Okay."

He starts counting, but when he reaches number two, he shoves me to the side and yells, "Run, cupcake!"

I am momentarily stunned. The Faceless *aren't*—they immediately launch at us, but I snap to my senses and strike

87

the flare in my hands. A bright burst of red illuminates the area and we have exactly four seconds of stillness.

The Faceless stumble backwards at the mere sight of the red glow from my flare. I hold it high above my head as I run toward the bus. There's a burning flare in my hand, a group of Faceless behind me, and a metro bus in front of me. I have no idea how I'm supposed to climb over this thing, but I've got to try.

9

Erik

When I take off running, I immediately hear footsteps behind me, and I know the plan is working. There is no time to glance over my shoulder. Every second counts. I hear RaShonda yelp as she makes it to the metro bus, but I can't focus on her right now. The only chance she has of getting away is making it over that bus. To do that, she'll need me to lead the Faceless away, so she has the time to climb up. Judging from the sound of rushing feet, I'd say everything is on track. There is a herd of Faceless sprinting behind me as I run toward the edge of the highway.

Awesome.

I yank my hunting knife from my waistband as I make it to the shoulder, it's a long drop to the ground below, but I can't run back in the direction we came from and I'm definitely not going down that interstate. I only have one option.

As I make it to the concrete barricade, I shift my focus to the sound of pursuing feet. There's at least three Faceless on my left, two on my right—I only need one.

When I'm just a few feet from the wall, I slow my pace so the Faceless can catch up. One of them gets greedy and lunges. Perfect. I pivot and raise my hunting knife, stabbing the wild man in the throat. He lets out a guttural cry, but it's cut off when I snatch him toward me and hurl us both over the highway wall.

We drop twenty feet to the ground, but I shift in time, so I land on top of the Faceless. His head whips back upon impact, bursting into a spray of red mist. I don't have to look at his eyes rolled to the back of his head to know that he's dead. But I stare into them anyway, just to make sure.

A loud thud goes off behind me, followed by a piercing shriek of pain. I look over my shoulder to find a Faceless with two broken legs. It just jumped off the interstate right behind me, but it's landing wasn't as pretty. Not that mine was all that great. Every part of my body aches, but I can't think about the pain right now. I've got to move.

There's a group of Faceless staring over the edge of the highway now. I grunt as I push to my feet and wipe off my blade, blinking away the sun to watch one more of the wild men throw themselves over the interstate. He meets the same end as the first guy—two broken legs.

The other Faceless smarten up and shock me by stealing my strategy. I watch in horror as one of the wild men grabs one of its own and leaps over the edge. The captive Faceless shrieks in fear, but his cries end abruptly when he hits the ground. The Faceless holding him down smirks at me as he steps over his dead companion and begins a new chase.

I take off running.

Over the thudding of my heart, I can hear more shrieks and thuds going off beside me. That could only mean I'm being chased by more freaks. The only part of that that doesn't make me panic is the fact that RaShonda is safe. The more Faceless coming after me means she's got a better chance of getting away. Especially since they're killing each other just to hunt me down.

I run as fast as I can, heading west toward the far end of the city. That's where the exit will spit RaShonda out if she took it. I can only hope she followed my instructions and made it over that bus. Even if she didn't, I'll find a way to track her down.

Minty wasn't lying when she said I was the best in the camp. After losing my son, I made it my goal to hone my skills in tracking. I made it my goal to be the best at hunting down my enemies.

RaShonda isn't my enemy, but I will find her if she gets off track.

The Faceless are relentless. They chase me through the roads, slipping on the uneven ground and running into abandoned cars. I open the doors of the cars as I run by, trying my best to slow them down any way possible. One of them runs right into a door and shouts as she crashes into the metal. The other Faceless resort to running like animals over the tops of the vehicles, jumping from car to car.

I run through an old gas station with at least three still in pursuit. They jump over the metal shelves and howl like monsters as I sprint for the door in the back. I barely make it inside and manage to close the door. My chest is heaving, but there's no time to catch my breath. The wild men are banging on the door, I have seconds before they tear it down.

The backroom is dark and partially destroyed, it looks like

it used to be an office. I grunt as I slide the heavy desk across the room, just as I get it in front of the door, one of the Faceless kicks it in, but he's too late. The desk is in the way, forcing the monster to shove against the wall a few more times to make enough room for him to squeeze through.

By then, I'm already running through the back exit, scanning the road left and right, trying to orient myself. I need to head west to find RaShonda, God knows she needs me, but I can't lead these monsters over to her. Otherwise, we'll both be dead.

A shriek cuts through my thoughts and I take off running in what I think is towards the west side of the city. I go through an alley and cut through an overrun neighborhood. Half the houses are scorched, which means this area was close to the initial explosion. I'm not surprised; if the Faceless truly were leading us to a nest, it would be near the initial bombsite, where the radiation is most concentrated.

I throw myself over a metal fence and sprint through the backyard of a destroyed house. The Faceless make it over the fence with ease, gaining speed as they run on all fours now. I spare myself a heartbeat to glance over my shoulder, the sight of them snarling in pursuit almost makes my legs buckle.

With a grunt, I hurl myself over another fence, but the strap of my backpack gets caught. It tears, but not enough to set me loose. I'm stuck to the fence, caught on the jagged wire by my bag. The Faceless are less than ten feet away, howling and shrieking in excitement as they realize that I'm trapped.

"Come on!" I shout, hacking at the strap with my hunting knife. The blade is sharp, it goes clean through the material, but I don't have time to hurl my bag over with me. It's nearly thirty pounds of supplies and it's hanging over my head. If I weren't so exhausted, I would fight for it. But I've been sprinting through the city, getting chased by a group of man-eating monsters for the last twenty minutes.

I don't have the strength.

With a frustrated cry, I tug on my backpack, jerking the entire fence, but it doesn't move. The strap just tears more, the fence somehow hangs on to my bag like it's got its teeth sank into it. A Faceless roars as it slams into the fence, grabbing the bag and ripping it away like it weighs nothing at all. It tears at the sack like it's just found a great prize, meanwhile, the others begin climbing the fence.

I let go of an anguished sob and turn to run with only my hunting knife in my hand.

This is bad. This is so bad. I can't outrun these wild men, but I can't fight them all at once. Not with just a knife. The only choice I have is to force them to separate, but I can't think of how I'm supposed to do that while I'm sprinting through a destroyed neighborhood with no clear goal in sight.

I take a chance and charge through the open patio doors of an abandoned home. I don't realize the doors have been shattered until I slip on the broken glass and land right on the sharp blades. A hiss slips from my lips but that's all the time I have before a Faceless charges through the door right behind me.

Thankfully, the exact same thing happens to him, and the woman behind him. They both slide on the glass and then fall, except they crash into each other—almost comically—and thrash around on the floor as they try to orient themselves.

I rise and limp away, running toward the staircase as my right leg burns in pain. I'm bleeding, I can feel the warmth of the crimson liquid running down my jeans, but I can't assess the damage just yet.

A thud behind me lets me know the Faceless are still

coming. I don't know how many there are, but I'm in a narrow hallway now. They aren't separated like I want them, but they've got to approach single file. That'll have to work.

The first one in the hall is a large shirtless man whose face is swollen and bleeding. He shouts like an animal as he throws himself at me. I brace myself and raise the knife, grunting as it sinks into his chest. He thrashes against me, blinded by pain and the animal instinct to kill its prey.

There is a Faceless woman behind him, climbing on his back and biting at my mask. Flecks of spit fly out her rotten mouth and dirty the glass eyeholes of my gasmask. Meanwhile, a third Faceless rams into her back and full on tackles her. The force sends all four of us toppling to the ground. I'm getting buried beneath three wild people who want to eat me.

The hilt of my knife rams into my ribs. I feel them bend inwards as all the wind is knocked out of me. I scream behind my mask, but I doubt anyone can hear it. Everyone in this hallway is screaming or howling or shrieking in both pain and anger.

The Faceless right on top of me is still alive. Thankfully, he's more focused on his injury than on eating me. He shoves onto his hands and knees and glares into my mask, but the woman behind him is still trying to climb over his back. In anger, he forces himself to his feet and reaches over his shoulder to grab the woman by her shirt. I watch in horror as he slams the Faceless woman into the wall. The plaster cracks and caves in with the force of the blow. The woman cries out in pain, clawing at the Faceless man's eyes and nose.

I frantically scoot away and scramble to my feet while the Faceless tussle amongst themselves. Another pang of defeat washes through me as I glance at my hunting knife still buried in the chest of the Faceless man. I've got a pocketknife in my boot, but it's nowhere near as good as that weapon. I have a distinct memory of the same thing happening to me not long ago. I am tired of losing my weapons to the very things I'm defending myself against.

But it's not like I can just walk up and yank my knife free from the Faceless man who is using his fists to pound on the Faceless woman's head. She cries out at each blow, but he's enraged and not letting up. The other wild man watches in fear as his leader kills one of his own companions. After a moment, the fretful man scurries away like a scared dog. I take this chance to do the same.

There's a window at the end of the hall, like the patio doors, they're busted out with glass littering the floor. My boots crunch on the broken shards as I swing my leg over the windowpane. All at once, the thudding sound of a fist hitting a face stops.

I glance back to see the angry Faceless man staring right at me. The body of the Faceless woman is in his hands; she's unconscious, or dead. I can't tell. But her face is smashed in, and her shirt is smeared with blood. Her left hand twitches as the man drops her limp body to the floor. She doesn't move.

A growl fills the hallway, it's all I need to hear before throwing myself out the second-floor window. I land hard, and roll to the side, trying to ease the jarring impact. My leg was already bleeding, I'm sure I just added a sprained ankle to my list of injuries. Regardless, I force myself to my feet and start limping away, wondering how on earth I'm going to escape the Faceless man behind me.

I hear the thud of his landing over my shoulder, it's accompanied by a painful cry that pulls me to a halt. When I look back, I see the Faceless lying flat on his back, arms splayed out like he's making a snow angel. He doesn't try to get up. He doesn't try to move at all. I can see his chest rising and falling, letting me know he's still alive, and in his chest is my knife. Four inches of sharpened metal buried in his lung.

I sigh with relief. He might be Faceless, but he still needs oxygen. Right now, he's sucking for air, but he isn't breathing. In fact, he's drowning in his own blood.

I limp back over to his heavy body and drop to my knees beside him. He glares at me, and huffs in anger as he tries to reach for me, but he's already too weak. He's lost too much blood, and he's drowning in whatever's left.

"You were human once," I say, though I doubt he can understand me. He might be wearing clothes, and he might be conscious enough to feel emotions like fear or anger, but his humanity is gone. He is an animal, hunting for prey, searching for food.

His hunt is about to end.

"You're not human anymore," I rasp, gripping the hilt of my blade. With one yank, it comes free, and the Faceless man lets out a whimper that is eerily human. For the first time, he doesn't sound like a feral animal, and the expression on his face doesn't look like the bloodthirsty man who'd tried to kill me and then killed his own companion in a blind rage. His hands are still covered in that woman's blood. I stare at his knuckles as he makes a fist, grabbing at the dirt in pain.

"Just die," I whisper.

Finally, he does. One last breathless gasp sucks in through his flared nostrils, then it comes back out in a whistle as his eyes roll to the back of his head and his mouth sags open. I am shocked to see a tear slip from the corner of his eye. Other than that, he looks like the monster he'd been a few moments earlier. Except now he's dead.

I let out a long sigh. I am so tired. So sore. But I've got to find RaShonda. There's still one more Faceless out there, but he ran off in fear and isn't likely to come back anytime soon. I could retrace my steps and see if the Faceless destroyed all my supplies in my bag. Then I'll get started on tracking down the woman. She'd told me she was tougher than I gave her credit for. Maybe she's right—she's killed two Faceless, after all. But only time will tell. Which means I've got to hurry.

10

Shon

When Erik shoves me to the side and takes off running, I immediately snap into focus. Despite the pounding of my heart, despite how badly my hands are shaking, despite the fact that I glance over my shoulder to see Erik throw himself over the edge of the highway, I run like mad toward the metro bus.

It's parked horizontally so it blocks the highway exit. The tires are deflated, and the windows are busted. I'm too short to reach up and grab anything, but I'm not too short to jump up and try.

With a shout, I use the momentum of my sprinting head start to jump onto the hood of the bus. I jam my foot into the gaps of the hubcap on the massive tire, thankful to God that I wear a size 7 and not a 13-wide like my good old country grandmother, bless her soul. Still, the gap isn't very large, and I have to reach up to hold on to the sideview mirror, so I don't slide right off the hood of the bus. This is awkward to do with a signal flare burning in my hand, but I manage to slowly crawl up the side of the hood and throw myself onto it.

I roll onto my back and allow myself to breathe for exactly two seconds before I sit up and begin climbing down the other side of the bus. That's when I hear it. The rattling of chains.

Two of the Faceless had chains tied around their necks like they were dogs on a leash. And now I hear their chains rattling somewhere nearby. Maybe they're chasing Erik. Maybe they're keeping guard. Maybe—

My thoughts are cut short when a Faceless appears above me, snarling as it shrieks. I scream and almost lose my footing, then the Faceless takes a swipe at me and I *do* lose my footing. I fall to the ground and drop the signal flare, it rolls back toward the bus, almost going underneath it, but I dive for it and manage to scoop it up in time.

When I look back up, the chained Faceless is right in front of me, and there's another climbing over the bus. I gulp and start backing up, trying not to make any sudden movements.

It doesn't matter.

The Faceless runs at me, letting out a piercing cry that is not human at all. Its mouth is a black pit in its face, its eyes are neon gems that somehow appear cold and dead. I can see the veins in its face as it leaps at me, they are just as bright and blue as the radiation of its pupils.

Without thinking, I raise my hands in defense as the Faceless tackles me to the ground. *It should be afraid! I've got a flare in my hands!* But this Faceless is naked and chained, it's completely mindless, unable to feel fear any longer.

I can smell the scent of decay on its body as it pummels me. Its hits aren't even as strong as I would expect, not like the Faceless that'd dragged me backwards out of a car just days ago. This one is half starved and its muscles have withered away. I'm fighting a skeleton—one I can overpower.

99

I let out a cry as I roll us over and grip the only weapon I've got in my hand. The signal flare sinks into the soft goo of its eye, burning that pretty blue iris away. It shrieks madly and bangs its head against the concrete in pain. I figure that's gruesome enough—plus, I hear the rattling chains of the second Faceless climbing over the bus—so I leave the monster there to die as I turn and sprint away.

Thank God for those chains. They're slowing down my pursuer, making it easy for me to gather myself and form a plan. I'm not going to get away from this thing; it might be mindless, but it's high functioning enough to chase down its target until it catches it. Like a dog after a bone. I'll need to face it eventually, but some part of me wants to hold off on that for as long as possible.

The Faceless are flesh-eating monsters, but they were human once before. I could end up as a Faceless. Erik could end up as a Faceless. Killing them is still taking a life. And I haven't decided how I feel about that yet. I've done it twice now—probably three times if that flare burned through that wild man's brains. But each time it was life or death. Kill or be killed.

Is there a way to shake off this Faceless? Could I fool it into chasing something else?

I shake my head at my own foolishness as I run down the ramp of the highway exit. It lets me out at a fork in the road. If I were driving a car, I could keep going straight, or turn left onto the main road. Erik told me to take the exit, but his instructions ended there. Where do I go now? What do I do now?

I hear the chains getting closer, so I make my decision and turn left. The area slowly becomes what looks like a once busy street. Little shops and storefronts, even a church sits proudly on this road, but I don't have time to look at any of the buildings. The Faceless is still running behind me like a dog. I'm panting with the effort to stay ahead of it, even though it's slowed down by restraints. I can't keep this up forever—not with my aching hip. I've got to stop and fight or throw it off somehow.

I duck into an old pizzeria and dash behind the front counter. The kitchen is lined with overturned boxes and tables that'd once been covered in flour and dough. It's obvious the place is old and has been looted; the register is totally gone, and the drawers are all open. The cabinets are the same, but I start closing them as I run through the kitchen.

When I hear the sound of chains enter the pizza shop, I yank off my backpack, toss it into a cabinet and slam it shut. Then I pull my hunting knife from my waistband and climb into a different cabinet. I swing it shut as quietly as I can, closing myself inside. Then I sit and wait.

Thank God I'm a small woman, even before the apocalypse began. The cabinet is small, but there's just enough room for me to fit if I hug my knees to my chest. There are slivers of light cutting into the darkness of the little space, I can see through them if I tilt my head to the side.

Over the sound of my beating heart, I can just make out the footfalls of the Faceless, even louder than that is the sound of the chain around its neck dragging behind. I hear it walking through the dining area of the pizza parlor. I hear it hop onto the counter and sniff around. When it begins walking through the kitchen, I hold my breath and fight the urge to squeeze my eyes shut.

I need to stay alert. I need to be ready in case it finds me. Judging from the way it's sniffing at the floor, I know it'll find me soon. It takes long breaths, inhaling the dust and blowing it around in a grey cloud. I can't see it fully through the tiny slivers on the sides of the cabinet door, but I can make out enough to know that this Faceless is a woman. She's on her hands and knees, thin enough that I can see her spine as she leans down and sniffs the floor. Without any hair, it's hard to make out her age; plus, the fact that she's malnourished and behaving like an animal.

When she lifts her face and inches toward the cabinet with my backpack inside, I get a good look at her front with her skin stretched taut over her small ribs. She can't be more than maybe fifteen years old.

I haven't seen many Faceless before but, for some reason, the thought of one of them being a child seemed a complete impossibility until now. I watch with tears misting my eyes as the teenaged Faceless hesitantly approaches the cabinet holding my backpack. My scent is in two different locations, throwing her off. She doesn't know which cabinet to approach, as she looks toward the one I'm in and then turns back toward the backpack cabinet.

I don't give her the chance to decide.

With a cry, I burst from my cabinet, wielding my knife. The Faceless is young, but she's still wild. She shrieks and runs at me, totally unafraid. The look in her eye is enough to make my steps falter. I slip just as she nears me, and instead of stabbing her in the eye, my blade slices across her face and cuts open her cheek.

She yelps as she tackles me to the floor, my head whips back and smacks the tile. Stars burst in my vision, but I'm shaken back to focus by the Faceless trying to claw out my eyes. Her attempts are unsuccessful since I'm wearing a gasmask that wraps around my head. After a moment, she gives up on clawing at my face and starts pounding her fists on my chest.

All the air rushes out of me in a painful shout. I curl up and turn on my side, which only makes the pounding worse as she starts hammering at my ribs. My hunting knife is still gripped tightly in my hand. All I've got to do is raise it and stab, but I can't get myself to move.

This Faceless is just a child. A teenager who didn't ask for this. Who wouldn't be fighting me right now if she were in her right mind. Even though she's hurting me, I can't gather the strength to look her in the eyes and take her life.

So I do it with my eyes shut.

I scream as I roll over, swinging my arm in an arc. The blade cuts blindly through the air—I have no idea where I've stabbed the girl, but I know I've stabbed *something* as I feel the knife connect and then I hear her shriek.

When the blade is yanked from my hand, my eyes pop open and I see the Faceless girl crawling across the floor as she wails in pain. The knife is buried in her temple. A trail of blood drips behind her, bright red drops plopping on the tile, mixing with the dust as she scrambles away in search of safety.

She won't find any.

I am not big on hunting. I've never had the stomach for it. But there were times my dad would drag me out on his weekend trips to try to toughen me up. One thing he always told me was to be brave. Not brave enough to pull the trigger, brave enough to pull it *twice*. Because if you miss your kill shot, then you've got an injured animal running wild through the woods. And it's your job to put it out of its misery. To end its suffering.

I was never brave enough to pull the trigger twice. So I never tried to kill anything when I went hunting with my father. I remember purposely missing a beautiful buck and watching with a smile as it dashed away to safety. My father had ranted and raged at me for my poor aim, but I'd been happy. I had shown it mercy. I had saved its life.

Right now, I've got to show a different sort of mercy. The sort that ends suffering for good.

I push to my feet and follow the droplets of blood through the kitchen. It doesn't take me long to find the injured Faceless. She's huddled in a corner by a rusted metal garbage can, lying on her side and staring up at the ceiling.

For a moment, I think she's already dead, but then her eyes snap over to me and I suck in a gasp. She doesn't move, just lies there staring, almost pleading for me to end her pain. With a breath, I step toward her and grant her this wish.

My hand closes around the handle of the knife and I tug it free. The Faceless whimpers in pain, squeezing her eyes shut. She seems so human right now, I almost break down into tears, but my sympathy seizes in my chest when she opens her mouth and says, "C-Cup … Kay…"

I stare down at her.

Cup Kay?

My eyes enlarge. She's trying to say *cupcake*, the nickname Erik gave me as an insult. He shouted it before he shoved me and ran off with the other Faceless chasing after him. I had no idea anyone else had heard—I mean, *of course* they'd heard. But I'm shocked that they understood. That there was enough comprehension left inside for them to remember. And to repeat it later.

Is she still human?

Does comprehension make you human? Does understanding make you less feral?

Worst of all… If she's human, is it alright to kill her?

I stand there with my hands trembling, my knees

104

threatening to buckle. I don't know what to do. This Faceless just spoke to me. She couldn't really say the word right, but she had said *something*. Is she still human inside? Has her brain somehow remained intact? If I raise this blade, would I be stabbing a wild animal or a teenage girl?

I can't get myself to move. I can't get myself to make a decision. This changes everything. Maybe Faceless can get better. Maybe they can return to normal. Maybe Minty is right and there is a cure for whatever this is.

Or maybe she's wrong. Maybe this isn't proof of comprehension or understanding at all. Maybe it's one last breath, the vestiges of her mind convulsing in psychological death throes. I'm not a doctor, scientist, or psychiatrist. I have no idea what this truly is. But I know what I heard and it's enough to leave me standing there as this Faceless child stares up at me, begging for a mercy I can't give her anymore.

I can't do it.

"I'm sorry." I drop the blade and fall to my knees beside her. "I'm so sorry."

She doesn't respond. She doesn't even move. When I look closer, I realize she's dead.

I sit there beside her lifeless body, wondering if I'm evil for murdering these Faceless people or if I'm a fool for even caring. Does it really matter that this particular Faceless was a young girl? Does it matter that she'd been trying to kill me first? I have no idea, but I pray to God for answers anyway.

Please… I beg inside. *What am I supposed to make of this? How am I supposed to live with myself after what I've done?*

I don't get an answer. But I wasn't really expecting one. I haven't prayed regularly in years, why would God answer me now that I've finally made time for Him?

I shake my head. God isn't like that. He's not petty like us humans. He'll answer in due time. At least that's the hope I plant in my heart as tears well up in my eyes. They blur my vision until they spill down my cheeks, but I can't wipe them away because of my gasmask. So I sit there in misery, sobbing like a child, wondering when this will end.

I have no idea how long I've been sitting in that spot when I hear something enter the pizzeria. I don't react at all. I don't have the will or the strength to get up and fight, to kill something or someone else.

Heavy footsteps limp through the dining area, stopping briefly at the counter.

I don't care. I just sit there, waiting for my fate to come.

Blankly, I blink around the dim room and realize how dark it is. I can barely make out the young body of the Faceless girl before me. *How long was I zoned out?* I wonder, as I take a deep breath. Those dragging footsteps are closer now, probably following the trail of blood. It's only a matter of seconds before another Faceless rounds the corner and eats me.

How pathetic that I traveled across the world in pursuit of God's Voice, only to die alone in the back of a pizza shop. That thought makes me angry. It makes every part of me come alive with rage. Not toward God. Not even toward myself. I'm ticked off at the barren fields. At the wild men and women who've succumbed to the madness of radiation poisoning. At the Faceless who've forced me to kill, cut, and maim the things I struggle to see as human.

That burning anger makes me reach for my knife. It makes me push to my feet and brace myself for the moment that monster rounds the corner. I'll swing with all my might and catch it off guard. Unlike the Faceless teenager, I won't miss the first time.

The steps grow nearer. My breath hitches in my throat.

Almost there…

I grip my knife and glance down at the floor. The moment I see the tip of someone's shoe poke around the corner, I launch like a madwoman.

The Faceless grunts and catches my wrist, shocking me with his reflexes, but I'm more shocked by the words that spill from his lips.

"Hold it, cupcake! It's me!"

I scream, and then I drop the knife and start sobbing. Erik pulls me into his chest and pats the back of my head. I hear the moment he sees the Faceless girl just a few feet away from us. He sucks in a gasp and his arms tighten around me.

"Oh, cupcake," he says miserably. "Oh, cupcake."

11

Shon

We've been holed up for four days now. We found an abandoned auto shop on the city strip, past an old mini mall and a Wal-Mart Supercenter. I suppose we could have stayed in the pizzeria, but I couldn't stand to be around that dead girl anymore.

It didn't take much convincing to get Erik to leave. Despite his rigid demeanor, he can be sympathetic when he wants. Perhaps *too* sympathetic. It wasn't until he nearly passed out on the road that I realized he was hurt.

Every part of my mind went into a frenzied panic when Erik toppled over, lying face-first on the ground. I had screamed and dragged him to the first building I could find. The auto shop was dirty and offered no sense of comfort with its hard concrete floors and metal lockers full of rusted tools. But it only had two entrances—one of which was a garage door I could close and guard easily. So I settled down there.

Erik is hurt. He's not dying, but he is in pain. I have no idea what happened while we were separated—he won't tell me anything except that he fought some Faceless. Honestly, I don't need the details. The bruises on his skin tell me all I need to know.

I stare down at him as he sleeps, chest rising and falling in a rhythmic pattern. His breaths are strained, and not because of the gasmask he's wearing. It's because of the purple bruises on his chest and abdomen. His ribs are bruised. I'm not a doctor, I can't tell. But the discoloration on his chest looks nasty, and I doubt the two aspirins we've got will make much of a difference.

Even if they *would* make a difference, Erik won't take them. Those two little white pills are the only medicine we've got, he says it would be a waste to use them on himself. That's flattering, but if I have to sit here for another day and listen to his ragged breathing, I'm going to lose my mind.

Erik grunts in his sleep, eyes squeezing tightly shut. I'm kneeling beside him, trying to decide if I should wake him or go out scavenging alone. I'm afraid to leave him alone. Afraid that I'll come back and find him dead. But I'm also afraid of the Faceless.

I sigh, staring at my companion. There are other bruises on his chest, scars with stories he'll never tell me. When Everett was twenty, he got stabbed by a wild man in the barren fields. There's a small scar where the knife punctured him, right above his naval. Erik's got a similar looking scar on his abs, only it's twice as big as Everett's and partially distorted by a tattoo. He's got a few of them that start at his neck and end at his hips, dipping into the waistband of his jeans.

Angelena—the name of a woman over his heart. An angel with one wing in the middle of his chest, words in a language

109

I can't read, and a collection of bold black lines that form a pattern I don't understand.

I wonder what story they tell.

Erik's a rugged man. Tall and strong with scars I don't understand and a story I'll never truly know. His hair is salt and pepper, his eyes are sharp when they aren't hard and cold, and his hands are big as mittens—calloused and always clenched into tight fists. I'm positive this man could kill me if he wanted. But he's chosen to protect me instead.

And now... he looks so weak. He looks so frail.

Somehow, I have become his only protection. I am the lifeline he'd once extended to me.

Tears prick the backs of my eyes. I'm so scared. I don't know what to do, but I've got to do *something*. We're low on supplies. Erik's bag was ripped by the Faceless he fought, they destroyed half his things, leaving us with only a fraction of the food and gear we'd left with. Thankfully, it rained yesterday so we were able to refill our water bottles. But it's not enough. We need more.

We've got maybe two days before things get dire, but that's not enough time. Erik won't be back on his feet in two days. Not without divine intervention.

I press my lips together. *God, if there was ever a time...*

Without thinking, I close my eyes and begin to pray. *I can't get through this without You. I don't deserve Your help, Jesus, but I'm asking for it anyway. Because I believe You're a God of mercy. As forgiving as You are loving. Please forgive me and Erik for our sins. Please help us... Somehow... In Jesus' Name, amen.*

When I open my eyes, I jerk backwards, shocked to find Erik's eyes open. He's looking right at me, a blank expression on his face.

"You're awake," I whisper.

110

He nods and starts to sit up, hissing through his gasmask.

"Take it slow," I say, but he doesn't listen. Erik struggles to a sitting position and then groans as he reaches for his shirt. I help him dress in silence, like this is our daily routine. His skin feels dewy from sweat, his abs flex at my touch. I can't tell if it's from the pain he feels or something else.

"How long did I sleep?" Erik's voice is so hoarse I can hardly understand him.

"It's afternoon now."

He nods once, green eyes blinking around the room. "You picked a nice spot."

"You told me yesterday." And the day before. He's been a little delirious these last few days, then again, he hasn't been eating or drinking much.

I pass him a water bottle. People can get crazy when they're dehydrated, I need Erik in the best shape possible if I want to survive the rest of this trip.

He takes the water and slowly removes his mask. The dark circles beneath his eyes make me catch my breath. He looks terrible.

"We're almost out of supplies. I want to go scavenging."

Erik shakes his head.

"We need food and water—"

"I know what we need," he says sharply. "I can get it—"

"Let me help."

His eyes snap to meet mine, and I feel his anger heat up the room. "You almost got killed."

"So did you."

He grunts, then hisses as he cradles his ribs. "I'm a *drifter*. I can handle whatever the Grey throws at me. But you—"

I bristle at his words. "I can't find my own food or water. I can't even read the map you've got. But I can fight." I lift my chin. "I'm not the one who can barely move right now."

For a second, I think he's going to start yelling. I even brace myself for the insults I know are coming. Erik might be injured, but he's still the man who called me useless and walked two days in complete silence because he'd rather pretend I don't exist than acknowledge me as a companion.

But instead of getting angry, Erik lowers his gaze to the concrete floor and nods. It's a small gesture that shouldn't mean much but, somehow, I feel like it's just given us a chance to possibly make it through this trip without killing each other. Erik doesn't like me, but I think he's just agreed to at least respect me.

"Maybe you're tougher than I thought," he admits.

I almost smile. "Maybe I am."

"But that doesn't mean you should be out there alone. It's dangerous."

"You almost sound concerned."

He laughs and then winces, clutching his abs. "I promised Minty I'd get you home safe. I intend to keep that promise."

I watch in silence as he finishes the water and replaces his gasmask. "Minty told me her theory," I say slowly, "a theory that the air is poisoned with something else, not radiation."

Erik just blinks.

"That Faceless girl in the pizzeria..." I shiver at the memory of her dead eyes, at her starved frame and her leathery grey skin. "She spoke to me before she died."

"What did she say?"

"She tried to say 'cupcake.' The name you called me before you ran away."

It's silent for a moment.

"Do you believe Minty's theory?" I ask.

Erik shifts on the sleeping bag he'd been lying on. "It

doesn't matter what's in the air."

"Yes, it does. If Minty's right, then there's a chance she can develop an antidote for the poison in the air. There's a chance she can reverse what's happened to the Faceless."

Erik laughs at me. "There's also a chance that Minty is wrong. And even if she's right," his eyes harden behind his mask, "there's a chance she *can't* produce an antidote. There's a chance the antidote only works for those who *haven't* been infected. There's a chance the Faceless are dead no matter what."

"You sound like you don't want them to have a chance," I whisper.

Erik grunts, and I can't tell if it's in pain or anger. "Do you know why we call them Faceless?" he asks me.

"The radiation makes their skin rot. It falls off and leaves them literally faceless."

He nods. "There's another reason. Before the radiation causes their skin to fall off, it takes their hair. It turns their eyes neon blue. It turns their skin grey." Erik wheezes out a sigh. "Before the Faceless die, they lose everything. Their emotions, their minds, and their identity."

He's right. If you lined up a hundred Faceless, you wouldn't be able to tell them apart. They all look the same. Grey-skinned humans with neon blue eyes and bald heads. They are faceless because they have the same face. The same features. The same lost mind.

Erik chuckles darkly. "They're dead, RaShonda. Accept it."

For a long moment, neither of us speaks. I stare at Erik, wondering what's got him so pensive and bitter. And then I remember the name I saw tattooed on his chest. Over his heart.

"She turned into one of them, didn't she?" I ask in almost a whisper.

Erik blinks, one tick of his eyelids that I almost miss. "Who?"

"Angelena. The woman whose name is tattooed over your heart."

The silence that follows is so suffocating, I want to scream. But I force myself to sit there and endure Erik's hot glare. He's too weak to hurt me. But he doesn't need his fists to relay his anger. I can feel his dark mood storming through the little shop as easily as I feel the sweaty heat of the Georgian summer outside. He hates me, this man I've saved. He hates me.

"Who was she?" I dare to ask.

His voice is a low growl. "None of your business."

"It is. We're stuck together. I've been looking after you these last four days, I think I deserve to know something about you."

"You don't deserve anything, cupcake," he sneers.

"You expect me to just travel in silence again? Like strangers?"

"I expect you to keep quiet and be thankful there's someone crazy enough to take you across the state." He leans closer to me, hissing through his mask. "I don't owe you anything. Not a story or an explanation."

I take a breath, trying to be brave. I don't know why this means so much to me. I don't know why I've got to have details about Erik's life, but the more he resists telling me, the more I want to pry. He's saved my life and I've helped him heal. We're even. We're partners. It's time he treats me as such.

"Was she your wife?" I ask, looking him dead in the eye. When he doesn't answer, I realize I'm right... and my heart breaks for him.

Erik looks away.

"That's why you don't care about Minty's theories. Because

114

it doesn't matter for Angelena whether there's a cure or an antidote." I swallow hard. "She's already dead. Isn't she?"

A shaky breath fills the space between us, and I watch in silence as Erik's walls come down, brick by brick. He closes his eyes and sags his shoulders, like he's just set down the weight of the world.

"She was the love of my life," he says. "Pretty, like you. Same dark brown skin and thick afro hair." Erik swallows. "We were married for thirteen years. Even had a son, an eight-year-old who wanted to be a pilot."

"Did you lose them in the explosions?"

Erik shakes his head. "When the bombs went off, the National Guard rolled in and evacuated the city. We were given ten minutes to pack, and then we were escorted to the shelter assigned to our neighborhood." He pauses, as if in thought. "The shelter didn't last long. Comms were down. Power was out. People were scared. It took less than a month for a group of people to attack the guards and raid the supplies for themselves."

That sounds horrible. Minty told me I'd lived a cushy life in the airport—for the first time, I believe her. I didn't experience the panic that gripped the nation. I didn't experience the fight for survival and supplies. I didn't experience the slow decline of government forces. But Erik did—with his wife and his eight-year-old son.

He shudders as he exhales slowly, like the memories playing in his head pain him. "When the guards went down, chaos broke out. I grabbed whatever supplies I could and left the shelter with my family. We hit the road and lived on the move for a month. I had no idea where to go or what to do. But I knew we had to keep moving."

I nod as I listen closely.

"That's when I met Minty. She took us in with her husband and her sister. For three months, everything was fine. Well…" he laughs, but it sounds more like a sob, "things were as fine as they could be. Minty taught me how to hunt and track things. We learned some skills along the way, but we did it together. We survived together."

I had no idea his connection to Minty went so far back.

Erik looks up at me, his voice strained as he says, "Then everything changed."

I feel a chill run down my spine.

"We bumped into some drifters. But they were bad folks. Horrible folks." His jaw clenches. "They killed my son… They killed Minty's husband… They tried to kill me. But they failed." He sniffles behind his mask. "I was stabbed and left for dead. Bleeding out on the ground as I watched six men drag my wife away, along with Minty and her sister. It took me a while to get better. It took me a while to bury my son. But when I got back on my feet, I set out again." Erik looks me in the eye, never breaking contact, voice never wavering as he says, "I tracked them down. All six of them. And I killed each one."

"Your wife," I whisper.

He shakes his head. "It took me months to find them. By the time I caught up… it was too late. My wife and Minty's sister were lost. Minty herself was broken."

"Broken?" I repeat.

"Why do you think those wanderers killed the men but took the women, Shon? What do you think they wanted with them?"

I gulp for air behind my mask. I won't believe it. Even though Erik had witnessed the horror firsthand, I just can't get myself to stomach the idea of human trafficking. The government had shut down, the world had been thrown into chaos. But had things truly been that bad beyond the safe walls of the airport? Had people truly fallen to that level?

Erik curses softly, his hands balling fists into the material of his sleeping bag beneath him. "They sold them like slaves. Used them like animals. And when they were done, they threw them out like trash. Minty's sister got infected and was left to starve as a Faceless. My wife was killed for trying to escape. But I found Minty alive. I got her out of there."

"And she still sent you away with me," I say without thinking.

Erik lifts his mask to wipe at his wet eyes. "She knows I'm strong enough to survive out here. And I think she just wanted space again."

"Space?"

He nods. "It's hard for her to be around me sometimes. It's hard to be reminded of everything we had, and how quickly we lost it. I feel it too. The pain inside, whenever I'm around Minty. We both lost everything."

"But you saved her."

He nods. "I guess that's why she trusts me with you."

I don't know what to say to that, so I try to change the subject. "Well, you're going to disappoint her if we end up starving to death."

Erik sighs. "What supplies do we have left?"

I reach for my bag and start randomly pulling things out. "A few strips of jerky, some duct tape, a lighter, three water bottles—" I pause as my hand brushes the Bible I'd stuffed into my bag. I hadn't even realized it was in there, but now that I'm staring at it, I remember the moment I'd pulled it out of my makeshift drawer at Rebirth Colony and crammed it into the bag.

Erik shifts beside me, trying to see what's in my hands. I

hear him make a funny noise when he realizes what I'm staring at.

"Fire starter?" he asks, eyebrow quirked.

I press my lips together. "No."

"Then why do you have a Bible?"

"Because I want to read it."

I can't describe the look on Erik's face except to say that he certainly was not expecting me to declare that I wanted to read the Word of God. I shouldn't be surprised; Everett didn't understand why I held on to my beliefs either. *I* don't even understand why I've held on, but when I think about it, I think maybe I haven't.

I don't remember the last time I read the Bible. Even though I packed it, I still haven't bothered to crack it open. I'm on this journey now because I believe God spoke to me. But there are days I have to convince myself that's really the case. That I'm not crazy.

Maybe I didn't hold on to my beliefs. But God certainly held on to *me*. He never left me and He didn't forsake me. He's always been there, just like He promised He would be. Right now, it feels like I'm literally in the valley of the shadow of death, but I can't let the fear of the barren fields or the look of doubt on Erik's face stop me from trying to rebuild what was forgotten.

I didn't hold on. But nothing says I can't take it back. Nothing says I can't believe again.

"God told me to go home," I say softly, running my fingers over the old leatherbound Book. "I had been living in Barcelona for three years when He spoke to me. Without hesitation, I packed my bags and caught a flight back to Georgia." I laugh. "The moment my plane landed, the explosions went off. I spent six years living in an airport.

118

Hiding from the job God sent me to do."

"God sent you to do a job?" Erik sounds like he's talking to a toddler, trying to make sense of some wild story I've just made up, but I ignore the doubt in his voice. I can't be mad at him for doubting when I hardly believe it myself.

"God told me to go home. I haven't made it there yet."

"What's at home?" he asks.

I shrug. "I'm hoping my family is there."

"What sort of family did you have?"

"I had a mother and a father. A grandmother who babysat me on weekends. And I had…" I hesitate as a child's face flashes before my eyes. "I had a little brother. I'm praying to God he's still alive."

"What if he's not?"

I sniffle. "I have to believe that he is. God kept me alive all this time. Why wouldn't He keep my brother alive too?"

Erik grumbles to himself but I can't make out his words.

"You don't believe in God," I say gently.

For a moment, he doesn't speak. Just when I think he isn't going to respond at all, Erik looks up and sighs. "My wife did." That's the only answer he gives me before he leans back on his sleeping bag, wincing all the way. "First thing tomorrow, we're heading out."

12

Shon

We walk for what seems like hours, moving at a snail's pace. After enjoying a can of peaches in heavy syrup together, Erik and I set out at the very crack of dawn. He walked without a limp, but his pace was slow, and his breathing was labored. Even though he hasn't complained at all, I haven't bought his tough guy act for a second. Then again, we are down to minimal supplies and two bottles of water. He isn't being tough at all; he's trying to survive.

Erik's drive makes me shove aside my own exhaustion and match his every footfall. We duck into abandoned buildings, searching for supplies. We open the trunks of rusted cars. We overturn crates we find on the street. Our day is slow and laborious and doesn't yield a profit at all.

It's early afternoon by the time we finally decide to take a break. We're on the outskirts of a new city, someplace I've never been, but a place that looks like it might have been beautiful six years ago. The entire country looks like the set of an apocalypse film, even though it's been less than a decade since the explosions. With the toxins and radiation killing everything, the world around us looks like the remains of a planet that died centuries ago. Everything is crumbling. Everything is dead.

Fields of neon blue daisies stretch out before me. They stick up like starbursts of unnatural color, effervescent beauty that gives me chills. I can't help but frown.

Beside me, Erik grunts as he sits on his butt and leans back on his elbows. "Another dead city."

I nod. "You ever been here before?"

He eyes me through his mask. "I've been a lot of places."

"I forgot you're a drifter."

"Even before then." He sighs. "I was a truck driver before the explosions."

Well, that explains why he's so familiar with so many places. I feel like a deer in headlights following him around, staring blankly at our map when Erik isn't using it. I have never felt so dumb in my life.

"What about you?" Erik's raspy voice fills the silence.

I blink at him. "Me?"

"What did you do before the explosions?"

"I was in college. A senior, actually."

"Which college?"

"It was overseas, in Barcelona."

"You went to college overseas?"

I nod. "I wanted to study abroad."

"I knew you were a cupcake." He mutters something behind his mask, but I can still hear him. "*Rich girl cupcake.*"

I narrow my gaze at him. "I didn't go overseas to live in luxury. I left because..." I pause, suddenly feeling exposed. Now I know why Erik didn't want to tell me about his wife.

It's not that I don't want him to know about my past, it's that I don't want to think about my past. I don't want to remember all the mistakes. The regrets.

Just like the day before, I see a child's face in my mind's eye. Jeremiah is his name, the most beautiful little boy in the world. I can't stop the tears that fill my eyes, they remind me that I don't regret Jeremiah at all. He's the best thing that's ever happened to me.

But I still left him.

I left him behind in Georgia while I ran away to Spain, and when I finally got the courage to return home, the world ended. Now I'm in a race against time, the Faceless, radiation, and everything else that wants to kill me just to have a chance at seeing him again.

Nine years ago, I fled the country to leave all my mistakes behind. Now I'm coming back because I've finally learned my only mistake was leaving in the first place.

"Shon," Erik's voice is calm—surprisingly gentle.

I look up at him and realize I never finished my sentence. "I left because my life had fallen apart."

"At age eighteen?"

I laugh. "Told you I wasn't a rich girl cupcake."

He laughs too and struggles to his feet. "Walk and talk."

I don't want to tell Erik about my past. I don't want him to think I'm a cupcake, but I also don't want him to realize I'm the bad batch of sweets. The cupcakes that turn stale and get tossed out at the end of the day. Or even before then.

Still … Erik opened up and shared the most brutal story I've ever heard, the least I can do is share something about myself too. Besides, whether I'm a cupcake or a stale loaf of bread, Erik has already judged me. It doesn't really matter what he thinks of me.

So I tell the truth. I admit that my boyfriend was my high school sweetheart and the love of my life. I admit that I gave him my virginity when he got the news that he'd received a football scholarship to a university right there in Georgia. I admit that I didn't regret it for a second.

Until I missed my period.

I'm a Christian girl who got pregnant at seventeen years old. I was a walking hypocrite, a canister of fuel for people to ridicule and mock the Faith. When I could no longer hide the pregnancy, I told my boyfriend about it, and he accused me of getting pregnant on purpose. He said I was hoping he would join the NFL and pay me millions in child support.

That wasn't the case at all. I wish I hadn't gotten pregnant. I wish I hadn't thrown away my values in the first place. I'd grown up Christian. I knew sex before marriage was a sin. But I'd done it anyway, and I thought it was okay because we were in love. I thought it was okay because we were planning on getting married. And then I was slapped back to reality with the pregnancy—and slapped again when I realized my boyfriend wanted no part of it.

He left for college without saying goodbye, so I was forced to tell my parents alone. News of their Christian daughter being pregnant at seventeen tore my family apart. My father shocked everyone when he recommended I get an abortion. The suggestion ignited a fire between my parents that threatened to burn everything in its wake.

My father filed for divorce the day Jeremiah Jr. was born, by then, I was a freshman in college, my parents were tied up in court, my boyfriend was long gone, and my faith was nonexistent. I felt cornered. I felt like my world was caving in. So I passed Jeremiah off to my mother and packed my bags. I was on a plane to Spain within months after my own child was born. I haven't seen him since that day.

Erik lets out a long sigh after I finish my story. "I guess you really aren't a rich girl cupcake," he says finally.

Not in the least.

"I left my own child."

"His father left him first," Erik says sharply. Even though he's wheezing for air, I can hear the anger in his voice clear as day. "Your boyfriend was pathetic."

"He did the same thing I did," I tell him. "We're both pathetic."

"You were both kids." Erik grunts as he steps over a pothole, we're in the inner city now, walking through a block of abandoned shops and corner stores. "Eighteen is too young for a kid."

"I wish I could go back and do things right."

"Is that why you're here now?" Erik asks. "To find your '*brother*.'" He turns toward me and uses air quotes.

I almost chuckle. I'd forgotten that I told him Jeremiah was my brother last night. I didn't want him to know the truth. I wasn't sure how he would react to it—so far, he's been surprisingly calm about it.

"I'm here because God told me to be. But I think it's time that I do the right thing."

"Which is?"

"Being a mother to my child."

"You have impeccable timing."

I laugh behind my mask. "It's God's timing."

"You really believe in God after everything that's happened?"

"The Bible says *trouble will come*. There is no promise of a perfect life in the Word of God, just a promise that Jesus would be with you when you faced hard times."

"The whole world is having a hard time," Erik grunts.

"And Jesus is still here. If you're willing to accept His help."

He bunches his shoulders like he's angry, but before he can say anything, Erik stops dead in his tracks. He halts so suddenly, I nearly walk into his backside, but I catch myself just in time and glance up to trace his gaze. He's staring straight ahead at an abandoned church.

For a moment, I think he's in deep contemplation—considering our conversation—then I hear something crash inside the church and my heart begins to race. But it's not the noise that sets me on edge, it's the sounds that follow the crash.

Inside the church, I can hear voices.

They drift out to us as if riding the breeze that blows through at that exact moment. We're both standing so still, the gentle wind is almost enough to knock us over. I'm frozen in fear, but every part of Erik's body is suddenly alive, suddenly alert. Despite his injuries, he looks ready to jump into action.

But he never gets the chance.

"Get to cover!" Erik hisses out a whisper as he turns to run, but before either of us takes our first step, a man appears on the steps of the church.

From our distance, the only thing I can tell is that the man is tall. He's wearing stained jeans and a hoodie with the words **KAPPA PI** printed on the front. I vaguely remember seeing **KAPPA** somewhere before, but the memory eludes me.

There is a gasmask over the man's face and a weapon in his hands. A large knife that looks like something I'd expect to belong to the villain of a slasher movie. The blade is easily as long as my arm, like a machete. It looks heavy, even as it rests over the man's shoulder. The sharpened metal winks in the sunlight as he slowly turns, casually scanning the area.

It's obvious from his demeanor that he does not expect to find anyone out here, but that doesn't give me any clues as to what he might do if he did find someone.

We are standing in the middle of the street right now, the man on the church steps hasn't spotted us but he's seconds away from doing just that. If we move, he will definitely see us. But if we stay, he will definitely see us. The only thing I can think to do is to give ourselves away.

"Help!" I shout, grabbing hold of Erik and pulling his arm over my shoulders as if I'm helping him walk.

Erik curses but immediately plays along. He's a drifter. He's used to changing plans on a dime. He's used to doing whatever it takes to survive. Including playing nice to machete-wielding strangers.

The man snaps his head toward us and almost topples down the stairs in shock. Great. He can't be *that* dangerous if he's this clumsy. My confidence starts to rise as we limp forward.

"We need help!" I say in my most pathetic cupcake voice.

Once the man has regained his footing, he points his machete at us and his voice booms through the air. "Stay right there!" he shouts, then he looks back through the double doors of the church. "We got company!" he barks.

It takes two seconds for four more men to join Machete Man on the church steps. They all stare at us in silence as I limp forward with Erik, but the way they look at us is nothing like the unintimidating way Machete Man had looked. They are as stiff as Erik who is reaching for the hunting knife sheathed at his side.

I press my hand into his ribs as we walk, and he grunts beside me. "That hurt."

"Stay calm. If they think we're hostile, then they'll be

hostile."

"I'm not getting any closer without a weapon."

"*Erik*," I hiss under my breath, but he doesn't listen. I can feel him fumbling for the weapon as we awkwardly walk together. My hope is that he's being as discreet as possible, reaching for the knife in a way that the men staring at us won't notice, but my hope shrivels and dies when Machete Man shouts, "Hands in the air!"

"He needs help!" I shout back. "If I let him go, he won't be able to stand."

One of the other men walks down the church steps. He's wearing a sweatshirt with a skeleton printed on the front, his strides are long and powerful, crossing the distance to us faster than I expect him to. When he's halfway to us, he pulls out a handgun and points it right at us.

I stop immediately.

"We said, *hands up*," Skeleton says.

The other four men join him now, and I get a good look at their weapons and gear. None of them are wearing tactical equipment. None of them have combat boots or great weapons besides the gun and the machete. The one on the end isn't even wearing a gasmask, he's got a bandana tied around the lower half of his face. But his skin isn't grey or rotting and he's moving like he's conscious and aware of what's going on—not like his brain is rotting. If he's this competent with just a bandana over his face, then these guys must be from nearby. Close enough that they feel comfortable traveling without masks.

Unless they just don't have them.

One guy has a baseball bat. Another holds what looks like a pipe. The last guy just has a chain that he drags behind him. They aren't the best weapons in the world, but I still don't want to take my chances in a fight right now. Erik's ribs are still busted, and we're tired and thirsty and hungry.

The gun clicks and gains my attention. I feel Erik go rigid beside me.

"Hands up. Put the man down."

"H-He'll fall," I try again.

"Good. That means he won't be a threat."

"We don't want any trouble," Erik says, but the gunman doesn't care.

He starts shouting, "HANDS UP!" and waving the gun around.

We both do as he says and, as promised, Erik crumples to the ground the moment I let him go. Of course, he can stand on his own, but it works in our favor to let the others think he's weak and useless. It works in our favor to let them think I'm weak too.

They don't know I've got a knife on my own hip, tucked beneath my thick hoodie. They don't know that I've used it before, and I'm not afraid to use it again.

So, I let the Skeleton man saunter forward and point his weapon right in my face. I pretend I'm afraid for my life and throw my hands up in defense when the barrel is pressed against my temple. Erik yells for him to leave me alone—I can't tell if he's sincere or not. It's hard to decipher the worry from the anger in his tone.

"What's a woman doing out here alone?" Skeleton asks. His voice is familiar, but like a distant memory, the familiarity is fragile and fleeting. Gone as soon as I begin to question it.

"I'm not alone," I whimper as he drags his gun down my face, from my temple to my cheek. He's standing behind me, trying to snake his free hand up my shirt. I squirm away before he can find my knife hidden under there.

"Please," I whisper.

He chuckles in my ear; it sounds muffled behind his mask—but I still get that niggling sense of familiarity. I still feel like I've heard this man's voice before. I just can't remember where from.

"Say please again," he orders.

My stomach churns as his dirty fingers play with the hem of my shirt. There are five men in total. Each with a weapon—one of them with a gun. And that gun is pressed to my cheek. I might be in over my head. I might have overplayed my hand. But I'm in this now, I can't go back. So I suck in a breath and do as he says.

"*Please*," my voice is breathy, little more than a whisper.

Skeleton grabs me roughly by the arm, his gun remains pressed into my face. He starts dragging me backwards as he announces to his lackeys, "I get her first. Watch the man and then you can all take turns."

Erik starts to yell, but his words are lost to the hoots of the men behind him. I can see his eyes bulging behind his mask. I can see the panic fueling his movements as he shoots to his feet and runs toward us. That's when the fear finally kicks in. That's when I realize my plan is not going to go the way I want.

Machete Man runs up and kicks Erik in the back of his knee, dropping him to the ground. For one horrific second, I think he's going to use that monstrous blade to hack his head off, but he's more interested in Erik's torn backpack and starts yanking at that instead. He's only using one hand because that gaudy machete is in his other hand. So he has no way to defend himself when Erik rolls over and sinks his hunting knife into his gut.

I scream which catches Skeleton's attention. He's still trying to drag me back toward an abandoned printing shop, but when he glances up and sees his friend doubled over with a knife in his abdomen, his grip on me goes slack.

I hear His Voice again. As distinct as it was when it woke me from my sleep and brought me back home. It is unmistakable, as powerful as it is gentle. I would know God's Voice anywhere.

Move.

I twist my arm away and pivot, pulling out my knife at the same time. I could slide this blade across Skeleton's throat before he even registered that I've moved, but I hesitate at the last second. God told me to move, but He didn't tell me to kill this man.

I can't, I realize, stopping mid-swing. *I can't kill him.*

The man sees my hesitation—it sparks a storm in his eyes that sets fire to whatever mercy he might have shown me two seconds earlier. In a flash, his free hand is around my throat, the gun is shoved into my forehead, digging into the leather of the gasmask.

"You little—"

"Jeremy!" one of the guys behind us shouts. "Jeremiah! He killed him! That old man killed one of ours!"

Skeleton stops and flicks his gaze to the dead man lying beside Erik. Erik's back on his feet now, glaring at the three remaining guys, daring them to make a move. They've got a bat, a pipe, and a chain between the three of them, but they just watched Erik gut a man like it was nothing. They're not taking any chances.

Neither is Skeleton. He's frozen, trying to decide what to do. Let his men kill Erik? Or stop to mourn his friend? And then there's me, still held in his grasp. I'm not struggling anymore, but it's not because I've given up. It's because I'm in shock. Absolute shock. And horror.

130

Everything suddenly clicks into place.

GO BACK. KAPPA AHEAD. The writing I saw written in the dust on the back of an abandoned car from the highway. It was a warning about Kappa Pi, the name of the fraternity from Octane University, a college I know is somewhere in this area. A college my ex-boyfriend attended.

Now this man's familiarity makes sense. His demeanor. The sound of his voice. Even the fact that he'd tried to assault me fits his persona.

"Je-Jeremiah," I croak, sucking for breath as his fingers press into my windpipe. He's still got me by the throat, and his grip only tightens as he looks down at me now.

"Do not speak," he orders, but I ignore him.

"It's me," I whisper. "It's RaShonda."

He blinks. I see his lashes flutter behind the glass of his mask. And then I see recognition roll over him like a storm. It's violent and angry, making him shove away from me like he's just touched acid.

"No." He starts shaking his head. "How? How is this possible?"

How is it possible that after three years of silence and then six years of an apocalypse that I would be reunited with the father of my child? I don't know. But I'm suddenly glad that I listened to God. I'm glad that I trusted Him to keep me safe, even when I hesitated.

I'm glad I didn't kill this man.

He was about to hurt me. He might have even killed me. But God had been looking out for me. *Thank You, Jesus*, I pray inside.

I'm not happy to see Jeremiah at all. I'm not happy with who he's become or what he was about to do just moments earlier. But bumping into him puts me one step closer to finding the rest of my family. I won't let this blessing slip away.

13

Shon

Jeremiah Sr. lives in a small community holed up in the remains of the university he'd been attending when the explosions went off six years ago. If I remember correctly, we were both seniors at the time, it would have been early March when the blue lights flashed. I was studying linguistics with a minor in sociology. I had no idea what I was going to do when I graduated.

Jeremy, on the other hand... He was a star athlete who'd gotten a full ride to Octane University. If he performed the way he had in high school, then I know he'd been looking forward to the NFL draft before the lights. He'd been wrong when he'd accused me of getting knocked up on purpose, but it would be a lie to say I hadn't felt giddy at the thought of calling myself a football wife.

I was seventeen when I'd gotten pregnant. I was eighteen when I'd given birth. I knew the baby would be a shock, but I never thought my son would cause so much damage. So much heartbreak. But... it wasn't Jeremiah Jr. who caused this. It was me—my own mistake of not honoring my body. And Jeremiah Sr.'s for making the same mistake.

I won't let myself feel bad for going forward with the pregnancy. As a Christian, I've never believed in abortion anyway. But I had no idea that my own Christian father had. And I'd had no idea that Jeremiah Sr. had. He blamed me for our baby. He tried to make me feel guilty. He tried to say I'd ruined his future.

Turns out, an abandoned frat house at a partially destroyed university was his future. A sort of failure and disappointment I had nothing to do with.

When it mattered most, I stood by my faith and had the baby. I chose life over death, and I don't regret it. I wonder if Jeremy regrets it as I blink around the small room I woke up in this morning. After recognizing each other, Jeremy stopped his guys from attacking Erik and invited us back to his home base. It was a three-hour walk to the university which we spent blindfolded and bound by our wrists.

Jeremy does not trust us. But I'm not offended because I don't trust him either. He might be the father of my child, but he is also the man who would have held me down and raped me yesterday—and then let his friends do the same—without hesitation or remorse. I remind myself of his cruelty as I stare out the window of the little dorm.

Most of the campus is relatively intact. A bomb went off not far from the school, but only the academic buildings were caught up in the explosions. The dorms were mostly left untouched, which meant a good percentage of the student body survived the attacks that day. I didn't get a good look around when I first arrived here yesterday because I was

134

blindfolded almost the entire time, but from what I can see from my window, it seems like most of the students stayed here.

There are people walking the cracked paths of the campus, going from building to building as they carry out tasks to keep the small community alive. I see a greenhouse in the distance, it was probably functional before the explosions. Students take boxes and crates from the little glass building into the small building next door. The sign on the front has been crudely painted over to say, *Green Storage*, instead of *Recreational Center*.

Beside the green storage den is an infirmary. The sight of it makes me suck in a little gasp. Jeremy had his men take Erik there when we arrived. The men grumbled their complaints, but Jeremy didn't budge. We are far from being friendly, but he promised to treat us as guests instead of enemies. This decision sparked an argument that nearly dissolved into violence.

I couldn't see anything from behind my blindfold, but I could hear their hissing voices, and their snarled statements. I didn't exactly blame the men who wanted to kill us. Erik had taken the life of that machete guy; they had every right to be upset about sharing their medical supplies with us. Although they would have killed *us* given the chance, but whatever.

To my shock, Jeremy stuck to his guns. He told the men to treat Erik's injuries and to have him fed before bed. He gave me my own room to sleep in and had food delivered by sunset. I had wondered about his position here when I noticed he was the only one with a gun, but all the arrangements he made without question from the men and women on campus solidified my musings.

Jeremiah is in charge.

There is a knock on my door that startles me. I immediately

135

reach for the knife at my hip, but I end up grabbing a handful of my hoodie instead. Jeremiah has treated me well so far, but he has also taken precautions. I was searched and stripped of my supplies when I arrived. I have no knife. I have no food or water.

My gasmask sits on the bedside table, I snatch it up and put it on—thankful Jeremiah didn't take that too—and then I face the door and say, "Come in."

The door swings inward and a tall figure fills the doorway. It takes me half a second to realize it's Jeremiah, and that's only because he's still wearing that sweatshirt with the menacing skeleton on the front.

He is bigger than I remember, but I doubt he looked this way before the explosions. We're all starved and slightly depressed. No one is in their best shape anymore. Still, Jeremiah had dragged me away yesterday without an issue. If I had fought, I'm sure I would've dealt damage, but I don't believe I would've gotten away.

I subconsciously pat my hip again, anger jolts through me as I realize—again—my weapon is gone.

"What's going on?" I demand.

Jeremiah closes the door behind him and leans against the cracked wood. "You don't have to wear the mask in here. The air is clean."

It's then that I realize he isn't wearing a mask. I blink at him. His dark brown skin and thick coils of hair; when we were in high school, he had dreadlocks that touched his collarbone. Now his locks are gone, and his hair is short, a small afro in desperate need of a pick. His eyes are tired and there are lines around his mouth like he's been scowling for the last six years. He doesn't even try to hide his annoyance now as he rolls his eyes and folds his arms over his chest.

136

"You don't believe me?" he says.

I stir, realizing I hadn't replied to his revelation. "How do I know you aren't lying?"

"If I wanted to kill you, I would have by now."

"You're right. You only wanted to rape me."

He swallows and glances away. "Look, Shon, that… Back there—that's not me."

"But it was you."

"And I didn't know who you were."

I shake my head. "That only makes it worse. If I had been a stranger, you would have…" I hug myself and shiver. I don't want to say the words again, but I've got to. I want him to hear what he almost did. "You would have raped me." I look him in the eye. "And you would have let your friends do the same. So excuse me for not trusting you."

"Let's not forget your boy killed one of my men. We're even now, Shon."

I want to argue. I want to scream that we will never be even, but he does have a point. Jeremiah would have hurt me, but in the end, I'm just fine. Meanwhile, there's a boy who isn't here anymore.

I slowly remove my mask and let out a long sigh. "I'm sorry about your friend."

Jeremiah nods, his brown eyes tracing the lines of my face. They're bigger than I remember, almost bulgy now. I guess he's been as stressed as I have, especially since he's the one in charge. Everyone here is his responsibility, and he's just brought in two outsiders. Two more mouths to feed.

We stand there examining each other until I can't take it anymore. I turn away and walk toward the little window again, reaching out to touch the plastic that's been duct-taped over it to seal it shut. It isn't much, but I suppose it keeps enough of the toxins out that the air is breathable for short periods of time. Minty had the same setup in that abandoned Amazon factory—the thought of her brings a question to my mind.

"How'd you clear out the toxic air indoors?"

Jeremy scratches the stubble on his chin. "Put up plastic and let the place sit until the daisies stopped reacting inside. We had to wear masks until it was safe."

I nod. "Where'd you get the masks from?"

"The chem building. The lab had a small stash of masks for emergencies—in case an experiment went wrong, I guess. There weren't more than a dozen or so; we had to share them, pass them around every few hours."

My eyes widen. I can't imagine hundreds of students surviving off two dozen gasmasks. It's a miracle any of them survived.

"Is your lab still standing?" I ask. Minty had been in search of one; I doubt a college lab has the resources she would need but it's better than nothing. Unfortunately, my hope dies when Jeremiah's shoulders sag.

"The lab is gone. Half of it was destroyed in the initial explosion. The other half burned down a few days after we looted it for the masks. An exposed wire caught fire."

I sigh. It was worth a shot.

"Shon, I didn't come here to talk about the chem lab."

"Fine. Where is Erik?"

He looks annoyed again. "Still in the infirmary."

"I want to see him."

"Maybe later."

I raise an eyebrow. "Why not now?"

"Because we're talking. I have questions, Shon." He pushes from the door and walks a slow circle around the little room. The heels of his large hands are pressed into his eyes, his voice

138

comes out strained. "I can't believe you're here. After all these years. I never thought I'd see you again. I never thought I'd see anyone again."

"*Have* you seen anyone?" I ask gently. I'm not sure I want him to answer or not. Jeremiah could tell me my entire family is dead. That would unravel everything I thought to be true. If my family is gone, then why did God tell me to go home?

Jeremy slowly drops his hands. His eyes are filled with an emotion I can't place. "No," he mutters. "I haven't seen anyone, Shon. I've never left campus except to scavenge for supplies."

I gulp. He's the same as me. All this time we've been sitting in place, letting the world rot around us. Maybe this is why God told me to return, not to find my family altogether waiting for me, but to gather them from their scattered places.

I take a step toward Jeremiah, ready to forgive him for the nightmare that almost happened yesterday, ready to ask him to join me and Erik on this journey, but his next words stop me in my tracks.

"How is he?"

I pause, heart fluttering.

"How's my son?" Jeremy asks.

My mouth feels like it's full of cotton. "Umm..."

The last time I saw this man, I was fat and pregnant, and he was packing for college. Jeremiah missed his son's birth, and he never returned for a visit. I mailed a letter to his dorm with information about our child. I told him his height, weight, and I was happy to report that Jeremy Jr. was perfectly healthy. I even included a photo of him.

Jeremiah never responded.

So he has no idea that I packed up and left too, just a few months after Jeremy Jr. was born. I haven't seen my son since he was the size of a watermelon. Jeremiah has never even met him.

We are the worst parents on earth.

I clear my throat. "I don't know how he is."

Jeremiah stares at me. "What do you mean?"

"Jere… I haven't been home either. I haven't seen my family in…" I pause. He expects me to say *in six years*, since the explosions, but the truth is that I'd left three years before that. It's been almost a decade since I've seen anyone from the States.

I sigh. "It's been nine years for me."

Jeremiah's face curdles in anger. "It's been *nine* years?" His hands ball into fists. "So who's been looking after my boy?"

Anger storms through me. How dare he? How *dare* Jeremiah act protectively like this? As if he has the right to be angry that I left.

I start to shake my head. "You never wanted Jeremiah Jr. to begin with. What does it matter who's been looking after him?"

Jeremiah takes a step closer to me. For half a second, I feel afraid, but I refuse to back down. "My life was complicated, just like yours. You don't get to judge me for leaving," I say boldly.

He glares at me, and I lift my chin. He doesn't need to know I'm holding my breath. He doesn't need to know that I'm afraid he'll get angry and take it out on me.

I relax a little when he turns back toward the door and runs his hands through his hair. "Then what are you doing here, Shon? I thought you showed up with Jeremy. I thought you were looking for me."

A coldness washes over me. Did he really think that after years of complete silence I would trek across the state—with our now nine-year-old son—just to see *him*?

Jeremiah has always been self-centered, but this is wild even for him.

"I'm here because I'm going home, Jeremiah," I admit. "I'm going to find my family."

He shocks me with a laugh, his head thrown back, his mouth open to reveal yellowed teeth. I suppose they did not have toothbrushes on campus.

"What's so funny?" I ask.

He cuts his laugh short to blink at me like I'm stupid. "Our families are dead, Shon."

"How could you know that? You've never left campus."

He waves his arms open, as if to say, *look around.* "Everyone is dead."

"You aren't. And I'm not. And Erik isn't either. Who's to say my family is? They could have hunkered down just like you. They could be drifters like Erik. Anything is possible."

"*Erik,*" Jeremiah says his name so hard I flinch like he's just cussed at me. "That white man tell you he's gonna find my son for you?"

"Don't even go there," I snap. My voice drops to a dangerous growl, shocking both of us. "Don't you dare talk about Erik. You don't know anything about him."

To my surprise, Jeremiah smiles. His brown eyes lazily rove over me from head to toe. Then he nods and lets out a low chuckle. "I bet you know him real good."

If I weren't a Christian woman, I would have slapped him. But Erik doesn't need me to defend his honor and I'm sure not about to defend my own to an attempted rapist. So instead of getting angry, I square my shoulders and say firmly, "I am going to find my family and Erik is going to help me. Thank you for giving us a place to stay and for treating Erik's wounds, but I think it's time for us to go now."

Jeremiah's smile vanishes. "That's the thanks I get? After giving you food and shelter and medical attention, you pack up and go—and I'm left with a thank-you?"

"You can keep our supplies—"

"A couple cans of beef stew ain't gonna cut it."

My nostrils flare in controlled rage. "Well, I don't have anything else to give you."

If I had more, I'd offer more. I'd give Jeremiah my left arm if he would just step aside and let me through. From the way he's looking at me, and from the hiss in his voice, I just want to get away from here as soon as possible. If I'm fortunate, he'll never leave this campus for another six years and we'll never have to see each other again.

A shadow darkens my view as Jeremiah stands before me. He towers over me at his height, standing so close I can smell his body odor. We all stink a little, but I have a hard time breathing with him this near. He smells sour. Like he's stinking from the inside.

"You got one thing you can offer." Jeremiah winks when I look up at him.

"That's not happening," I almost snarl.

He chuckles and backs toward the door. "I'm just messing with you, Shon."

"That's not funny, Jeremiah."

"You're right. I'm sorry." He turns and grabs the doorknob. "Why don't we both cool off for a bit? We can talk about what happens next after lunch."

I want to remind him that I haven't even eaten breakfast, but he's out the door before I can say anything.

Now that I'm alone, I want to break down and cry, but I can't let myself be so weak. Erik would never let me live it

142

down if he caught me crying over this.

Speaking of Erik… That man has saved my life and killed someone on my behalf. I've got to make sure he's okay.

I strap on my mask and limp to the door—my bad hip aches all the way. Then my heart stops when I grab the knob.

It doesn't turn.

I jiggle it and put some muscle in it, grunting as I yank at the door, but it doesn't budge. I'm locked inside.

Jeremiah was lying. He isn't *messing* with me at all. He's keeping me prisoner.

14

Erik

The only thing I hate more than Faceless is people. The kind whose minds *haven't* rotted.

For what it's worth, Faceless are honest creatures. You know exactly what they want when you see one. And it's always the same thing—to eat you. They don't have to fool you, lie to you, or trick you. Faceless are open and upfront about what they want, and they make it very clear they're willing to do anything to get it. I don't like Faceless, but I appreciate their honesty.

Humans are different.

We feel safe when they smile at us. We feel trusting when they're nice to each other. We feel like there's nothing to worry about when they offer a hand. And we believe the ones we call our friends are the people we can trust without thought or question.

That couldn't be further from the truth.

Jeremiah and his men told us they would treat us well and give me whatever medical attention I needed to get back on my feet again. They even had a little argument about it outside so Shon could hear and be convinced that they were looking out for us—despite me killing that kid.

All of that was a lie.

This is not an infirmary. I haven't seen a doctor or a nurse since they shoved me in this room... and handcuffed me to a metal pole in the wall. I'm sitting on the floor with my legs folded and my arm hanging a few feet from the floor. I can't really lie down because I'm cuffed to an old rusty pipe, so I'm just leaning against the wall, blinking wearily at the tiled floor.

This room is hell.

It's so hot, I want to claw at my own skin. And it's small enough to make me feel claustrophobic. Think of a walk-in closet ... And then cut that in half.

My ribs are doing better, but I'm still in a lot of pain and I'm starving. Someone has come in to give me exactly one cup of water and five peanuts once a day. When I first got my bearings, I thought they were keeping me in this condition because I'd killed their friend. I thought they were angry. I thought they hadn't decided whether they wanted to kill me or not. But then I got a closer look at the young man who serves me my humble meal every day.

The door to my little prison opens just now with a creak and I see my new buddy waiting with my peanuts and water. Same time. Every day.

His hands tremble as he passes me the paper cup. My hands are steady as I take it. The water is sweet on my chapped lips, I'm sure I'm *this* close to dying of dehydration. I savor the liquid, ignoring the sour flavor in it. It tastes like they used dirt to filter it. I hate dirt filters.

145

When the kid passes me the peanuts, he hands them over one by one. I stare at his face as I chew, trying to make the food last longer. He's young—even younger than Shon—maybe early twenties. I wonder what year he was in when the explosions happened. Poor kids. Most of the ones staying in the dorm were from out of town or even out of state. They had no choice but to stay put with the hope that the military and the government would figure things out.

That never happened. And like Shon, they never got to return home.

The kid has olive skin with hollow cheeks and eyes that bulge from his sockets. When he blinks, it looks like it hurts. But I can't stop myself from staring right into his fully dilated pupils.

Shaky hands. Bulgy eyes. Dilated pupils.

That's three red flags. Flags I have seen on the most desperate drifters. Flags that mean the worst form of betrayal has happened somewhere on this campus, and from the looks of this boy, I'd say it's been happening for a long time.

Jeremiah's folks have a base set up that has been running for six years. But they are not prospering. There are too many people and not enough resources. I imagine scavenging and looting has turned up less and less these days. They have two options, pack up and become drifters, or take drastic measures.

They did not become drifters.

These people ... they're cannibals.

That would explain why they haven't bothered to give me much food, they need to keep me alive long enough to make sure I'm not infected. I've seen what happens when people eat people, but I have no idea what happens when people eat *infected* people.

The rule of five states humans will show signs of Faceless

146

transition within the first five days of untreated exposure or bites. This is day number four. I've got one day left to figure out an escape, or else they're going to kill me and eat me. But even with this death threat looming over my head, I can't find it in myself to worry about that.

I need to get to Shon.

The boy passes me my last peanut and I debate asking him about Shon. Even though Jeremiah clearly lied about what he was going to do to me, I don't think he's going to starve and devour his ex-girlfriend.

Assault her? Sure. But eat her afterward? I don't think so.

He stopped his disgusting attack when he realized who she was, I'm hoping the fact that they have history, and that Shon is the mother of his child, will be enough to keep her alive. But we're dealing with a man who was moments away from disgracing her body—and letting his friends do the same. RaShonda might be alive now, but there is no telling whether Jeremiah will change his mind or not.

When I've finished my last peanut, the kid begins his daily examination. He checks every inch of my body for bite marks and scratches—I forgot to mention that I'm butt naked right now—and then he peels my eyelids back with his dirty thumbs and stares into my eyes. He's searching for any hint of neon blue, but he's not going to find any. I'm not infected—they've even let me keep my gasmask, which has been resting beside me while I eat.

Rule of Five.

In five minutes, you're contaminated.

In five hours, you will lose the body part that was contaminated.

In five days, you will begin to transition into a Faceless.

All of this can be avoided if you find shelter from

contaminated air and undergo deep cleansing. Minty told me when she worked in a lab and anyone was exposed to radiation, they would shower for forty-five minutes with an examiner present to make sure they washed properly. They even locked the showers so the contaminated subject could not leave until they had been thoroughly cleansed. After that, they were quarantined for five days and then examined for signs of deformity, illness, or delusional behavior.

I am personally convinced it was Minnesota herself who developed the Rule of Five.

Either way, these people want to eat me, so they've got to be meticulous. They've got to keep me alive for at least five days to make sure their meat hasn't spoiled. That means I'm stuck here.

As long as I'm healthy.

When the kid has my eyes peeled back with his thumbs— which hurts—I suck in a breath ... and cough.

He flinches away so fast, you'd think I'd spat acid at him. But that's good, panicked cannibals are not as dangerous as calm ones.

I cough again.

He stares at me in horror. "I—I'll be right back," he says in a raspy voice, and then he scrambles out the door. But he leaves it open.

I struggle to my feet. I'm tired and hungry and probably two days from death whether they eat me or not, but I have enough strength to stand on my own and get ready for what's going to happen next.

A woman with glasses appears in the doorway, blinking at me like she has no idea what to do. Her eyes are bulgy too, but nowhere near as scary looking as the young man who's been feeding me. Her brown eyes narrow as she steps into the hot room, but her movements are slow and wary. She's afraid. That's good.

"Are you sure he's infected?" she asks the kid like I'm not even there.

"He coughed."

"Could have been the peanuts."

The kid shakes his head. "No … His cough was different."

That's because I'm dehydrated, injured, and starving. Anyone in my condition would have a hoarse cough. But this kid is too stupid to realize this—maybe unintelligence is a side effect of cannibalism. Either way, this works in my favor.

I cradle my ribs as I hack out another dry cough that honestly hurts my throat. Both the boy and girl back away with panicked frowns on their faces. After a moment of silently staring at each other, the young lady curses under her breath.

"This is the only one Jeremiah came back with."

The boy shakes his head. "There was a woman."

"She's locked in the dorms." The girl curses again. "Jere isn't letting anyone near her."

"So … He's all we've got?"

Now the woman shakes her head. "We don't have *anything* now."

It all makes sense. They weren't looting for supplies out there; Jeremiah and his buddies were waiting for *us*. They were scavenging for *people*. But I'm not afraid, because now the young lady is telling the boy to uncuff me so they can take me around back to slit my throat. I'm naked and unarmed, but I'm not going to let them kill me. I've just got to get out of this room.

And now I know where they're keeping Shon.

I'm glad it's the kid who uncuffs me, because when I grab his arm and twist it behind his back, the young lady just squeals and stands there like she's going to wet herself. If I had taken the girl hostage, the kid might have gotten brazen enough to try something stupid just to play hero.

"How many are in the building?" I rasp.

The girl shakes her head. "You won't make it out of here alive."

I twist the kid's arm and he yelps, "Four! There are four inside besides us!"

"Connor!" the girl snaps. "Be quiet."

"Keep talking," I order, but he tries to play tough, so I twist his arm again. This time, it pops.

He screams, but I cover his mouth with my free hand to muffle it. I also have a feeling this little room is soundproof; it would be hard to keep their cannibalism a secret if anyone heard their victims screaming all day. Then again, I'm not so sure their cannibalism *is* a secret. I wasn't around Jeremiah for long, but from the few moments I was close to him, I picked up whiffs of the same sickly scent I smell on the kid squirming in my grasp.

They stink. But it isn't a normal musty body odor. This stench is different, coming from the inside. Like they're all decaying. The smell is so strong with us close like this, I almost feel dizzy, but I keep my bearings and focus on the girl in front of me.

She looks like she's thinking now, weighing her options. If she turns and runs, my plans are over.

So I act before she does.

"Sorry, kid," I mutter. Then I release his arm and wrap him in a headlock. It takes me two seconds to break his neck.

Now, the girl turns to run.

But I'm faster than she is, and they've made the mistake of closing the door that guards the larger room outside. Before she's taken five steps, I grab her by the hair. Her hand is extended, reaching for the big metal door, but I've got her now. She isn't going anywhere.

My ribs ache as I back us both away from the door, clamping a hand over her mouth so she doesn't scream, and hissing in her ear, "One word and I'll do the same thing to you."

She whimpers.

Honestly, I don't want to kill this young woman—I didn't want to kill the boy—but I also don't want to have my throat slit so they can eat my corpse.

"Where are the four others?"

I slowly lower my hand for her to answer.

"Two are at the exits—"

"And the other two?"

"One is at the front desk. The other is treating an injured scavenger."

Huh, so this place *is* an infirmary. I guess I just got the short end of the stick.

"Which exit is closer?"

"The southern exit," she says in a shaky voice, then she hiccups and adds, "please don't kill me."

"How many have *you* killed?"

She sobs in response.

I don't spare her because I'm a gentleman. I decide not to kill this girl because I know Shon would be upset if I did. She wouldn't even know that I killed her, and I really shouldn't care if she's upset, but I do. So instead of snapping this young lady's neck, I drag her back to my tiny prison—which I realize is truly a walk-in closet now that I'm seeing it from the outside—and I cuff her to the pole I'd been chained to.

She sobs as she drops to her knees, shrieking at the sight

151

of her companion's body. I don't feel sorry for her. They were going to kill me and eat me. This is more mercy than she deserves.

I kneel and begin undressing her friend. We aren't the same size, but I'm not about to walk out here naked. His pants are a squeeze, the t-shirt fits snug, I don't even try his shoes. But it's better than nothing.

"Where are they keeping RaShonda?"

She looks at me with a puzzled expression, watery eyes blinking behind her glasses. Her skin is dirty, like everyone else's, and I can pick up that nasty odor wafting from her bare arms as she wrings her hands. She's a pretty girl, looks Asian, with jet-black hair and smooth skin. But none of that matters to me right now.

I reach out and grab her roughly by the shoulders. "The dorms," I say urgently. "Which one is she in?"

The young lady sobs until I shake her.

"Tell me!"

"The Kappa Pi Fraternity! That's Building C!" she says. "I don't know which room, but she'll be on the third floor."

I stare at her face, trying to tell if she's lying, but all I see is her dilated pupils and the swollen veins of her bulgy eyes. She's a lost cause.

With a sigh, I cock my fist and hit her once, right on the temple. She crumples like a leaf—not dead, just passed out. I don't need her screaming for help, whether the room is soundproof or not.

When I close the wooden door to the little closet, I look up in time to see the big metal door swinging open.

"Sakura, Connor, you done yet?" a masculine voice calls into the room as a tall Black guy appears in the doorway.

He takes one look at me and starts to turn away, but I'm

152

across the room before he realizes it. I don't know why he changes his mind on escaping and decides to turn back and fight me instead, but I'm grateful. Running hurts my ribs. Fighting is easier—when you know how.

The guy whirls back around and steps halfway into the room, his fist is up—like he might have been swinging at me? At the last second, I realize there is a canister in his hand. He isn't throwing a punch at all; he's trying to pepper spray me.

I close my eyes and throw my body against the door, smashing the metal barrier right into his arm and chest. With a shout, he drops the spray, giving me the chance to grab him by that same arm and drag him into the room.

This is perfect.

As the man trips into the room, I immediately wrestle him into a chokehold. It isn't easy. He's big and strong, considering he's half my age and has probably had more than five peanuts to eat today. But I'm desperate and angry and fighting for my life. I've got adrenaline pumping through my veins, giving me an edge over him—not a big edge, but enough for me to overpower him.

My ribs are screaming but I ignore them as I kick the metal door shut. He has a knife sheathed at his hip. I'm going to assume from the pair of cuffs at his side that he's one of the guards Sakura mentioned. Since he came to check on his buddies, I'm also going to assume he's the guard from the southern exit—the one closest to us. Which means that exit is now unguarded.

That's the exit I'm going to take.

"Please," the man begs, but I ignore him as I reach for his knife and whack him over the head with the hilt. It takes one more hit to knock him out. His body falls to the floor with a thud. I'd like to search him for more weapons or at least take his shoes, but this guy screamed pretty loudly when I slammed the door on his arm. Someone will be coming soon. That means I've got to move fast.

I leave him there as I move to the door, peeking out into the hall. Mercifully, it's empty. So I take a breath and step out, moving toward the southern exit as swiftly as I can.

15

Erik

I have been locked in a closet for the last three days. I have zero sense of time when I push through the exit doors of the infirmary, so I'm completely shocked to see the sun setting in the distance. There is a faint orange-red glow that blankets the campus, it's accompanied by dozens of torches that are being lit and set on poles on the sidewalks.

I blink until my eyes adjust to the darkness, then I begin a casual walk toward what I think is a cluster of dorms. I never went to college, but I have an idea of what dorms look like. Plus, there's a partially destroyed sign that helps point me in the right direction.

My feet dig into the pavement, sending sharp pain through my toes each time I step over gravel or rocky dirt. No one seems to pay me much attention, so I grin and bear it until I reach Building C, just like Sakura said, and take the side entrance.

Inside, the place is quiet. My breaths echo around the concrete stairwell, and I try very hard not to make any more noise than necessary.

My feet hurt by the time I get to the third floor, but I have no choice but to keep moving. When I peek into the hallway, I see a guy exiting one of the rooms. He's wearing a baseball cap, so I can't see his face, but I don't think he's Jeremiah. I hold my breath as he closes the door behind himself and turns...

To my relief, he turns in the other direction and walks away from me.

For the first time, I'm thankful for my bare feet, because the man doesn't hear me coming when I approach him from behind.

He gasps when my hand wraps around his mouth, but the sound is cut off as I slide my blade across his throat. I take my chances and kick in the door right beside us—the room is empty, which almost makes me smile as I ease his body down to the floor. He's bleeding everywhere, but I don't have time to care. He's a big guy—bigger than Connor—so I strip him of his pants and shoes—the shirt is soaked in blood—then I take his baseball cap and brush my hair back with my hand before placing it on my head.

Once I'm dressed, I quickly search the room. The dresser comes up empty, but there is a cardboard box beneath the bed with a granola bar in the bottom and an empty backpack. I slip on the bag and stash the bar in my back pocket. This'll have to be enough for now.

Right before I leave, I hear someone shouting outside. The noise draws me to the window, and I blink into the torchlit night to see people scrambling from the infirmary and pointing at the dorms. Even if Sakura is still unconscious, it doesn't take

156

much to assume where I'd go once I managed to escape.

I don't let the sight of people running toward the dorm send me into a panic. If anything, it just lets me know that Shon is definitely somewhere in this building.

With a sigh, I tuck my knife into my waistband and exit the dorm. It's not until I'm back in the hall that I realize the guard I killed had been armed with a crowbar. It's lying on the carpet right outside the door. He must have dropped it when I grabbed him. I was too busy trying to drag him away to notice it.

I scoop up the weapon now, hefting it in my palm, testing the weight. Just as I decide it's good enough, I glance up to see a woman exiting the stairwell on the other end of the hall.

She's holding a torch and smiling. "Ready for the night shift, Michael?" she says so casually, I pause, momentarily stunned. Then again, I am wearing Michael's pants, shoes, and baseball cap. And, more importantly, this woman is blinded by the torch so near to her face. She cannot see me fully, not unless she moves the light further away or I step closer.

She looks up when I don't answer right away. I may be wearing Michael's clothes, but I doubt I *sound* like Michael. So I feign a yawn behind my mask, giving me an excuse not to speak for a few more seconds. By now, I'm less than ten feet away.

When I finish my yawn, the girl has a look of surprise on her face—it's replaced by a look of fear when I raise the crowbar … and swing.

She steps to the side and dodges the attack. Her swiftness shocks me bad enough that I can't regain my footing, but I pivot as I trip to the side and catch her in the hip with the bar as she tries to run away. She yelps and falls, the torch spills from her hands and fire immediately begins a slow crawl down the hallway.

Great.

The only good thing here is that the woman is not interested in fighting me. She scrambles to her feet and runs in the opposite direction, sobbing all the way. That works out fine for me.

I immediately turn and start kicking in doors, screaming Shon's name. "SHON! RASHONDA!"

No one answers, but a few doors swing open to reveal people with panicked faces. They all stand in their doorways for a moment, eyes flicking between me and the orange glow lighting up the hallway. They're torn between trying to stop me or trying to escape the flames.

Every last one of them turns and runs.

That helps an awful lot.

I make my way down the hall, kicking in the doors that are still closed. The first two dorms are empty. The third door swings in to reveal a woman frantically getting dressed. She's pale and very tall—not Shon at all—and she shrieks when she sees me.

"Please!" she screams, covering her chest with her dirty t-shirt.

"The woman you took in three days ago, where is she?" I say quickly.

Her eyes grow big, like she's just realized what all the chaos is about. "The last room on the right side."

I nod. "Get out of here. The hall is on fire." Then I turn and run to the end of the hall.

The flames have grown, making the hallway so hot, it's almost unbearable. But I welcome the heat, this fire is the only thing keeping my pursuers at bay. By now, I should have been caught by those kids I saw running from the infirmary. But chances are, the guys who've escaped so far have probably spread the word about the fire. Even if they haven't, there's smoke everywhere, so thick I can taste it even through my gasmask. No one is coming after me in this mess.

"RASHONDA!" I scream.

Outside the last door on the right side, I hear a small voice in the room. I can't make out who it belongs to or what's being said, but I know Shon is in there when I kick the door and feel biting pain shoot through my ankle.

The door doesn't budge. It's locked.

"RASHONDA!" I holler, jamming the sharp end of the crowbar into the strike plate of the door. That soft voice comes back again, I still can't make it out, but I can tell it sounds more urgent now. With all my strength, I stab at the wood surrounding the plate and—finally—the door slides open.

What I find when I step inside makes my knees buckle.

RaShonda is lying on the tiny twin-sized bed. It's been completely stripped of its linen, so she's pressed into the stained mattress. I cringe at the dirty bed, but that's the least of her worries…

Shon is completely naked and one of her wrists is cuffed to the headboard with duct tape sealing her mouth shut.

Bitter anger burns through me as I march through the room. Her eyes are so big, they're like to pop from their sockets. But they're not filled with tears, they're filled with a rage that rivals my own.

When I cover her with the blankets I find on the floor, her gaze meets mine and for a split second I see RaShonda for who she is. She should be broken by this. She should be sobbing and screaming and begging for help, but I know the look I see in her eyes. I recognize the anger that is as powerful as it is fragile. I have felt that anger every day.

Shon cannot afford to let her fear take over. She cannot focus on her grief or self-pity. Right now, white-hot rage is the only thing that will keep her sane.

I peel the tape from her mouth as gingerly as I can. "That sick monster!" she shouts.

"If I find him, I'll kill him," I promise her.

"Do you have the key to the cuffs?"

I shake my head and raise my crowbar. "But I have this."

The headboard is made of wood. It splinters after three good jabs, then I'm able to kick it until it gives and the wooden bars crack in half. Shon immediately sits up and starts directing me around the room while she gets dressed.

"My gasmask is in a box beneath the bed. He taped my mouth closed after I bit him. I guess as punishment."

"You bit him?" I pass her the mask, trying to move as quickly as possible. Shon's already wearing a baggy t-shirt, now she's sliding into a pair of men's jeans.

She nods at my question. "I did everything I could."

"Right," I say awkwardly.

She bends and grabs a pair of sneakers from the box that held her mask. They look too big for her, but neither of us are complaining. "Ready?" she asks.

"The building is on fire."

She hesitates for only a second. "The whole building?"

"No. We're right next to the exit, actually."

Thank God she was locked in the last door at the end of the hall, the stairwell is right beside us and it isn't surrounded in flames. Yet.

I pass her the knife from my waistband and heft the crowbar. "Let's go, cupcake."

She walks right behind me until I step outside the room and come face to face with the only man insane enough to

160

battle flames just to find Shon. Well, the *second* man insane enough to battle flames just to find Shon.

"Jeremiah." I point the sharp end of the crowbar right in his face.

He underestimated the state we'd be in. That gun he likes to wave around is still holstered at his hip instead of gripped in his hands. His fingers twitch as he stares at the point of the bar. I *pray* he makes a move so I can ram this thing right through his eye. I'm in the middle of calculating how much time I'd need to do it when Shon shifts beside me.

At first, I think she's backing away to hide from him in the room, but then I see the metal of her blade glint in the smokey darkness, and I suck in a gasp.

She stops short of stabbing him, pressing the tip of her knife into Jeremiah's throat. A trickle of blood runs down his neck, staining the collar of his skeleton sweatshirt. "We're leaving," she hisses.

"You can't go," he says.

"Say the word, cupcake," I tell her.

"And what?" he growls.

"And I will *nail* you to that wall," I snarl.

I don't know if he believes me or not, but it doesn't matter because Shon places her hand on my forearm and says softly, "Don't."

That's the only word she says, but it's enough for me to lower my weapon. I hate the guy for what he's done. I hate him for kidnapping and eating people. But I don't have time to convince Shon to let me kill him, so I swallow my pride and grab her hand.

"We're leaving," I say firmly, then I kick open the exit door and we sprint down the stairs together.

Jeremiah doesn't follow us. He's got bigger things to worry

161

about—I realize this once we make it outside and I see the flames bursting from the third-floor windows. People are screaming and frantically running back and forth; men wheel carts with barrels of water over and stand there staring up at the building, trying to figure out what to do.

That water is their life source. They can't afford to spare it on a fire. So they've got two choices: Use the water and save their housing, or save the building and deplete their water supply.

I don't stick around to see which decision they make. Shon and I keep our heads down as we walk quickly down the sidewalk, passing another guy who's pushing a cartful of water. There are at least two dozen gallon-bottles jiggling around in the cart—when he rushes past us, I swiftly turn and grab two. It's not until I glance back to make sure Shon is with me that I realize she grabbed one as well.

Neither of us speaks, but we share a grin that says, *Ha!*

We did it. We got out of this hellhole.

We have a crowbar, a hunting knife, a granola bar, and three gallons of water between us. But we made it. And we aren't ever going back.

It's not until we've cleared the parking lot with our stolen goods that I look over my shoulder to see the flames lighting up the night. Smoke billows into the sky, blotting out the stars.

I glance over at Shon, she's keeping pace with me despite her shoes which are at least two sizes too big for her. The handcuff on her wrist dangles wildly, filling the empty night with a metallic click as she moves as quickly as she can. We remain silent and we keep moving until the fire is nothing but an orange dot behind us.

Then, Shon bursts into tears.

16

Erik

We walked for hours. I'd say half the night was spent on our feet. I marched ahead, clutching Shon's hand because it was so dark, we couldn't even see each other anymore. She stayed beside me, sobbing softly, letting her tears drip down her chin because her gallon of water was in her other hand so she couldn't wipe them away. I pretended not to notice.

When I was sure we'd put enough distance between ourselves and the university, we laid down to rest. I had no idea where we were, but both of us were too tired to care. We stumbled into a destroyed neighborhood, picked a house, and slept in the basement, snoring through our masks.

That was two days ago. Now, we're back to walking, staring into the distance and filling the silence with our heavy breathing. Shon hasn't said much since I marched her out of that burning building. She won't talk about what happened in her dorm. She won't tell me if she's okay, though, it doesn't take a genius to tell that she isn't.

I found her cuffed to a bed, stripped naked, her mouth taped shut. You don't need a big imagination to know what was going on in that room, especially since Jeremiah had already tried to force himself on her once before.

Pain swells in my jaw and I realize I've been grinding my teeth. Every time I close my eyes, I see Shon on that bed again. And I think of my wife. I think of the horrors she must have experienced before she passed on. And I hate myself for arriving too late. I didn't get to save her.

I glance over at Shon as she stumbles over a dead tree root, she glares at it like it tripped her on purpose but keeps walking.

At least I made it in time for her.

Or did I?

Maybe Jeremiah never touched her. Maybe he just tied her up and left her there to shame her. Maybe he enjoyed the psychological torture more than the physical. The sexual. I don't know—because Shon won't talk to me.

I get that she's hurting, but I'm hurting too. It wasn't easy to see her like that and being left to my thoughts—wondering about it—ain't been easy either. I *need* her to talk to me. I *need* to know if I was on time. Or if I failed … again.

"Shon…" I stop walking and turn to look at her.

She blinks behind her mask. "Yes?"

"We need to talk."

"Erik…"

I shake my head. "I'm just saying. You can't experience something like that and not talk about it. Shutting down isn't any good for anyone."

For a moment, we just stare at each other. I feel like an idiot for pressing her like this. What I saw has been giving me nightmares, but she's the one who experienced it. I can't force her to talk. And besides… I've been shut down for the last five years. Asking her to open up right now is such hypocrisy I could almost laugh at myself. But I don't see anything funny.

"Shon—"

"He hurt me," she says, cutting me off. "Is that what you want to hear?"

Now that it's out in the open… No, I suddenly realize I don't want to hear it at all.

"Let's set up camp," I say, just to change the subject.

Shon scoffs. "With what?"

When we left the university, we had three gallons of water and a granola bar, not to mention the crowbar and hunting knife. During our first rest, we drank an entire gallon straight down. I told Shon how I'd been locked up and starved, she balked at the details about cannibalism, telling me how bad Jeremiah had smelled up close. Apparently, he hadn't been giving her much food or water either, but that was all Shon said about it.

I tried to split the granola bar with her, but she claimed to have a bout of nausea and encouraged me to eat the whole thing. Considering all I'd had was a grand total of twenty peanuts over the course of four days, I didn't argue with her about the food. But that left us with nothing to eat once it was gone.

We went an entire day without food at all. But the day after that, we found an abandoned outlet mall and spent a little time looting. There wasn't much there, but we didn't walk away emptyhanded. Shon found a Slim Jim inside the cash register of an Old Navy store. We split it right away. The Old Navy also produced an expired pack of sunflower seeds which we devoured, shells and all. Then we sipped our water and found Shon some new shoes.

They were mismatched and covered in dust, but they were only a half-size too big compared to the men's shoes she'd been walking in before. I got a new t-shirt with a rip in the armpit. We both found jackets from the dried-up bodies that littered the parking lot.

Since then, we haven't had any fortune finding food. And we're down to our last half-gallon of water.

Shon folds her arms across her chest as she waits for me to answer her.

"What are we going to set up camp with?" she repeats.

I bunch my shoulders. This is not how our trip was supposed to go. I knew we would eventually bump into Faceless, I knew there was a chance something bad might happen along the way, but I did not consider the possibility of getting tricked into a cannibal camp by Shon's ex-boyfriend and leaving with the clothes on my back and a crowbar in my hand. My arms still itch from being exposed to the toxic air for so long, the filter in my mask desperately needs to be changed, and I have no real way to hunt down any food.

Not to mention the fact that there isn't anything to hunt. Almost everything is dead.

I drop my gaze to the ground; *we can't go out like this.*

"Erik?" Shon says.

I sigh and shrug off my backpack, then I hold the crowbar and stare at the cracked earth, digging my toe into the dirt. I take a deep breath, and then I stab the ground.

"What are you doing?" Shon asks.

"Finding us food," I grunt.

It takes me longer than expected to dig a hole. A crowbar is not suited for this job. By the time the hole is deep enough for me to lose my crowbar if I drop it in there, Shon has finished setting up our 'camp.' She laid out extra clothes we took from the mall bodies as sleeping mats and set the last jug of water out like it was being served for dinner. I can tell from her deep sighs that she's tired and anxious to know what I'm digging for.

She's about to find out.

I lie on my belly, still feeling a burning pain from my ribs, and I reach as far into the hole as I can. When I feel the ghostly legs of something whisper over my fingers, I close my hand and yank my arm out.

I've got a handful of cockroaches.

Shon screams and runs away.

I roll my eyes.

I have to shake off the roaches and gently step on as many as I can to kill them—without squishing them—before I dash off to go retrieve Shon. She yells at me and says she's not eating bugs, but when I tell her this is as good as it gets, she gives in and agrees to try one.

"It's good protein," I say, biting the head off one. It tastes awful, but it's nothing I haven't had before.

Shon grimaces like she's in physical pain at just the thought of eating a cockroach. I don't blame her. At least the ones I've had before this were cooked.

"Eat it quickly so it's not exposed to the surface air for too long," I tell her.

She nods and then picks up one of the roaches I'd stepped on earlier. Its head is flattened, but the bulbous body is still intact, its spidery legs look like bent whiskers jutting out. I can see her hand shaking as she brings the bug to her mouth and uses her other hand to lift her mask. She's still wearing the handcuffs I found her in, we have no way of removing them for now. The free one dangles from her arm, gently clanking against the one that's still latched around her wrist. I stare at it as she takes a bite.

Her face curdles into despair, and she actually lets out a sob. "This is *horrible!*"

"It's better than starving," I tell her. "Don't be such a cupcake."

She looks at me, her expression warming, lips curving into the ghost of a smile. I suppose it's too early to expect her to surrender any real smiles.

Shon rubs at her handcuff, exposing the bruise on her arm hidden beneath the metal. "He locked me in that room because I said I was leaving," she says suddenly. "I told him I wanted to go back home and find my family." She presses her lips together. "He said they were dead and trying to find them was a waste of time."

I nod, careful not to interrupt her now that she's finally talking.

"Jeremiah wanted me to stay there with him. He told me I could leave the room if I agreed to do that. But I said no. That's when he changed."

He didn't change. That monster's always been that way, Shon just didn't know.

"He said I was staying whether I wanted to or not. When I told him he couldn't keep me there forever, he laughed in my face." She looks up at me, fiddling with the half-eaten cockroach in her hand. "So I spat in his face."

I raise both eyebrows, shocked.

"That's when he stopped feeding me. On the second day, he sent a pair of handcuffs to the room with a message—I'd get food if I used the cuffs." She shakes her head. "I tossed them onto the dresser and went hungry. The next day, the offer changed. I could use the cuffs, or I could watch them kill you."

My heart stops. Part of me wants to know what happened

169

next, the other part is screaming for her not to tell me. I can't be the reason this happened to her. I can't be the reason she put those cuffs on her own wrist.

I swallow, but my throat is suddenly dry, and my mouth tastes like dirt. And cockroach.

"I put the cuffs on," Shon admits in a shaky voice. "And I stared at the ceiling until he was finished. The only solace I found was in the bowl of soup he gave me afterward."

A tear slides down her cheek as she stares at her wrist, like her bitter glare could unlock the restraints and reverse the damage that's been done. I watch her for a moment, wondering if there will be more tears, but Shon is stronger than I give her credit for. Instead of crying, she frowns and squishes the cockroach between her fingers. Then she tosses the carcass onto the ground and kicks dirt over it.

"It's over," she whispers. "We escaped. That's all that matters."

"Shon—"

"That's all that matters," she snaps.

I sigh as I put my mask back on, I haven't had a good meal in a while, but I don't have an appetite anymore. Shon puts her mask back on too.

"Why didn't you let me kill him?" I ask.

She doesn't respond for a moment, like she isn't sure herself.

"Killing people is wrong," she says softly.

I cock my head to the side. "What?"

"Killing him would have been wrong," she says louder. "God wouldn't have wanted me to kill him."

I suck my teeth behind my mask. "Jeremiah was killing people and eating them, Shon. He tried to rape you once—then he *did* rape you."

170

"I know that!" she shouts, bolting to her feet.

Shon is a small woman, but right now she towers over me with her fists shaking at her sides, her breaths coming out in choppy pants.

I flick my gaze away. "I—I'm sorry. I didn't mean to go that far. I just…" I sigh. "I don't see how you can forgive him for what he's done. Just because your Bible says so."

She shakes her head. "I never said I forgave him. But… I know I'm supposed to."

"How is that fair?" I snap.

"It's fair because God forgives *us*."

"No," I grunt. "That ain't right. Men like Jeremiah don't get to kill people and walk away. That's not fair."

"How many people did *you* kill?"

I stare up at her, my heart beginning to pound. I don't know how many I killed at the university. I don't know how many people I've killed at all. But this isn't about me.

"I did what I had to do," I say defensively. "If your God didn't want us to kill anyone, then why'd He let us fall into that mess in the first place?" I don't realize I'm yelling until Shon takes a step back, but it's too late. The dam's been broken, I can't stop the flood of words that pours from me.

"Why did He let us get taken by that monster? Why'd He let you get cuffed to a bed?"

Shon sways on her feet, like the weight of my questions are about to crush her. It dawns on me then that she's been wondering the same thing. The same question so many have asked before. Why do bad things happen to good people?

She hiccups and clutches at her chest, tears plop onto the ground below. "Being a Christian doesn't mean bad things won't happen to you." Her voice trembles. "In fact, the Bible promised that we'd get hit by storms when Jesus said, *Trouble will come.*"

She looks up at me through a watery gaze. "Bad things happen to good people because that's how the world works. Everyone faces trouble."

I scoff. "Then what's the point in being Christian?"

"The point is that when you're in the valley of the shadow of death, God is right there with you." She lifts her chin, and it's the most defiant thing she's ever done. Like she's directly rebelling against everything I've just said, fighting against every doubt in my head. No matter what I say, Shon will always believe that God is good. It's a strength—a *faith*—that I envy. Though I'll never admit that aloud.

"I believe that everything happens for a reason," she says confidently. "Even the bad things."

"Yeah? Well, what's the reason this happened?" I challenge. "What big plans did God have for you to be tied to a bed?"

She lifts her mask to wipe her runny nose. "This happened so you could see what true forgiveness looks like. And learn from it yourself."

My chest hurts at the sound of her words, like my heart is reacting despite my mind throwing up walls of rejection. I place a palm over my chest as I close my eyes, sucking in a gasp at the images of my wife that flash in my mind's eye.

She was taken from me. My son was taken from me. Minty's sister and husband were taken from her. I've lost so much… and I thought hunting down the men responsible for all that death and all that pain would make things right, but it didn't.

I spent a year of my life on a vengeance trip that only hardened and destroyed me from the inside out. I haven't forgiven the men who've hurt me. Not even in their graves. I

172

don't know if I *can*. But seeing Shon stand there in tears after what she experienced… Hearing her say that she still believed in God. That she still knew it was her duty to forgive Jeremiah for what he'd done. I … I don't know what to say. I don't think I have the strength to do what she's trying to do. I don't think it's possible for me to forgive the men who murdered my wife and son.

But if Shon can try to forgive Jeremiah, then I can try too.

The worst part about all this is that it's my fault. If I had found it in my heart to forgive my wife's killers five years ago, Shon wouldn't be here now. She wouldn't have been dragged into this mess, used as a demonstration just so I can learn a lesson I'd been taught since Sunday School.

I look at her now, tears streaking her cheeks. *You chose the right woman*, I pray for the first time in years. One strong enough to handle what she's been through. And one who loves God enough to still cling to Him when it's all over.

Shon doesn't blame God for her grief, instead, she's looking to Him for His comforting Hand.

"I… I'm sorry, Shon," I say in a surprisingly weak voice.

She looks at me like she pities me. It tears me apart.

"There's nothing to be sorry for."

"How can you truly forgive Jeremiah?"

"I don't know," she admits. "But I trust that God will help me. He'll heal the emotional wounds as well as the physical."

"You're not mad at God for letting this happen?"

She pauses. Takes a deep breath. "I don't know. I'm still human. And the human part of me wonders if sometimes God expects too much from us. If it's fair to test us like this. To use us as demonstrations."

"It isn't fair," I say.

She shakes her head. "God didn't *let* this happen, Erik."

173

"But He knew it would happen and He didn't stop it."

She looks at me dead-on. "He did the same thing to Jesus. God sat back and watched—He did not intervene—as Jesus was beaten, whipped, stripped and shamed, as His beard was torn out, as He was mocked and ridiculed and nailed to a Cross."

I stare at the ground.

"God valued His plan. He valued salvation over Jesus's pain. So what makes you think we are so special that He would not do the same with us?"

"That He would watch us suffer?" I challenge.

Shon smiles. The sight makes me shiver. "That He would trust us with the pain we suffer."

"I don't understand."

"Think of the people in the Bible. Paul spent years in prison. He was stoned and left for dead. King David lost his infant child. John the Baptist was beheaded. Dinah was raped." She sighs. "They faced unspeakable horrors, but if none of them had experienced these things, I wouldn't have an example to live by. I wouldn't understand forgiveness at all, and I wouldn't know how to turn to God in my pain."

I shift uncomfortably.

"Beneath my pain and grief, I have an odd sense of pride. God used me as an example unto others, just like the men and women of the Bible. God never plans for bad things to happen. He doesn't just step back and let His children suffer, but He does value His plan—He sees our salvation as more important than any trouble we face."

A gentle smile works its way onto her face as she whispers, "These light and momentary afflictions..."

I'm not that familiar with the Bible, but I'm certain she just quoted a Scripture from It.

174

"Paul said the pain he faced in this world was nothing compared to the glory that awaited him in Heaven. For the first time, I understand what he meant by that. I understand that sometimes God doesn't prevent bad things from happening, sometimes our experiences are horrible, and they hurt beyond belief. But the pain is not for nothing."

She lifts her chin.

"Paul's pain left him in chains, but it was in those chains that he wrote over half the New Testament. And through his chains that I learned what it means to be a base and what it means to abound." Shon nods like she's thinking to herself. "Paul had to suffer so that others could learn from his experience. God trusted me the same way. Like Paul, He knew no one else could have survived what I have with their faith intact." Shon lets go of a breath. "All this time, I thought God told me to return home so I could find my family." She meets my gaze. "But He wanted me to find *you* all along."

"Even though teaming up with me brought you trouble."

"It wasn't fun. But it's over now. And I know I'll never have to suffer again."

"What makes you think that?" I ask.

She straps her mask in place again. "Because this time, you got the message."

I blink away. I did get the message. I know I'm supposed to forgive. I just...

I palm the back of my neck. "My wife was Christian, like you."

I had called myself Christian back then too, like a lot of people did. But I never read my Bible, I never paid any tithes or offering, and I don't think I've ever prayed outside of church. I hardly ever went to any services, except when Angie would beg me to go. I think we both knew I was only there for her, not because I genuinely believed anything I heard during service. I never took it seriously. And now it's come back around to lay me flat.

I close my eyes and take a deep breath. "I think my wife would be proud of you for trying to forgive Jeremiah."

Shon nods slowly.

"And I think my wife would want me to forgive the men who hurt her."

"I think you're right."

"I don't know if I can, Shon. I don't know how *you* can."

"We can try together." She reaches for my hand, and I let her take it. "Do you know how to pray?"

Fear stirs inside of me. This is such a big leap. Not long ago, I was mocking Shon for believing in God, now we're holding hands about to pray. But prayer brings you closer to God and being close to God gives you hope.

I'm afraid of hope. Because hope allows disappointment and disappointment brings heartbreak. I can't experience that sort of pain again. I won't survive it.

I slowly tug my hand away from Shon, ignoring the sad look on her face. "I'm not ready to make any big commitment," I say weakly.

She nods, though I know I've upset her.

I guess … as some sort of way to make her feel better, I say, "My wife used to love the Psalms." I clear my throat. "Do you know any Psalms?"

Shon stares at me.

I stare back.

I know it sounds crazy. I never thought I would ever ask anyone to give me scriptures from the Bible, let alone in the middle of a makeshift camp while eating cockroaches for dinner during an apocalypse. But here we are. I suppose this is as good a time as any to try to understand my faith. To try to learn something about Jesus. It's what my wife would want.

Judging from the look on Shon's face, it's what she wants too. I can't see her smiling, but I can make out her bunched cheeks behind her mask as she says, "Yes, I know a few Psalms." She settles down and clasps her hands in her lap as she thinks, then she nods and takes a breath. "This is one of my favorites, it's from Psalms chapter sixty-two."

"Okay." I nod like I know what that means.

"Truly my soul finds rest in God," she says calmly. "My salvation comes from Him. Truly He is my rock and my salvation; He is my fortress, I will *never* be shaken."

I lean back on my elbows as Shon keeps going, delivering the verses like she's reciting poetry. The words sound beautiful, they sound so calming, and they stir something inside me that I can't explain. The only thought in my head as I stare at the sky is a curious wonder.

How does it feel to *never* be shaken?

17

Shon

It's been weeks. Weeks since I saw my crazy ex. Weeks since I had that tough conversation with Erik. Weeks since the shell around his heart splintered. He's been quiet lately. But not in his usual broody way; it's been different. Like he's thinking. Contemplating.

There are times when we're walking together that I find myself staring at the back of his dark hoodie. I wonder what he's thinking. I wonder if he still remembers the night he asked me to recite a verse from the Book of Psalms. And then, all at once, Erik will turn around and smile through his gasmask, and say, "Keep up, cupcake."

So I do.

I've made it my goal to carry my weight, because it's clear that Erik's carrying more than just the bag on his back. His shoulders are heavy with guilt, sorrow, anger, confusion, and so much more...

Unless he gets saved, he doesn't have God to give him

strength. Courage. Comfort. It's just him—literally. Erik's wife is gone. Erik's son is gone. He has a brother he hasn't seen since before the lights. And he left Minty back at that abandoned Amazon factory. Right now, it's just Erik. It's been Erik for a while.

But I'm here now.

I trip over a rock and immediately hear Erik's deep voice grumble a complaint ahead of me. I roll my eyes behind my mask.

"Walked a hundred miles and still haven't figured out how to place one foot in front of the other." Erik turns, hands on his hips, and gives me a mock-disappointed face. His shoulders drop as I adjust the strap on my bag. "Getting tired?"

I shake my head, but Erik's not convinced. He's been very careful not to overwork us. For the sake of my sore hip, I appreciate his concern and the frequent breaks, but I have to admit they also bother me. This kind version of Erik is much better than the mean-old-man version I met weeks ago. That guy wouldn't have cared if I needed a break. That guy had barely spoken more than ten words to me in two days.

We've moved on from that—from square one, when Erik hated my guts. But I haven't decided if this new territory of friendship we've entered is any better. Because I know Erik is only being kind because of what he saw in that dorm.

Me. Naked and handcuffed to a bed. We never really talked about it except when he was yelling at me about God. Since that night, we've avoided all conversation surrounding the university. I haven't overlooked the fact that we've also avoided talking about the Lord. But I won't press the issue. The Truth went forth, that much I know. When Erik's ready, he'll come back for more. I'm sure of it.

Just like I'm sure of my purpose here now. I thought God

had called me home to reunite with my family, but now it's clear as day that Erik's been my mission all along. I think I've completed that mission.

It wasn't my job to save Erik. It was my job to give him the chance to be saved. To tell the Truth when it was asked of me. To be honest, even in the midst of my pain.

I did it, God, I pray inside as Erik leads us to an abandoned cabin nearby. *I told him about Jesus. I gave him the Truth. It's up to him now.*

The sun is setting by the time Erik's done scouting the area. I've got a small fire going when he enters the cabin. The place is small, a hunting shack left for campers and other nature enthusiasts. There's an old wood-burning stove in the corner with two logs sitting beside it. I used them both to start the fire, and I opened one of the three cans of mixed vegetables left in the cabinet above the stove. The best thing about hunters and campers is they know the wild can be a struggle. This is the second shack we've found in the area stashed with a few supplies.

There wasn't any water anywhere in the cabin, but there is a single bed with linen, and I found a map in the bedside table drawer. Apparently, we're not too far from my hometown—if the little X someone marked on the map is truly our location.

Erik sits on the bed and sighs tiredly. "You checked everything in here?" he asks.

"Don't I always?" Since leaving the university, we've developed a routine that works for us. Erik leads the way, since I can't navigate worth a darn, I keep an eye out for Faceless and wanderers. When we find a place to settle for the night, I set up camp while he checks the perimeter.

It's my job to clear out any Faceless indoors. I'm still carrying the hunting knife Erik gave me, but I've added a nice metal baseball bat to my weaponry since we set out. I found it in an abandoned stadium—of course—where we also found a crate of jerky, expired packages of peanuts, unopened bottles of Gatorade, and a bolt cutter to snip off the handcuffs that'd been latched around my wrist. I can't express the joy I felt when I finally took those things off. But getting those bolt cutters—or any of the supplies we found—wasn't easy.

We had to fight for our lives in that stadium. It looked like there had been a game going on when the bombs went off, leaving thousands of people exposed to the radiation of the explosions and the chaos of the aftermath. The good thing was that most of the bodies in the stadium were dead. They never transitioned because they died in the fires of the bombs, or they died getting trampled by the panicked crowds trying to escape.

Still, there had been plenty of Faceless left. Enough to dissuade wanderers and looters from entering the building, and enough to give us trouble once we found a way inside.

With our supplies, we gorged ourselves on jerky, expired snacks, and bottled energy drinks. I would have loved to stay in the stadium, but I still want to find my family. Even though they weren't my true mission. I don't care what Erik believes; I'm choosing to believe that God is good, and that He will reward me for my troubles. I know my family is alive somewhere. And from the way Erik is enthusiastically reading the map from the bedside table now, I'd say we aren't far from finding them.

"Update?" I request, stirring the hot vegetables. I add a single strip of jerky to the little pot; we're down to our last pack so I'm trying to stretch it.

Erik grunts across the room.

"Erik, what's the map say?"

"We're about three days out. I think."

My heart skips a beat. "Three days?"

"I *think*, Shon. Don't get too excited. I could be wrong—this map could be old—"

"I haven't seen my family in almost ten years!" I exclaim excitedly. "I can't believe we've made it!"

"We haven't made it yet."

I glower at Erik, but the look doesn't last long because the vegetables start to boil over so I'm forced to return my attention to the stove. There aren't any spare bowls or utensils; I'd used a small stick to stir the pot, so Erik and I huddle by the cooling stove and pass the food back and forth.

While we eat, Erik starts explaining how we could be closer or further away than we think, but I'm not listening. I'm busy thinking of my family. Wondering how they've been. How my son has been.

Jeremiah Jr. will be nine years old now. I haven't seen him since he was young enough to breastfeed. I wonder if he remembers me at all. If he's been waiting for me to come home and be the mother I should have been years ago.

"*Shon.*"

Erik's rough voice snaps me back to attention. When I look up, I realize I've been staring into space for longer than normal.

"You good?" Erik asks.

I nod and pass him the pot. He greedily digs in with his dirty fingers, and I try not to feel grossed out. Erik is oddly comfortable with being dirty. I hate to admit that Minty was right when she'd called me spoiled for staying holed up in the airport, but I can't stop my nose from wrinkling as I watch Erik eat with his hands, sucking the salty jerky-flavored broth off his fingers like it's the best thing he's eaten all week.

Considering we've had to dig for cockroaches three times

182

since leaving the university, I guess this dinner isn't so bad.

"You think my family is in a settlement?" I ask, lifting my mask and setting it on the floor beside me.

Erik chews in silence. "RaShonda…"

I start shaking my head. He never has anything good to say when he uses my full name.

"They're alive, Erik. I know it."

"Did God tell you that?" he asks. I want to feel offended, but his voice is soft, and his eyes are full of sincerity as he looks up at me. He's being serious right now. He isn't mocking me.

"No." I sigh. "God hasn't said anything about my family, honestly."

"Then maybe—"

"They're not dead!" I snap.

"I wasn't going to say they were!" he snaps back.

We sit there stewing for a good five minutes before Erik stands abruptly and starts pacing the room. His arms are folded over his chest and his jaw is clenched. When he opens his mouth to speak, his voice is shockingly gentle.

"They could be alive. I wasn't gonna say they were dead, you hear?"

I nod slowly.

"I'm just saying, they might not be where you left them. They could have ended up as drifters, like me."

"My son would have been three years old when the bombs went off. My mother wouldn't have set out with a toddler."

Erik looks sad for some reason. "If she loved him, she would have done whatever it took to keep him alive. Even if that meant braving the Grey together."

I swallow. My mouth tastes like jerky and green beans.

"If they're not there—"

"I'll help you find them." The words leave his mouth so

183

quickly, even Erik looks surprised for a moment, like he can't believe what he just said.

When I expect him to recant his statement, he presses his lips together and nods. "I'll help you find them," he says again.

"Shouldn't you go back to your group?"

Erik doesn't speak.

I hadn't really thought about what would happen once I found my family. Will Erik just say goodbye and leave? Start his lonely trek back home all by himself?

"Minty will be expecting you," I say pathetically.

Erik grumbles something I can't make out, but when I open my mouth to ask him to repeat himself, he sighs loudly and stalks toward the door.

"Where are you going?" I ask.

He pauses, hand on the knob, shoulders tense. "To take a leak." Then he snatches the door open and marches out. Angry. Brooding. And I have no idea why.

Radiation settles on things. Objects absorb it like sponges, even solid metal. So it doesn't matter if I sleep on the bed or the ground, both are relatively contaminated. The good thing about radiation—if you could call it good—is that it's surprisingly simple to get rid of it.

Time and water.

Minty wasn't lying about getting scrubbed down at her lab. Washing contaminated surfaces helps get rid of radiation; but I can't wash the entire bed in the cabin, so I'm left with option B.

Plastic, lead, and aluminum foil.

Radiation has a hard time penetrating those materials, which is why we cover windows and doorways with them—

also to keep out the contaminated air. I don't have any foil or lead, but there was plenty of plastic and tarp in that stadium. I packed away a large curtain of it when we left, so I unfold it and lay it over the bed now. Normally, Erik would do this with me, the sheet of thick plastic is large enough for us both to fit on it, but he isn't here right now. His little bathroom break started an hour ago. And apparently, it's still going.

Maybe he got diarrhea. Maybe he got jumped by a Faceless and is lying dead right outside the cabin. I don't know, and I'm too tired to care. Erik will always be Erik. Chasing after him won't bring him back or change a thing. He'll come back when he's hungry or tired.

With a huff in annoyance, I climb on top of the plastic and try to get comfortable. It crinkles the entire time, but I'm so tired I hardly notice the sound. I'm asleep before I even realize it.

When I wake up, it's the middle of the night. I've grown accustomed to short sleep cycles, waking up every three to four hours to change shifts with Erik. As I swing my legs over the bed, I blink around the room and find Erik sitting by the stove. There's a low light glowing in its belly, keeping the night's chill away. When he looks over at me, I can see his green eyes glowing in the dim moonlight. During the ashen grey day, they look bright as mint leaves. But right now, his eyes are two emeralds in his face.

"The bed is all yours," I say softly.

He nods and stands. I hear his knees pop.

"Wake me—"

"At sunrise. I know."

He holds my gaze for a long moment. Then, before I can think of something to say, he turns and walks away.

Somehow, we've fallen back to square one.

185

18

Erik

When my son looks at me, I see death in his eyes. I know that he knows this is his last moment alive. His death doesn't tear me apart. If I'm being honest, I'd been surprised we'd lasted as long as we had. It was the look in his eye that sent a chill slithering down my spine. As the ruthless wanderers held him down and pressed a gun to his temple, it was the fact that he knew he was dying that left me short of breath. The knowledge that he knew this was the end, and the fact that there was nothing I could do to save him.

When I glance up and see my wife, the pain in my heart multiplies. Her shrieks pierce the air as the men drag her away, my own shouts ring out, screams that are off key and incoherent. I don't even know if I'm speaking English. I'm just screaming. Mindlessly. Painfully. Lost in the void of despair.

There is a gunshot that quiets the chaos. And all that's left when I can see past the blurry tears in my eyes is grief.

It is raw and heavy, and it stinks. Grief smells like death.

"Erik!"

My wife's voice…

"Erik!"

My eyes snap open and I blink at the inky darkness above me. I'm lying on my back on the crinkly plastic-covered bed. A layer of sweat leaves my jeans sticking to my legs, my shirt clinging to my chest.

I'd been dreaming; the same nightmare that has haunted me for the last few years. I thought I had finally escaped it about a year ago when it stopped coming back to terrorize me. But now it's returned.

Maybe it's because of the madness we experienced at the university. Maybe it's because I told Shon about my family not long ago. Maybe it's because of *Shon*.

She has her own family, they're the reason we're even out here now. That's the part that leaves me panting as I sit up in bed. We have no idea what we're walking into. Shon could be right. God could have protected her family. They could be waiting for her right now. Or she could be wrong. Her son could be dead and gone. Just like mine.

My hand shakes as I wipe it through my sweaty hair. I have to focus on my breathing or else I fear I might stop altogether.

"Erik!" My name again, this time, it isn't the sound of my wife's voice.

My gaze lands on Shon, crouched by the door, baseball bat in hand. She's fully dressed, but her backpack still rests by the unlit stove. The embers in the belly of the stove have died, but there is a sliver of sunlight peeling in through the plastic-covered window that gives me just enough light to see.

I can make out the wrinkle in Shon's forehead as she cracks the door and peers out, then quickly shuts it. "You awake?" she whispers, not looking at me.

188

"What's going on?" Every hair on my body raises, one by one.

"Faceless," Shon whispers.

I slide off the bed and slip on my boots. "How many?"

"A lot."

"Where?"

Shon pauses to look over her shoulder at me. "Everywhere."

What?

My eyes bulge when I peek out the window. Shon is right, there are Faceless everywhere.

The only way I can describe what I see outside is to say that a massive grey herd is walking through the dead woods right now. The trees are grey and slanted; bare, crooked branches jutting out like spider limbs. The ground is dotted with those wretched neon daisies, and the feet that crush them are cold and grey.

The Faceless walk through the barren fields in the same direction, like a dead army, their movements are not the same as the ones I've battled with Shon recently. These grey creatures are more dead than alive, almost catatonic.

Normally, any Faceless in the area would be scratching at our door by now. They would have sniffed us out and chased us down just like they'd done on the highway weeks ago. But when a human first transitions, their mind doesn't just rot... It reverts. They lose all sense and fall into a primal, animalistic state. That feeds their craving for flesh. That gives them the mindless desire for human meat and blood.

But the process is slower for some than others. The brain remains intact longer, allowing some Faceless to hold on to their minds and think beyond the craving for flesh. That's why there were Faceless wielding weapons while others crawled on all fours. That's why some Faceless were in chains—enslaved by their own kind.

There exists a sort of hierarchy amongst the mindless and the grey. There is order in the barren fields. That order does not include healthy humans.

Somehow, though, these Faceless are different. None of them are wielding weapons or guiding other Faceless on chains like wild dogs. Every single wild man and woman in this herd is walking slowly, shuffling in the same direction whether on all fours or upright. They pay the cabin no mind, walking around it like it doesn't even exist.

This is the most extraordinary thing I've ever seen. It's all I can do to stay indoors instead of running out to witness this up close. I'm too afraid of making any noise and snapping them out of their hypnotic trance.

"What's going on?" Shon asks, still peering through the cracked door. Her voice shakes with fear despite her brave curiosity. "Why haven't they attacked us?"

I lift my mask to scratch the stubble on my chin. "I don't know."

"Have you ever seen this before?"

"No. I haven't."

Shon slowly closes the door and looks up at me. "Maybe they're all tired?"

That idea switches on a lightbulb in my head. "Faceless are stronger at night," I whisper.

"That means they rest during the day," Shon adds. "Or at least *part* of the day."

I glance back out the window. It's just before sunrise.

"You're right. They're literally tired. They're going to find a place to sleep—away from the sun."

"What place though?"

190

I bunch my shoulders, trying to think. "I don't know. They have nests, but I've only seen a wild nest once. I thought it might have been a unique thing, you know? I never thought *all* Faceless stayed in nests."

Shon rubs her hands up and down her arms like she's cold. "This is freaking me out."

"You should be happy," I say quietly, like I'm afraid of waking the Faceless from their groggy stupor. "If this herd had passed through here any other time, we'd be in trouble."

"The fact that they *are* passing through here means their nest is somewhere nearby."

Now I start feeling a little anxious too. I can feel sweat pushing through the pores of my forehead, dampening my face. "We need to move as soon as this herd is gone."

"Maybe we should travel *with* the herd," Shon suggests.

I blink at her like she's crazy. "You want to go out there and walk with hundreds of Faceless?"

"If they were going to chase us down, they would have done so by now."

I shake my head. "There's a difference between not sensing us in this cabin and not sensing us standing right beside them." I sigh. "Besides, it's safer to travel during the day when they'll be gone."

"There's no promise they *will* be gone." Shon clutches her baseball bat tightly. "We've bumped into Faceless in the middle of the afternoon before. For all we know, they could go rest for an *hour* and hit the road again. That means we could get tracked down and eaten by the first wild men to wake up."

She has a point.

We don't even know where their nest is located. For all we know, we could start walking right toward it, even stumble upon it... As soon as they wake up again.

191

Shon seems to read my mind. "At the very least, let's follow the herd and see where the nest is located so we can avoid it."

I don't know what to say. This sounds like a really stupid plan or a really brilliant plan.

"There is no guarantee they won't chase us down as soon as we step outside this cabin."

Shon nods, slowly moving past me toward the bed. I watch in confused silence as she neatly folds up the plastic, returns it to her backpack, and then begins to strip the linen from the mattress.

"What are you doing?"

"What makes us different from Faceless?" she asks.

I shrug. "We aren't mindless and feral."

"Why is that?"

"Because we aren't pumped full of radiation."

Shon turns and smiles at me, clutching the stained sheets in her hands. "Exactly."

"Start making sense, cupcake."

"I don't think Faceless hunt us down by tracking us the way we track animals. I think they can smell us," she explains.

"Of course they can."

"No." Shon holds up the sheets. "I think they can smell our *health*."

I tilt my head to the side.

"We smell different because we aren't full of radiation." She lifts the sheet and wraps it over her shoulders like you would a warm blanket on a cold winter day. "If we cover ourselves in contaminated materials, we'll give off the same scent as them. We'll smell infected."

It's just like the neon daisies, leaning toward pockets of radiation so they could feed on it. That *is* brilliant.

"How do we know this will work?" I ask as Shon passes

me a sheet to wrap around myself. For all we know, this cabin has been sitting here for six years in the radioactive air. These sheets should be full of toxins. But that isn't a promise that Shon's theory is correct. We could walk outside in these contaminated sheets and still get hunted down.

"We don't know for certain," Shon says. "Faceless might have an instinct to ignore certain levels of contamination. These sheets may not have enough radiation in them to totally cloak us. Maybe they'll fool some Faceless for a while, throw off our scent until we're spotted."

That makes sense. We can hide our healthy scent, but nothing can fool a Faceless looking right at us. And also…

"If this truly works, why hasn't anyone else tried it in six years?"

Shon smiles, tying the sheet tightly around her neck. "Because it's not a good idea to wrap yourself up in a sheet contaminated with radiation."

Another good point. We're going to have to decontaminate once this is over. If we didn't have long sleeves and gasmasks, wearing these sheets for too long would make us sick. And then the Faceless would be the least of our worries.

I nod as I lift my sheet over my head. "Move quickly and quietly."

Shon moves toward the door, but I reach out and grab her wrist just as she touches the knob. I can hear Faceless shuffling by outside as I warn her, "Stay by me, Shon."

She nods and my grip tightens.

"I mean it. Don't you leave my side."

For a heartbeat, I see my wife standing in front of me instead of Shon. I see her nod and I feel her grip my hand. When I suck in a gasp, the vision dissipates and I'm back in the cabin, staring at Shon, a gasmask covering her face.

193

My throat feels dry when I swallow. I don't want to lose Shon just like I've lost everyone else. But we don't have a choice right now except to keep moving. I don't have a choice except to keep fighting.

Shon tugs on my sleeve. "Ready?"

"Yeah," I grunt. And then we leave.

I thought walking through the herd would leave me anxious and jittery—ready to fight or flee at any moment. But it has the exact opposite effect. I feel every part of me relax in the flow of Faceless traffic. I am as uncaring as the monsters themselves, melting into the crowd, secure in the safety of my anonymity.

Shon's theory is right. The contaminated sheets work as a cover, even though we're in plain view of the Faceless, they're too tired and their minds are too numb to distinguish us from any other infected person. To them, we probably smell so much like radiation, it doesn't matter how we look. That, and the fact that they're so catatonic, it's like walking through a crowd of hypnotized zombies.

Shon stays by my side the entire time, even reaches out to take my hand once. We walk like that for almost a mile, until I have to pull out the map from the cabin and try to pinpoint our location.

I want to enter the city so we can loot and find landmarks as guidance, but the herd is moving further west, going into the countryside. Should we follow them and locate their nest? Or should we follow the map and keep moving toward our destination?

Before I can make a decision, Shon darts forward through the crowd like she's lost her mind. I reach for her, but she's faster than she looks and slips right by me. I'm left with no choice but to chase after her, slipping between Faceless as I go.

Whatever bit of calm I'd had while moving with the herd evaporates instantly. I'm in full-blown panic mode now, sweating behind my mask and wheezing for air as I try to keep up with Shon. I have no idea where she's going or why she's running, but I can't lose track of her. Not in this crowd. Not in these dead woods.

I take a chance and call her name, holding my breath as a Faceless shifts toward me. Its dead eyes seem to gaze right through me, wearing an expression that is oddly reminiscent of someone who just woke up. We're in the very first hour of sunlight now, these wild men and women should be about to pass out. I don't want to be the reason they come to their senses and try to murder us, so I forget about calling for Shon and decide to outright sprint after her.

By the time I chase her down, snatching her roughly by the arm, she's standing in front of a dilapidated building. Her head is tilted back, and her eyes are misty, even behind her mask.

"What is wrong with you?" I growl, not trying to hide my anger. "You could've gotten us caught and killed!" I'm yelling now because we cleared the herd—they continued west, still unaware of our presence, while we ran toward the city. But I'm not just yelling because we're safe now, I'm yelling because I'm ticked off.

I get in Shon's face, wishing we didn't have these masks on so she could see the grimace I'm wearing. Not that it makes a difference to her. Even though I can't see her mouth, I can tell from her wide eyes that she's smiling.

Shon has blown up on me for not talking to her, the fact that she's totally calm and smiling while I'm yelling in her face makes me pause. I whirl around to stare at the partially destroyed brick building, a question forming in my head just as Shon answers it.

"This place… I recognize it."

Oh crap.

"Seriously?" I fumble for the map, trying to make sense of where we are. I thought we wouldn't reach her hometown for a few more days; there's a chance I could've been off by a few miles, but this is shocking.

Shon just found a place from her home. She knows this building.

We're closer than I thought.

"What is this place?" I ask, folding up the map again.

"It's a corner store." She turns to me. "I used to stop here all the time on the way home from school."

I want to smile as I think of teenage Shon buying snacks after school, but something over her shoulder catches my attention. Movement. A blurry figure that's too quick for me to make out. One second it was right there, standing in an alley between two buildings—the next second it was gone. Like it'd vanished. Or entered the building.

I snatch off my sheet and take a step in the direction where I saw the figure.

"What's wrong?" Shon asks, turning around as I keep walking. When I don't answer her, she discards her sheet too and jogs over to grab my sleeve. "Erik."

"I saw something," I tell her. "I think I saw *someone*."

"Are you sure? It could have been a Faceless."

"A Faceless would have attacked us by now."

She hesitates. Shon, who's killed plenty of Faceless and fought her way out of a burning building full of cannibals looks afraid now. She's a tough cupcake, but I understand her fears. We're *this* close to finding her family. We don't need any more

196

drama. Considering the last people we ran into wanted to eat us, I feel a small bit of the same fear I see claiming her features. But I can't let that stop us.

"I'll check it out," I say, turning away.

Shon's grip on my sleeve doesn't give. She jerks me to a halt and turns me back to face her. "I'm coming with you."

"This town might not be a ghost town, Shon. There could be dozens of people in that building."

"That's why you shouldn't go alone." She walks away before I can stop her, speaking over her shoulder. "Besides, if there are people here, they might know where my family is."

I seriously doubt that. But we've got to check it out anyway, so I keep my mouth shut.

When we get to the building, Shon lets me take the lead, though she keeps her baseball bat raised high—which I appreciate. I clutch the crowbar in my hand as I grip the doorknob to the building. There aren't any signs outside, and the walls are all painted over with graffiti so it's impossible to tell what this building had been before the explosions. We could be breaking into a restaurant, an office, or even a church. I have no idea.

"Stay close," I mutter as I turn the knob. Shon doesn't answer, but I don't need her to. When I shove the door open, we rush inside together. We've cleared enough buildings to fall into an unspoken routine. I clear the east while she swings west, if there are stairs then we sweep the first floor and move up as one.

The building is dark inside when the door opens, but the light that spills in splashes color around the room. I can see a counter and metal shelves, there's a grimy looking vending machine in the corner, and a cluster of overturned chairs. The space is small, so I'm able to see almost the entire room from where I'm standing by the door.

It's not until I start my sweep of the west side of the room that I see something move from behind the counter.

I pivot, swinging my crowbar. Shon shouts something—but her voice is cutoff by an explosion of pain that erupts in the back of my head. Stars burst into my vision and darkness is all I see next.

19

Shon

Erik finally wakes up an hour after he was knocked unconscious. It is not a peaceful event. He violently jerks upright as he heaves for air, blinking around the room in confusion. I can tell the moment he realizes he's alive and safe when he spots the man tied up in the corner of the room. His shoulders tense while his face relaxes. It's the strangest thing I've ever seen, like he's placed a mask over his features, lied to himself to appear calm. Even though I can feel the rage coming off him from across the room.

I step into the light, peeling from the wall I'd been leaning against. Erik immediately snaps his gaze over to me, adjusting his mask to see better. "Shon?"

I nod and walk over to him. "You okay?"

"What happened?"

"You got hit over the head." I jerk my chin at the discarded piece of wood behind him. "I think it's a chair leg."

Erik glares at the stick, then he shifts back toward me. "Are you okay?"

"Perfectly fine."

Turns out, Erik did see someone in that alley. And they saw us. Except that stranger wasn't running away to lure us into a trap, he ducked into this building to hide from us. So when we walked inside, he fought for his life.

It was not a mistake to attack us. It was a mistake to assume Erik was the greater threat.

When my comrade crumpled to the floor, I launched like a madwoman. It took two good slugs from that baseball bat to drop our attacker to his knees. Like Erik, he never saw it coming. I got him tied up and dragged him to the corner of the room. Been sitting around waiting for one of them to drift back into consciousness for over an hour now.

Erik came around first.

After I explain how he got his butt handed to him, he tugs off his gasmask and takes a deep breath. The air in here isn't so bad. I think this place has been locked up for a while, but Erik still coughs and then returns his mask.

"Has he said anything?"

I glance over at the man lying on his side, his hands tied behind his back. His gasmask is on the counter a few feet away—I'd taken it from him to use as collateral in case he doesn't want to cough up answers to our questions. On cue, he groans and turns over, his eyes blinking open.

"He might say something now."

Erik slowly gets to his feet, I don't know if it's his ribs, his head, or his age that's got him moving so slowly but once he's up, he's crossing the room so fast I have to leap to my feet to grab his arm.

"Hold on," I say quickly. "He attacked us out of fear."

Right before I hit him with the bat.

200

Erik tries to pry his arm free, but I hold on. "He won't talk if you beat him up. And he won't talk if he's still afraid."

"I'm not afraid," the man stupidly speaks up. I turn to see him sitting up, a smirk on his bruised face. He's got tan skin and dark hair, his jaw covered in the first stages of a beard. Any other time, I might have seen him as handsome, but right now his face makes me want to punch him. "Bring it on, old man," he taunts.

Now Erik wants to punch him too. He tugs his arm free of my grasp and storms across the room, grabbing the man by his collar and yanking him to his feet. Now that he's standing, I realize he's almost the same height as Erik. I can also see how much younger he is, and thinner.

"Go ahead," the man says in a thick Spanish accent. "You already took my mask. Might as well just get it over with."

Suddenly, he doesn't seem so angsty or mean. He looks like he's given up.

I walk over and place a hand on Erik's shoulder. "Don't hurt him."

"Shon—"

I cut him off and address the man in Spanish. "*What's your name?*"

He cocks his head to the side—so does Erik. Both of them ask in English, at the same time, "You speak Spanish?"

"I lived in Spain for three years. It's not as difficult to learn a language when you're surrounded by native speakers all day every day for years."

Erik looks mildly impressed but the man beams ear to ear. All his attitude from earlier is gone; he suddenly looks boyish. As young as Everett.

"My name is Arya," he says happily.

"And what were you doing out here, Arya?" I ask.

He looks at Erik and then glances down at his hands still gripping him by the collar. "Wanna let me go, *amigo*?"

Erik grunts. "No."

"Erik."

"I don't trust him."

"I don't trust you either," Arya snaps, though it's hard to take him seriously while he's got that smirk on his face.

"Were you following us?" Erik asks.

"I wasn't following anything but my map," he answers. His gaze finds mine; he looks pleading. "I'm just trying to find my sister."

Something tugs at my heart. I know what it's like to be separated from your family. I know what it's like to spend time wandering around in search of them. Not knowing if they're dead or alive.

"Let him go, Erik," I say softly. My hand digs into his hoodie, balling up the material bunched on his tense shoulder. My grip is tight enough to drag his attention away from Arya for half a second. When he looks at me, he must see all the emotion that's gathered in my eyes because his voice comes out as little more than a whisper.

"Alright."

Just like that, he lets Arya go and takes exactly one step back. He isn't going to pummel him anymore, but he's not going to give him much space to breathe. Fine. I can live with that.

"Tell me about your sister," I say.

Arya shakes his head. "Can't you untie me first?"

"No," Erik grumbles beside me before I can even answer.

Arya glowers. "There are two of you and one of me."

"I can count," Erik says.

"You're seriously that afraid of me?"

202

I decide to interject before Arya gets himself choked out. "Erik is paranoid. We've bumped into bad company before. I hope you understand."

"Actually, I do understand." Arya sighs. "Bad company is how I got separated from my sister."

"What do you mean?"

"We crossed paths with some thugs a little ways back and we got separated while trying to get away from them."

"How long ago was that?" Erik asks.

Arya shrugs. "Three or four days."

"Shouldn't you double back to find your sister where you left her?"

He shakes his head. "We agreed to meet up at the next destination. Keep going. No matter what. That's the code we live by."

For a moment, no one speaks. I'm too busy trying to think of whether that's a good code to honor but Erik is contemplating other things.

"What's the next destination?" he asks.

Arya shakes his head again. "You want me to give more information, you're gonna have to start handing out some too."

"You're not in a position—"

Arya spits on the floor. "Untie me or walk away. I'm done talking."

Erik stares at the spit, then he abruptly turns and snatches Arya's gasmask off the counter. He holds it at arm's length by the straps. "You've been out for an hour. That means you've got four left before you'll need a new lung." Erik takes a slow step forward. "Start talking."

Colorful Spanish words fill the air as Arya glares at us. I thank God Erik has no idea what he's saying.

203

"The next destination is a church, okay?"

"What church?" Erik asks. "And why?"

"Fire Baptized Ministries." Arya huffs. "We were going there because we heard it's got a community established. Like a settlement. A *mask-free* settlement."

"There's no such thing." Erik rolls his eyes behind his mask. I want to roll mine too. Even in Rebirth Colony I heard rumors of mask-free settlements—places free of radiation, where you could freely breathe in the air and not worry about getting contaminated.

No one ever had any concrete directions to these places or evidence of their existence, but they had plenty of stories and what we dismissed as myths. But I believe what Arya's saying. Not just because I'm Christian, I believe him because I know where Fire Baptized Ministries is located.

"That's my old church," I say without thinking, silencing the argument going on between Erik and Arya. Erik had waved off Arya's claims about the settlement, Arya had responded by calling Erik stupid—then he'd changed his mind and called Erik's *mother* stupid when Erik challenged him to say it again. They were *this* close to fist fighting when I spoke up.

Now, both men are just staring at me, eyes wide and unblinking.

"You know where Fire Baptized Ministries is at?" Arya asks.

I nod. "That's the church I grew up in."

I can remember going to Sunday school there as a little girl. I remember Hallelujah Night every year instead of Halloween. I remember Victory Day instead of Valentine's Day—and I remember getting asked out on a date for the first time when I was fourteen on Victory Day.

When I was fifteen, I was fire baptized by Pastor Anne-

Marie. I remember my mother tearing up and my father crushing me in a hug. And I remember my mother tearing up again and my father crushing *her* in a hug when I sat in Pastor Anne-Marie's office and confessed to being pregnant at seventeen.

I shiver at all the memories that follow. The destruction of my parents' marriage. The arguments over abortion. Pastor Anne-Marie even delivered a sermon about the meaning of life when she heard about my father's response to the situation.

More than anything, I remember how close my mother was to our Pastor. I remember her helping out at the church so much, she was invited to join the council. Pastor Anne-Marie had dinner at our house multiple times, and she never judged me or demeaned me for the mistakes I made.

That's why news of this church community sparks a fire of hope in my heart. Because I know if my old church stuck together and built a community led by Pastor Anne-Marie, then my mother will definitely be there. I have no doubt in my mind.

"RaShonda," Erik says, snapping me back to attention. He looks at me like he's concerned, and I realize he asked me a question.

"Do you know where Fire Baptized Ministries is located?" Erik repeats.

I nod and slide my gaze over to Arya. "I do know where it's at. And I'm going to take you there."

20

Erik

I don't think it's much of a shock that I'm not a big fan of Arya. Not just because he's annoying, I don't like him much because I think he's full of crap. I don't believe this secret mask-free community exists, and I'm only half convinced he's even got a sister out there.

Listen to this.

Arya has been travelling with his older sister for the last three years. Before that, they were hunkered down with their entire family, but their mother passed away and the family split shortly after. Half of them wanted to stay in Mexico where they felt safe, the other half wanted to set out and see if the rest of the world had truly been destroyed.

Turns out, whoever set off those bombs weren't looking to destroy just America. Arya told us he heard whispers of Canada being attacked less than a week after the US was hit. But I don't trust a word he says because he also claims he heard whispers of Fire Baptized Ministries being a safe haven. A

Christian haven.

He says he found out about the community through his mother before she passed away. Lolita Valentin was a lady Pastor who had her own church in Puerto Vallarta—that was where Arya and his family had taken up shelter for three years until everything fell apart. Just before his mother shut her eyes for the last time, she told him there were other churches like theirs. Places that were mask-free, holy ground untouched by radiation.

With that little lie in his head, Arya and his sister set out to track down these safe zones. They went from church to church until the family couldn't take the constant moving around anymore. With a group of 13, I couldn't blame them for breaking up and setting off on their own. I came from a group of drifters that had pushed 75 people at one point. I know the struggles of travelling in large groups.

Arya and his sister set off on their own, church hopping for years until they ended up here.

Part of me wants to at least try to believe Arya's story, especially with Shon clinging to every one of his words. She too had set off on a ridiculous journey because she'd convinced herself that God had a job for her to do. I suppose she believes that job is to get me saved, but that hasn't happened yet. And with Arya blabbing his nonsense, I feel like I've just taken two steps further from God.

If God is real and wanted all these people to magically meet up, why did so many have to die along the way? Why did Arya have to lose his mother? Why did Shon have to face any of the struggles she's gone through so far?

And what's the *point*? What does God want with all these people gathered in one place? It's like He's rallying Christians together.

"That's not a bad suggestion," Shon says as we walk through the empty streets. We'd left that abandoned building a few hours back, walking side by side at a pace that's slower than I like.

Shon glances over at me through her mask. "God really could be doing just that. Gathering His children."

I shake my head. "So, He's just bringing everyone together."

She nods.

"But why?"

"Because He's got a safe place for us all to live."

I stare at her like she's crazy. She *is* crazy if that's what she believes. Before I can tell her how nuts she sounds, she starts talking again.

"The Bible repeatedly prophesies that Israel gets scattered and then gathered together again." She shrugs. "Who's to say the same can't happen for us?"

I want to sigh but I know showing any sort of frustration will only make her get defensive. Right now, I don't want to fight. I just want to track down this church so we can all see that there is no secret safe zone community for Christians and go on about our business.

"Don't you think it's a little cruel to just gather all the Christians and leave the rest of the world hanging?" I challenge. "And why wait until now?"

"First of all," Shon says, "I'm sure these communities are open for everyone. They're not going to turn you away just because you don't like God."

I grumble behind my mask. I don't dislike God; I just don't understand Him.

"And anyway," Shon goes on, "God has always made a distinction between His children and those who have rejected

208

Him. Whenever the Israelites faced trouble, God took care of them. *Only* them. Because they were His. That's one of the perks of accepting God as your Father." She looks at me, and I know she's smiling behind her mask, though I don't see what's so funny right now. "Second of all, God didn't wait six years. For all we know, Fire Baptized Ministries has *always* been a safe zone. We just didn't bother seeking it out until now."

I can't argue with that. Shon has repeatedly admitted that she got the message to return home before the bombs ever went off. She has repeatedly admitted that she stayed holed up in that airport for far too long—until she'd had no choice but to leave.

Still...

"It just makes no sense to me."

"Good," Shon says confidently. "If everything about God made perfect sense, we wouldn't need faith to believe in Him."

"Okay, but how can an area be free of toxins?" I ask. "How can the rest of the world around your little church be filled with poisonous air? What's keeping the radiation out? What's cleansing the air and the grass around the church?"

Shon stops walking to look right at me. "God."

Her expression has *duh* written all over it. It's all I can do to keep myself from flying into a rage. I really hate talking about this stuff. Just when I think I've said something she can't argue with, Shon hits me with a perfect scripture or a perfect response. I've never left her speechless, never asked something she didn't have a ready answer to. I don't know if I'm annoyed or impressed. Either way, I just wish Arya wasn't here to witness it all. He's been walking on the other side of Shon all this time, smirking at me behind his gasmask every few minutes.

It has been so difficult not to beat him senseless with my

crowbar.

"So, you think it's your mission to find this community too?" I ask Arya.

He shrugs. "Maybe not my mission. But I know it's a place that's supposed to be safe. I believe it is. With all my heart."

"Because your mother said so."

"Because my church was safe too. We never needed masks, not until we left. We never went hungry. We never worried about Faceless. Everything was fine until we lost the church."

A moment of awkward silence looms over us until Shon bravely asks, "How'd that happen?"

Arya hesitates.

"Some of the members of the church got restless. There was a dispute over rations that rolled into a storm. Before long, a fight broke out and my mother jumped in to break it up. But someone pulled a knife…"

He doesn't finish his sentence, not that he needs to. I don't like Arya, but even I can see how much pain he's in while retelling this story. Each one of us has lost someone or something to the Grey. We get it. We understand his pain. So no one speaks as he breathes deeply for a few moments, his shaky breaths filling the stale air.

When he's ready, he speaks again. "My family left after that."

"Looking for my church?" Shon asks.

To our surprise, Arya shakes his head. "My mother never actually mentioned Fire Baptized Ministries. She only told me to search for places like our shelter—which happened to be a church. My family went all over Mexico, stopping at every church we found. None of them were safe."

"Why not?" I ask.

"Because God wasn't present at every church." He sighs

210

through his mask. "Sitting on a pew listening to a Bible sermon doesn't make you a Believer. *Believing* the Bible, believing in Jesus Christ, is what makes you a Believer."

Shon nods enthusiastically. "These people honor Me with their lips, but their hearts are far from Me."

"Matthew chapter fifteen," Arya says softly, "verse eight."

I blink at them, amazed at how easily they can finish each other's sentences. Amazed at how quickly they'd connected with each other over something that seems like nonsense to me.

We were going to kill Arya not long ago. And now they're reciting Bible verses together like old friends. While I'm just here.

I can't help but glower.

"Entire churches operating without the presence of God." Shon shakes her head. "I can't believe it."

"I can," Arya says, and he leaves it at that.

"So, if your mother never mentioned Fire Baptized Ministries, how'd you hear about it?" I ask.

"I never heard about it," Arya admits, which pulls me to a complete halt.

I stand in the middle of the road and blink at him. "What?"

Arya stops walking, so does Shon.

"I never heard anything about Fire Baptized Ministries," he repeats, then he reaches into the sack slung over his shoulder and pulls out a torn map. "My sister and I have checked every church in this area. Fire Baptized Ministries is next on the list."

"Wait a second..." I swallow the anger I feel rising inside of me. "You can't be this stupid."

"Call me stupid again," Arya dares.

I rise to the challenge, stepping past Shon to get into his

face, but she shoves an arm between us, and I'm forced to step back a little bit.

"Calm down," she orders firmly. "There's no reason to start fighting."

"We're wasting our time!" I snap. "Can't you see, Shon? This is a wild goose chase! Checking off churches on a bogus list based on something this guy's dead mother told him three years ago."

I feel Arya punch me, but the pain doesn't register until I'm stumbling backwards. By the time I regain my footing, he's charging me again. But I'm ready now.

He swings hard with his right, and thinks he's slick when he counters with his left. I'll give him credit, he's faster than I expect, but he isn't as strong as he thinks. I take the right hook like a man—admittedly, it does hurt—but when Arya counters with his left, I lean into the blow and grab him by the shoulder. My other hand latches onto his wrist, and before he can gasp behind his mask, I jerk him toward me and headbutt him straight on.

The hit is so hard I see a flash of white light burst into my vision, there's even a ringing in my ears. Beneath the noise, I can make out the sound of Shon's voice, she's yelling for us to stop but neither of us listens. We both stumble sideways and then hold up our fists again, swaying from the force of the blow. I bet we look like drunken idiots, staggering to keep our feet beneath us.

Arya crumples first, dropping to one knee as he holds the side of his head. With that, I drop my fists and stand there, breathing deeply. I feel dizzy. Maybe headbutting him wasn't such a good idea.

Shon is by Arya's side, pulling up his mask to look at his pupils. She doesn't care if *I've* got a concussion. I try not to feel jealous but the feeling slithers through me before I can stop it, slippery and fast as a snake, sinking its fangs into my heart. I have to look away from the two of them or else I might kick Arya over and storm off in silence.

As I blink into the distance, I try to focus on the shapes of the buildings to help clear up my vision. I swear I must be seeing things. There are three people standing in the middle of the street. Naked. Grey. Hairless.

Then it clicks.

"Get up," I say, grabbing Shon by the arm.

She yells at me and tries to twist away but I tighten my grip. "Faceless!" I hiss, and everything freezes.

Shon stares in the direction of the group of wild men, speechless. Arya looks too, but no one says anything. There isn't much *to* say. We've been found. We've got to run.

There's no telling if those Faceless are from the herd, fully rested and ready to hunt, or if they were already in this area before we arrived. But it doesn't matter. Now that we've seen each other, there are only two options. Kill them or escape.

There is a third option, but it involves getting eaten by them and I don't want to think about that. I'm tired of people trying to eat me.

"Let's go!" I bark, dragging Shon to her feet. She complies without argument, tugging her baseball bat from the strap on her backpack. Arya slips on a pair of brass knuckles that I must admit are quite intimidating, but I hope we don't have to use them.

"Keep moving. Stick together no matter what. You hear?" I duck into an alley as one of the Faceless lets out a bellowing cry. The voice is deep and feral, like the call of some untamed beast. It sends a shiver down my spine, but I ignore the chill as I pick up my pace.

213

We run two blocks before I hear the sound of rushing footsteps. They've closed in on us, going for the kill.

I stop running and glance back at Shon and Arya. They're both panting, wearing wide eyes as they gulp for air. "There's three of them," I say. "We can take them."

Shon nods. Arya glances back and forth between us. That's when I realize how young he is, that his tough guy act is just that.

"We'll stick together—"

Something crashes to my left. I glance up to see a Faceless running so hard, when he tries to round the corner and enter the alleyway, he ends up slamming into the brick building beside him. Another Faceless rounds the corner and does the exact same thing; for a second, the three of us stand there staring at them, stunned. Then we hear another cry ring out around us, and I whirl around to see a wild woman standing at the other end of the alley. They've cut us off, blocking us in this little back street.

"Run!" Arya shouts, violently shoving past Shon. He sends her crashing to the ground, but I'm not about to let him do the same to me.

I see the panic in his eyes when he nears me, and I use that against him. He's too distracted by the charging Faceless to notice when I place my foot in his path.

Arya trips and goes headfirst into the ground. He screams in terror, but he doesn't realize I've just saved his life. The Faceless woman at the end of the alleyway is faster than she looks. By the time Arya hit the ground, she was in the air, launching at him like a missile.

She lands on the sharp end of my crowbar. Up close, her face is grey and ugly. Saggy skin that looks far older than her youthful neon eyes. I wonder how long she's been alive in this

214

state, her skin is so rotted when I shove her off my crowbar, her stomach tears open, and her innards gush out onto the ground.

I want to vomit, but Shon's screams snatch my attention away. She's managed to whack one Faceless in the head with her bat. He's so decomposed that his head is actually bat-shaped now, but he's still moving, mindlessly clawing at Shon as she tries to fend him off. The other Faceless is prowling on all fours, searching for an opening.

Arya's back on his feet again. In a panic, he runs to the door on the side of the building and yanks hard—it doesn't budge. He tries the next door, then moves on to the boarded-up windows, trying to find an escape for us. I can only hope he doesn't run inside and leave us. For now, I've got to focus on helping Shon.

She hits the first Faceless again, grunting with the force. It's enough to literally knock his rotted head off. That gives the other wild man the courage to dive in for the kill. He runs and leaps at Shon and she readies herself like an actual baseball player. This time, when she swings, the Faceless takes the hit and tackles her to the ground.

That's when I run over, crowbar in hand. The wild man is on top of Shon, pounding her with his fists, but she's got her arms up to protect herself. I kick him off her and swing the bar in an arc, but he dodges backwards and screams—spittle flying from his rotten mouth.

"Arya, how's that door!" I shout. When he doesn't respond, I chance a look over my shoulder in time to see him pry a board from a window—as soon as the slab of wood is gone, a grey hand juts out of the broken window and grabs him by the collar.

He screams so loud I want to cover my ears.

215

"Save him!" Shon shouts, shoving me back.

I blink at her, then at the Faceless. I don't want to leave her alone but, admittedly, Arya needs my help a lot more than she does.

With a huff, I turn and sprint down the alley to find the kid punching at the hand that holds him. When he sees me coming, he cries, "Help! It's got me!"

I roll my eyes and lift the crowbar high. When it comes down on the Faceless arm, I hear a painful shriek inside the building and it miraculously lets go.

That's when Arya takes off. Just turns and sprints away like a madman. I have half a mind to just let him go, but I know Shon would never forgive me for that, so I take a breath and run after him. He clears the alleyway and runs down the main road, when he sees more Faceless crawling from the shadows, he ducks down a side street. I follow him, but my pace is slower. I'm distracted by the Faceless swarming the streets now, but I notice figures in the crowds.

People running away from them, just like us. Either this town isn't deserted or the thugs that chased off Arya and his sister have finally caught up. And brought company with them.

I don't have time to think things through. When I chased after Arya, I thought I was leaving Shon alone with one wild man to fight. I didn't think we were surrounded by dozens of grey men and women. Plus, other survivors trying to get away.

This is bad. This is really bad.

I pick up the pace and throw myself at Arya. We both tumble to the ground in a mess of tangled limbs and grunts. I'm so angry, I could pummel this kid, but I'm more focused on surviving, so I drag him to his feet and yank him into the closest building.

"Let me go!" he shouts.

216

So I do. I shove him to the ground and step on his chest, holding him in place.

"Get off!" he screams.

"Calm down!" I bark, increasing the pressure on my boot.

He punches my foot, but it does little damage. I step down harder, making him yelp.

"Chill out," I say sternly.

"You're going to get me killed! The Faceless are coming!"

"You're going to get us *all* killed!" I say sharply. "I left Shon alone because of you!"

"I don't care!"

I kick him. Hard. He rolls onto his side, and I grab him by the collar and shove him into the wall. "Listen, you little snot drip, my friend is out there *alone*. You can go out and help me get her or I can knock you out and leave you to the Faceless. What's it gonna be?"

"Please don't make me go out there!" he cries, then he starts blubbering incoherently as tears gush from his eyes.

I slap him. "Get it together! There are other people out there with the Faceless. We might be able to use them as distractions to circle back to Shon, understand?"

He blinks. "Other people?"

"I saw someone." I step back and let Arya go, convinced that he won't run again. "I don't know who it was, but it wasn't a Faceless. If we're careful, we can use these strangers' presence to keep ourselves hidden."

Arya shocks me by stepping forward, adjusting his brass knuckles. "One of those people could be my sister."

"Exactly—"

"So I can't help you."

"Arya," I swallow, "I need to find Shon just as badly as you need to find your sister."

217

Arya shakes his head. "I'm sorry."

"We need to work together!" Arya flinches at my tone. But before he can say anything back, I hear Shon's voice outside.

"Erik!" she screams.

I'm out the door before I even realize it.

Shon is running up the middle of the street. She looks fine—in fact, she's dragging someone with her. A woman in tattered clothing and matted hair. She's leaning on Shon to keep herself upright and holding a flare in her hand to stop the Faceless around them from attacking. The crowd of grey men hisses and growls as they follow the two women. Some even run forward and snap their jowls at them.

Shon isn't afraid. She keeps marching up the street, a determined look in her eye. I want to tell her to leave the woman behind, she's only slowing her down, but I know from her expression there's no way she will ever give up on this stranger.

If things weren't so dire, I'd laugh at myself. In a panic, I had run out like a hero trying to rescue Shon. When she had been out here playing hero the entire time. She didn't need my help at all.

"They're coming!" Shon shouts to me like I can't see the Faceless surrounding her. Then I glance up and see a figure moving through the crowd of grey men.

That's who she's talking about.

A man in a black sweatshirt, running swiftly through the streets. He stays on the outskirts of the Faceless crowd, relatively undetected by the distracted monsters. It's not until he steps into the street, just a few feet away from the women, that I recognize him.

"Run!" I shout to Shon, darting forward. Arya takes off beside me, but I yell at him, "Get to the women!"

He nods and runs toward Shon while I sprint past them, right up to the man chasing after them. The Faceless sneer at me, striking out to attack as soon as I've cleared the safety of the dying flare. I stab one with my crowbar and dodge another. The man isn't far from me; when he realizes I'm coming right for him, he turns and starts running the other way—but not before I see the unmistakable skeleton on the front of his hoodie.

I don't have time to wonder how he caught up to us. All I can think about is whether I can catch him now. He's quick, darting through the Faceless who have turned their attention to us now. But I'm fueled by rage and adrenaline.

My feet carry me right up to the man and I snatch him backwards by his hoodie. He shouts as he falls, and I pivot with him, bringing down my crowbar right on his head. He crumples like a leaf.

And now I've got to drag him away while surrounded by Faceless.

21

Shon

When Erik left to chase after Arya, I wasn't worried. Until I killed that Faceless and stepped out of the alleyway. That's when I saw the Faceless crawling from the shadows, drawn out from all the noise of our fight.

My first instinct was to run. In fact, I took off in the same direction I saw Erik running when I left the alley. He was too far ahead to hear me calling for him, and I'd hurt my leg wrestling with the Faceless so I wasn't fast enough to catch up. But I also fell behind for another reason.

I saw a woman in the crowd of Faceless.

I had no idea who she was. But she was being chased by three men—three normal, uncontaminated men. They had weapons in their hands and frowns on their faces. Meanwhile, the wild men were surrounding us, running on the sidewalks, and climbing out of windows to join the hunt.

I had two choices; help that woman or catch up with Erik. I don't think I have to tell you what choice I made.

It's not until we make it inside an abandoned building and Arya is boarding back up the door that I realize the choice I made was the right one. Arya recognizes the woman immediately.

With a sob, he falls to his knees and cradles the woman's face in his hands. "Arianna," he whispers. "You're alive."

She groans as she leans on him for support. I give them some privacy while I run to the door, prying the wooden board loose to peek out. Just as I poke my head out, Erik charges up the steps, dragging a man behind him. I have no choice but to back away and then quickly slam the door shut behind him before the Faceless can get in.

"Arya, help me!" I shout, slamming my body against the door. The Faceless are relentlessly tearing at it, trying to get inside. Not to mention the ones clawing at the boarded-up windows around us.

Arya is beside me in a flash, grunting as he shoves his full weight against the barrier. Even with both of us holding it, it's obvious this won't last very long.

"Find something to barricade it!" Arya shouts.

I nod and turn around to find the room behind me has erupted into chaos. Arianna, who I thought was half-dead, is on her feet now, wielding a shard of broken glass like a knife and screaming at the top of her lungs. When I step closer, I realize she's actually pointing the glass at the man in Erik's arms. He's passed out, but even with his head tilted back and his gasmask still on his face, I can tell who he is.

I recognize the skeleton printed on the front of his hoodie. I recognize his dark brown skin. I recognize the size and shape of his body.

It's Jeremiah.

"How?" I whisper, but I never get to figure things out.

Arya screams as the door bursts open and Faceless pour inside. "Run!" he shouts, tripping away.

I don't remember Erik passing me his crowbar, but it's suddenly in my hands and I'm swinging like I've lost my mind. I want to reach for the hunting knife at my hip, but there isn't any time to think or switch weapons. Mercifully, Arya stays back with me, and we stab and slash at the monsters while Arianna and Erik run deeper into the building, dragging Jeremiah with them.

The Faceless throw themselves through the doorway and it acts as a funnel, clogging up when too many of them try to charge through—that's when Arya and I take off. There are still stragglers chasing us, but the bulk of the masses is stuck in the doorway. Still, that doesn't give me any sort of peace as I sprint through what I realize is an old furniture store.

We hop over bedside tables and overturned chairs, trying hard to follow the rushing footsteps of our friends who are ahead of us. I hear a door scream as it creaks open and switch directions to run left, through the mattress section. The sudden change leaves two Faceless sliding across the floor, but the place is carpeted so they regain their footing faster than I'd like.

In the mattress section, there are sheets hanging from the ceiling, sectioning off the open space as if someone had lived here and tried to hang curtains for privacy. I slap at the sheets as I try to catch up with Erik and Arianna. My field of vision of obscured, white linen swaying back and forth, cutting off the scene. The Faceless don't have it much easier; one of them runs right into a sheet—snatching it from the hook in the ceiling and getting tangled up as it drops on top of it.

There are a handful more Faceless still chasing us, but I hear them running into things and tripping over themselves. I can see Arya from my peripheral. We're all still alive. There's a chance we can make it out of this.

"Over here!" I hear Arianna shout and it gives me a new surge of energy.

I burst through a curtain of sheets to find her holding open a metal exit door. My legs feel like they're on fire as they carry me toward the door. Arya is a step behind me, nearly running me down once we make it out and Arianna slams the door shut behind her.

Without needing to be told, Arya and I both turn and lower the metal latch over the door while Arianna holds it shut against the pursuing Faceless.

We're outside now, panting, staring at each other, smiling because all the Faceless are locked in the building behind us. There are no guarantees of our safety, but we feel secure enough to burst out laughing altogether.

My adrenaline turns into uncontrolled joy, and I smile ear to ear as I watch Arianna and Arya embrace. Then my gaze slides over to Erik and my smile fades. Jeremiah is still unconscious, his entire body folded over Erik's strong shoulders.

Neither of us speaks. I can't think of any words to say. Erik just nods and I nod back. Then he turns in the other direction and says, "We're not out of the woods yet. Let's find somewhere else to rest."

We walk for an hour in silence. Arya helps Arianna as her adrenaline rush fades and the pain of her injuries catches up to her. By then, Jeremiah has regained consciousness, but we stopped to tie his hands and feet before setting off, so none of us are worried. But we are tired.

With a grunt, Erik drops Jeremiah. He falls six feet three

inches to the ground and lands with a thud that makes me wince. I don't feel sorry for him.

"Let's get this over with," Erik grumbles, taking his mask off. He sucks in a breath of air and then squats in front of my ex to tug his mask off too.

His face is bruised and burned. Lip swollen, his hair singed off, and one of his eyes has turned grey. I guess the building wasn't the only thing that burned in that fire.

"How'd you find us?" Erik asks.

Jeremiah looks defiant as he struggles to sit upright, but he opens his mouth to answer anyway. "Did you honestly think we wouldn't come after you?"

"You hadn't left the university in six years," I say.

His hateful eyes drag over to me, and his voice comes out as a venomous hiss. "That was before it was burned to the ground."

I swallow.

"With nothing left, we had no choice but to set out."

"You didn't have to set out after us," Erik says, folding his arms over his chest.

"We had no supplies. We had no weapons. We had no reason to live." Jeremiah's eyes never leave mine. "Except vengeance."

"You took what you had left and decided to hunt us down instead of trying to survive?" Erik shakes his head. "You're more pathetic than I thought."

"I'm not pathetic," Jeremiah growls.

"Yes, you are!" Arianna screams. She limps forward, pulling free from Arya's grasp to get in Jeremy's face. This close, I can see her resemblance to her brother. She's closer to my age, but she's still got his tan skin and chocolate brown hair. Her Spanish accent is thicker than his, but it's easy enough to understand her when she shouts, "You're a disgusting human being! No better than the Faceless!"

Jeremiah holds his chin up. "You deserved what you got."

My heart stops. For the first time, I take a good look at Arianna. At her great height and long legs, at the cords of muscle in her sleeveless arms. She is clearly strong enough to handle herself, yet… she is covered in dried blood. Her clothes are ripped. And her hair is all stuck to her head in a crust of mud and blood.

I can't even begin to imagine what happened to her before I saw her in the street. Arya had said he'd gotten separated from his sister when they ran into some thugs. But I'd never guessed those thugs were people from the university. People who only crossed their path because they were hunting *us* down.

This is all my fault, I realize with a gasp. If I hadn't burned down the school, Jeremiah wouldn't even be here now.

I shake my head.

The school was burned down because we were trying to escape his madness. And he's only out here now because his madness drove him to vengeance. I refuse to blame myself for the misery he's been spreading. But I can take responsibility for stopping it.

I step forward, clutching Erik's crowbar.

"You two know each other?" I ask slowly.

Jeremiah suddenly looks like he doesn't want to answer, but Arianna speaks up boldly. "He ambushed us in the woods! An entire group of them!"

"How many?" Erik quickly asks, glancing around in every direction. We're on the outskirts of the city now, nothing but highways and factories around us. If there was someone following us, we'd never know it unless they stepped out for

225

us to see them.

"They're dead now," Jeremiah admits. He spits on the ground at Arya's feet. "He killed two of them. Which is why we took his sister."

"You said you two were separated." I look at Arya who's glaring at Jeremiah.

"We were. I thought Arianna got away while I was fighting. I saw her run."

"But you didn't see me chase after her." Jeremiah smirks, but it's wiped away by Arianna's foot. She kicks him so hard he topples over into the grey dirt.

None of us move to help him up.

"What did you do to her?" I grip the crowbar so tightly I wouldn't be surprised if it was shaped like my palm when I let it go.

Jeremiah looks me right in the eye, sucks in a breath through his cracked lips, and says, "What do you think?"

When he cries out in pain, I don't react. Arianna's kicked him again, and she's lifting her foot to stomp on him once more when her brother grabs her and pulls her back. She collapses into a fit of tears as he whispers into her matted hair.

Jeremiah watches silently from the ground.

"Shon," Erik says softly. It isn't my name that gets my attention, it's the gentleness in his voice. The sympathy. It makes me want to scream. Like every sin Jeremy has ever committed is staring me in the face right now... And laughing.

This isn't fair, I pray inside. *God, I'm not strong enough to deal with this.*

I'd boasted a great game to Erik weeks ago, preaching about forgiveness. Telling him I'd been sent to set an example in his life. To teach him what it means to move on. To let go. To cling to God through the storm.

226

But my storm has returned now. Like a challenge from the grave, it's latched its skeletal hands around my throat and now it's squeezing.

I feel like I can't breathe as I stare down at Jeremiah. I feel like I want to tear my ears off as I hear Arianna's sobs behind me. What do I do? What *can* I do?

"Shon," Erik says again. He inches closer to me. "What do you want to do?"

When I look over at him, I see the real question he's asking written all over his face.

Do you want to kill Jeremiah?

He's tied up and literally lying at my feet. Two victims stand before this monster, knowing that if I let him live, there will be a third victim. It would be so easy to drive my crowbar through his eye and end his streak of madness right here. It would be justified if I stabbed him and watched his life drain from his eyes. But it wouldn't be right. It wouldn't be *righteous*.

I squeeze the crowbar in my hands, lifting it above my head. I thought I had forgiven him. I thought I had gotten over the pain in these last few weeks. I thought God had washed away the nightmares. But they're all still there, bubbling up inside of me as I grip the metal in my hands.

I could end those nightmares in one swing. I could lay to rest all this violence and pain.

My hands shake as tears rush down my cheeks. I can hardly see past them, but I don't need clear vision to make out the monster before me. Flashes of those days I spent cuffed to his bed play out in my mind and I gasp, letting go of a wretched sob.

I hear Erik shuffling beside me, giving me space. Letting me make this decision myself. I can hear Arianna screaming for me to do it. I can hear Arya begging her to calm down. And

227

I can hear Jeremiah laughing. A low chuckle that sounds like the devil's lullaby.

Beneath all of that, I hear my own voice. A prayer I don't say aloud; it's alive in my heart. A silent plea to God.

Help me...

The last time I heard God's Voice was when He protected me during my fight with Jeremiah before he recognized me. Now, I hear His Voice again.

My peace, I give unto thee.

The words of Jesus Christ hit me like a storm. A reminder of who I am and Whose I am. The peace is more violent than the pain, crashing into me and wrestling away the fear, grief, and sorrow. It chases off the nightmares in my head, leaving the memories, but capturing the heartache that'd been attached to them.

I feel a weight lifted from my shoulders as this peace floods my entire being. And with a cry of victory, I drop the crowbar and fall to my knees.

I don't need vengeance. I don't need pain to justify pain.

"Shon?" Erik is beside me, a heavy arm draped over my shoulders.

I yank off my gasmask to breathe, and to wipe away my tears. My eyes land on Jeremiah as he stares up at me with a confused expression on his face.

"I told Erik I'd forgiven you weeks ago," I whisper. "But I realize now that maybe that claim hadn't been as true as I thought it was. It wasn't as easy as I thought it was." I sniffle. "But now I know without a doubt ... I'm done here. I'm not letting your sins control my emotions anymore." I take a deep breath. "I forgive you, Jeremiah."

On shaky legs, I stand and reach for the crowbar, but I'm suddenly shoved to the side. When I turn, I see a brown blur,

228

and it's not until I hear Arianna scream that I realize she'd stepped forward…

And grabbed the hunting knife from my hip.

It sits in Jeremiah's throat now, jutting from the side of his neck as blood spurts out in rhythm with his heartbeat. His eyes are large and round, his mouth is gaping open. When he tries to scream—in pain or for help, I don't know—all that comes out is a horrible gurgling noise. And then he curls up in a ball and squeezes his eyes shut, like he knows he's dying.

In that moment, Jeremiah is not a monster. He's not my captor. He's not my rapist. He is the father of my child, and he's dying right in front of me.

My hands are stained crimson as I reach for Jeremy's neck, trying to stop the blood from flowing, but it's pointless. I know it's pointless. There's so much red. And it's pooling around his body now, thick and sticky and hot. I'm sobbing as I hold him, though I don't know why. I can't place my emotions, not a single one.

I'd just forgiven him. I'd just set down the crowbar. And now he's dead. Like none of that mattered. The struggle I'd gone through to let go of all the pain is draining out in my arms. I peer down at Jeremiah as he sucks in wet breaths, and I stare into his eyes as the life fades from them.

"Why?" I whisper into the stiff silence. "I said I'd forgiven him. Why did you stab him?"

Arianna's voice fills the air. It's hard and cold. "Because *I* hadn't."

22

Erik

I dream of my wife. This time, she is smiling and laughing, and her slender fingers are interlocked with my own. I call her name and she glances at me, but the smile fades from her face and she suddenly looks sad. Her grip on my hand begins to slip away, I cling to her, but she shakes her head.

"I've got to go," she says solemnly. And I have no idea how to respond to that.

When I wake up, Shon is staring at me. She's sitting across the campfire with her mask off; her eyes are huge and her mouth is pinched into a frown that she tries to hide. As I shift to sit up, she looks away.

"What happened?" I ask in a hoarse voice.

She swallows, meeting my gaze for half a second. "You were mumbling in your sleep."

"Oh."

She gazes at the fire, absently poking it with the burnt stick in her hand. "You said her name… Angelena."

A cold sweat breaks out on my forehead. I'm thankful for the mask I'm wearing, otherwise, Shon would see my cheeks burn. I don't know if I'm embarrassed because she heard me mumbling in my sleep or because of *what* she heard me mumbling.

I shouldn't care at all. But I do. And I wonder what she thinks of what she heard when I look at her across the flames. The light dances over her face, illuminating her nut-brown skin and round nose. She reminds me so much of my wife, it aches. And it confuses me.

Do I want to protect her because it's my job or because I genuinely care?

Before I can think things through in my head, or form a response to Shon's statement, Arya pushes through the metal gate that surrounds the abandoned car lot. The sight of him immediately makes me glower. He lazily drops his sack of mystery loot he collected on his scavenging trip and sits beside Shon by the fire. Arianna enters the room shortly after him, but she goes straight to her sleeping mat in the far corner of the room.

I look away when Arya scoots closer to Shon, tugging off his mask to reveal a crooked smirk I've come to hate. He's young—barely twenty-one—and his snarky attitude and youthful physique is a painful reminder that I am long past my prime.

For over a month, I have been travelling side by side with Shon. Just the two of us. For over a month, we have survived together. Fought together. Bled together. And argued the entire time. Shon has given me numerous headaches, and I know I've given her some too. But I'd still give my life for that woman.

Now, as I watch the two of them bump shoulders and

smile at each other, I feel like nothing but an angry old man—watching from the sidelines. Arya and Shon have been spending time together since we found this place. We've been camped out here for the last two days after leaving Jeremiah's dead body on the road. We're so close to Fire Baptized Ministries, but we needed to stop and heal from that last encounter. All of us.

Arianna had injuries, Shon hurt her leg—not to mention the emotional and psychological scars we're all carrying around. Shon and Arya have been holding hands and whispering prayers together every day. I guess that's how they're coping. I usually sit and watch from my place near the fire. To my surprise, Arianna takes that time to find some sort of excuse to leave.

I don't question it. Things have been complicated enough as they are.

Across the fire, Arya pulls a Bible from his backpack. Shon's face lights up. She lost hers back at the university when they confiscated all our stuff. We hadn't found another one since, so I'm not surprised by how thankful she is for the Book. I'm just irritated that she shows her gratitude by wrapping her arms around Arya's neck and hugging him tightly.

I look away. Again.

At this point, I should just roll over and go back to sleep. I even consider grabbing my hunting knife and giving myself a shave. My beard is getting thicker. But I don't want to sit here while those two cuddle up. It's slowly making me angry.

With a grunt, I push from my sleeping mat—which is actually a pile of beaten up car seat cushions covered in noisy plastic wrap—and walk past the fire. Unsurprisingly, Arya stops me as I stalk by.

"Headin' out, old man?" he says, a grin on his face.

I ball my hands into fists but then quickly unclench them. There is no point in getting angry at his childish remarks, it's what he wants anyway. So I calmly exhale through my mask and shrug my sore shoulders.

"I've got first watch," I say, then I turn away before he can reply, and walk into the shadows.

I'm not really enjoying all the new company, but it isn't all bad. We've split the night watch into four shifts, so we all get more sleep now. When it was just me and Shon, we'd split the shift in half and barely get more than three or four hours of rest per night. Looting is easier now, and we share all of our supplies. Arya and Arianna had extra filters to share so when I take a breath through my mask, the air smells as clean as possible, given the state of the world.

Absently, I lift my arms into the air and groan as I stretch every muscle in my back and legs. It feels so good, I hardly notice the shadow that creeps up behind me until I hear the voice it belongs to.

"Tired?"

I whirl around to find Arianna leaning against a rod of the metal gate. The door is bent so it's always ajar, but we tied rope to it with tools from the shop hanging from the cord like loose laundry. They act as chimes, clanking together whenever they're disturbed. Now we'll hear any Faceless approaching.

There is a wrench, a handful of large nails, and a pair of scissors tied to the front part of the gate. They clang together as Arianna opens the metal door and walks out of the car lot right toward me.

"Tired?" she asks again, folding her arms over her chest.

I blink at her, studying her. She isn't wearing a mask, but the expression on her face is just as blank and difficult to read. I can't tell what her aim is here, so I give her the blandest response I can think of.

"I just woke up. I've got first watch."

"Mind the extra company?" She leans against the fence and tilts her head to the side so her wavy hair falls into her face. That's when I realize what she's doing.

Arianna is a pretty woman. Tannish brown skin and dark hair that makes her look exotic, there is a speckling of freckles across her nose that gives her a youthful appearance. It collides with her hard exterior and leaves me in a silent stupor as I fumble for words. She is older than her little brother, but I'm not sure how much older. She's never said her age aloud—she's never said much of anything. If there is anyone in our group as antisocial as me, it's this woman right here. But, suddenly, I've become the focus of her attention and I know exactly why.

Her brother is getting cozy with Shon, I guess we're supposed to become nice friends too.

She's about to be disappointed.

"You should rest while you can," I tell her.

Arianna purses her lips. Shamelessly, I watch them pucker, but when she starts to smile at the attention, I pry my eyes away and face forward. "We're setting out at sunrise," I grunt. "Rest while you can."

She sucks her teeth beside me. "Am I the only one here who isn't psyched to go to the church?"

Her question stuns me. I'd noticed she made an excuse to leave every time Arya or Shon started praying, but I thought it was to give them privacy. Not because she didn't believe.

"Didn't you and Arya set out to go church-hopping in the first place?" I ask.

She shrugs one shoulder. Her sweater is oversized and hanging off, so I can see the muscle in her arm that flexes with

234

the movement. Arianna looks so strong, like she could fist fight me and expect to win.

"I had no other plans. No idea what else to do. Going from church to church kept us moving—that was all that mattered to me."

"So you never actually expected to find this Christian haven."

A long moment of silence passes between us.

Arianna sighs. "I did at first. Our church was mask-free. Even the parking lot had clean air to breathe. We started a small garden out back, and there was a nearby pond on the property that gave us fresh water. Everything was pure and clean. God really protected us, just like He protected the Israelites everywhere they went."

She pauses.

"And then what?"

"And then He let my mother die."

I drop my gaze to the concrete. I understand Arianna's pain. I know what it's like to lose someone you love. Someone who was good and kind and innocent, and then they're suddenly snatched away so violently that nothing else in the world ever makes sense again.

But then I remember all the stuff Shon told me about bad things happening to good people. The reminder makes me look at Arianna again, taking in her angry expression, the thick wrinkle of frustration in the middle of her forehead. She's so hurt. That much is obvious, but she's also mad and confused and bitter. She lost her mother, and then she was taken by Jeremiah, just like Shon.

Unlike Shon, however, she sought vengeance. I'd watched as she stabbed Jeremiah with Shon's knife. I'd watched as she had callously stood over his body when we'd finally packed up

235

to leave. Arianna didn't regret her decision, but she also didn't gain anything from it. She's just as hurt as she was before.

I want to tell her all the things Shon said to me when we fought over her faith. But I'm pretty sure I'll end up butchering any attempt to explain it all in a way that'll make sense to this broken woman. So I let go of a stale sigh and lift my mask so Arianna can see me fully.

"It'll get better," I tell her.

"Sure." She kicks a rock. "But what happens when we get to the church tomorrow and we find out the truth?"

I don't want to talk about this, but I guess we need to. Shon and Arya won't accept the notion of being wrong. They won't even consider that the church could be empty. Maybe they're right. Maybe there *is* a clean-air Christian community somewhere out there. But if there isn't … What happens next?

"Whatever happens tomorrow," I say to Arianna, "we'll get through it together."

"So, this is it? We're a group now?"

I nod. "Is that a bad thing?"

Arianna gives me a smile that makes every muscle in my body stiffen.

"That's not a problem at all," she says with a wink.

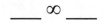

The next morning, we set out as planned. It's an hour before we hit the city, and then another 90 minutes of walking before we hit the right neighborhood. Shon is brimming with excitement; it takes every ounce of self-control she's got not to take off into a sprint. If there's anything we've learned on this journey, it's that anything could be hiding just around the corner. So we all keep calm—even when the steeple to the church comes into view, we approach the building cautiously and as one.

Arya flanks left while I take the right side. The women travel up the center toward the front doors, weapons gripped and ready. I've got the crowbar again, Shon lost her baseball bat in our last fight so she's down to the hunting knife and a screwdriver she got from the car lot. Arya is still wearing those brass knuckles and Arianna carries a hunting knife of her own.

We move silently, visually sweeping the area and checking around the corner of the church. I don't see anything suspicious, so I give the cue to move forward.

Fire Baptized Ministries is a building large enough to have comfortably held a thousand congregants. The outside looks like it used to be white or beige stone and there are windows cut into the side of the building that would have been beautiful before the explosions.

The outside is grey now. I can see scorch marks on the sides of the building and some of the windows are boarded up. The parking lot is cracked and the tubs that once held shrubbery and flowers out front are all overturned or broken. I don't know how Arianna's old church looked, but I'm sure if God protected it then it looked nothing like this.

Whatever tiny speck of hope I'd held on to for Shon's sake is snuffed out when we approach the double entrance doors. Miraculously, they're intact despite being made of glass. It seems almost every other window is blown out or splintered.

"Ready?" I ask Shon, peering up at the building. The sign on the front has been crudely spray-painted over so it only reads, *Fire*. The 'Baptized Ministries' part is covered in a bloody red paint. I shiver as I stare at the single word. I know Shon and Arya have seen it too, but nobody comments. Nobody wants to acknowledge what it could mean.

Shon reaches for the door and tugs. It comes loose after two hard yanks, crying out in misery. Arianna lifts her knife as she glances around.

"Better get inside quick. If there are any Faceless nearby, they definitely heard that."

We all agree, and hurry inside one by one.

The church is dark and painfully empty. That much is obvious just from walking through the lobby. I can hear our footsteps echoing through the empty halls, but it's what I see that confirms my beliefs.

The place has been torched.

The black scorch marks I saw on the outside of the building are on every surface inside. The tiled floor is stained black, the walls are dusted with smokey debris, the ceiling holds the pattern of scattered burns as if pockets of flames had crawled up some of the walls and licked at the roof.

I am not a religious man, but even I feel terrible as I look around. There are human remains in some of the rooms, dark red stains on the floor beside the dried-up bodies that I imagine had once been pools of blood. It's hard to tell how these people died. There aren't many bodies, but the ones I do see are so old and dry I can't find any obvious injuries. The walls are also pocked with what look like bullet holes. They could have died to the fire or the guns. There's no real way to tell.

I hear a gasp behind me, and I turn to see Shon hugging herself. I suddenly feel like an idiot. I was out there exploring, studying dead bodies, while Shon was taking this all in by herself. I can see the tears swelling in her eyes as I walk over to her, but before I get close, Arya appears by her side and wraps an arm around her shoulders.

I stop in my tracks, feeling anger bubble inside me.

238

"Shon?" I call from my stance a few feet away.

Arya looks up with a frown, but Shon sniffles and says, "I don't get it."

"It'll be alright," I tell her, coming closer.

Arya's arm tightens around her shoulders, and he turns her away from me so they're facing the doors to the sanctuary. I want to snap at him for the obvious move he just pulled, but Shon speaks before I get the chance to.

"Let's check in there," she says, pulling away from Arya's grasp. She's through the doors before either of us can stop her. Arianna doesn't even bother trying to join this scene, she maintains her distance by the entrance, staring outside like she's just waiting for this show to end. I don't really blame her.

Inside the sanctuary, I find Shon running up the middle aisle. She stops right at the steps that lead to the pulpit. A giant golden cross waits on the stage area, there is a destroyed piano off to the side and a drum set that's burned and useless now. Miraculously, the cross is not burned or damaged in any way, but it has been marred by spray paint.

Unlike the crude red splotches on the sign out front, the spray paint on the cross was done in white and it isn't a design or even vandalism. It's a message. A scripture, to be exact.

Exodus 15:22-27

I'm staring at the scripture when Shon drops to her knees and catches my attention. Before I can help her, Arya is there by her side, kneeling and whispering in her ear, but he's still wearing his mask so he's speaking quite loudly. Loud enough for me to hear what he's saying.

"It'll be alright. We'll move on to the next church on the list."

"You don't understand!" Shon nearly yells.

She's right. Arya doesn't understand at all. To him and

239

Arianna, this was just another church on their list. But to Shon, this was her hope. She grew up in this church. She had believed that her family would be here waiting for her. Now… the place is destroyed, and no one knows if the bodies scattered through the building belong to her family and friends.

"Shonny," Arya says kindly. I cringe at the nickname. It's been two days. Not long enough for them to have nicknames for each other. But Shon doesn't seem to mind. When he calls her name, she blinks up at him like he's got all the answers in the world. It makes me sick.

Without thinking, I step forward and interrupt their little moment. "What's that scripture mean?" I ask loudly.

Shon and Arya both stare at me, then I point at the cross and they look away at the same time.

Arya shrugs. "Don't know. Exodus was one of those long books in the Bible."

I squint at him.

"It's about Moses and the Israelites," Shon says softly, then she pushes to her feet and slowly walks up the steps of the pulpit until she's standing right in front of the massive cross. "In that passage, Moses leads the nation of Israel from the Red Sea into the wilderness. They travel for three days before they get thirsty."

"Yeah, I remember that," Arya says, though I doubt he remembers anything at all.

"In the end, the Israelites are led to Elim. Where they find…" Shon's voice trails off as she stands there with her head tilted back. "No way…"

"No way, what?" I ask.

"Twelve Springs Campsite."

"Huh?" Arya and I both speak at the same time. Our confusion makes Shon turn around to face us; she's smiling ear

240

to ear, I can tell even with her mask on.

"Every other summer, my church had a big retreat. It was organized as a camping trip at a site called Twelve Springs."

"Um, okay," I say slowly, trying hard to connect the dots. It must be a Christian thing because Arya steps forward and says, "Twelve springs and seventy palms!"

They start excitedly jumping up and down together. I'm really glad Shon isn't in tears anymore, but I still have no idea what the heck is going on, so I wave my arms around and say, "Care to explain to the Gentile over here??"

My comment makes Shon snort.

"In the Bible, after God delivers the Israelites from Egypt, they travel through the desert and need God's help and provisions. After He provides them with water, they're led to Elim. A place described as having twelve springs and seventy palms."

I tilt my head to the side. Still confused.

Shon sighs. "The campsite my church went to is called Twelve Springs."

I bunch my shoulders. Still confused.

"Don't you see?" Shon asks, waving a hand at the cross. "The scripture written on that cross is a message! My church wasn't destroyed, they relocated to Twelve Springs Campgrounds!"

I place my hands on my hips. "I don't know, Shon. That seems farfetched."

"It's not farfetched at all," she argues. "Twelve Springs is three days from here, just like the Israelites. They spent three days in the desert before God gave them water. We'll walk three days through the barren fields before we find our twelve springs. The clean-air haven of Fire Baptized Ministries."

I have to admit, it's a good theory. But there's so much

241

stacked against it. Like, if the church relocated, where did all these bodies come from? What happened here before they left? And what if someone else left that scripture on the cross—some thug just trying to throw people off?

The cynical part of me wants to ask these questions but seeing Arya and Shon celebrate and start talking about Bible verses together makes me lock my lips. If I start sowing seeds of doubt, they'll get angry. Then Shon will drift that much further from me, and Arya will get that much closer.

"So, I guess we're heading to this campsite?" I say, shifting my weight from one foot to the other.

Shon pulls away from Arya, who'd been hugging her *again*, to walk over to me. "Of course! Don't you think that's a good plan?"

I could tell her what I really think, that we're part of some wild goose chase, but that'll only drive us further apart. So instead of being honest, I let go of a tired sigh and pat Shon on the shoulder. She frowns behind her mask and looks at the spot where I touched her.

It was a detached gesture. Something so far away from the friendship we'd had before that it stuns both of us. A few days ago, she was *Cupcake*, now I'm treating her like a stranger and for the first time since Arya's let her breathe, Shon has finally noticed the distance between us.

"Erik," she says, but I shake my head. That little action is the most that I've said to her in days. Without any words, she understands everything. The frustration over Arya butting in, the confusion over where to go next, and the pain behind it all.

The miserable memories I have of my wife.

Shon calls my name again, but I'm turning away now, walking toward the exit. I don't want to hear anything else. But I don't want to just leave her hanging, so I say over my

242

shoulder, "We'll camp here and make plans. Then we'll set out tomorrow or the day after."

Shon doesn't respond and I don't turn back around.

23

Shon

We stay at the church for another two days. The only place that doesn't have any bodies lying around is the sanctuary, so we all set up in there, hanging plastic and curtains from the church to give ourselves some privacy.

The whole thing is so awkward.

When it was just me and Erik, we had no problem sharing space or giving each other space. For the most part, he was asleep while I was awake keeping watch and vice versa. So we never had to decide who would sleep where or how close or for how long. But there are four of us now and only one stays up to keep watch, so the other three are left to themselves.

I can't help but notice that Arya has set his space up right beside mine. He pokes his head behind my curtain with a smile and sits with me on my sleeping mat sometimes. For lunch, he brought me a bowl of stew and shared his canteen of water without me even asking. It's like I can't get away from him.

But the same can be said for Erik and Arianna now.

As much as I've tried to ignore her tent right beside his, I haven't been able to stop myself from glancing in their direction whenever I see Ari strolling toward his makeshift room. She never asks for permission to enter. Every time she visits—which is more often than I'm comfortable admitting—she boldly pulls the curtains aside and goes into his space wearing a smile she's never given anyone but Erik.

Last night, I entered the sanctuary to wake Arya for his shift and saw Arianna leaving Erik's tent … wearing nothing but his flannel. She'd only looked at me and smiled before stepping behind her own curtain.

I had no idea what else to do except simply climb into bed and try to get some rest.

Things have changed between us—all of us—and it's hard to pinpoint when the change happened or why. But it also doesn't matter. We've got to get to Twelve Springs no matter who is cuddling up together at night. We're all adults here. Whatever happens between Erik and Arianna is none of my business. And nothing is going on with me and Arya. He's sweet, but he's still young and it doesn't matter to me that he's Christian. I didn't set out on this journey to find a boyfriend, I set out to find my family and I'm finally this close. This tale is almost over.

I pull back my curtain with a sigh and realize the sanctuary is empty. My mask is beside me, resting on the pew with the rest of my meager belongings. The air in here is slightly better than outside so I don't have to wear my mask all day if I don't want to. I slept a few hours without it and my throat isn't burning, so I guess I'm fine.

I leave the mask where it's at and step into my boots, then I strap my knife to my hip and walk down the long aisle of the church. Despite the destruction, the place is more or less the

245

same as I remember. Purple décor with gold finishings, paintings on the wall depicting scenes from the Bible.

There was a really gifted lady who donated one of her works to the church called *Eden*, it depicts what she imagines the Garden of Eden would have looked like. I used to love it. But now it's covered in dust and partially burned. I stare at the ruined artwork as I stand by the entrance to the sanctuary, wondering what else about this church, this town, these people who used to live here, has changed.

I wonder how much *I've* changed.

Seven weeks ago, I hadn't stepped foot in the barren fields at all. I had no idea how to navigate or survive. Everett had been my only family and one stupid decision had ruined everything between us. But now I've got so much more. I'm stronger—mentally, emotionally, even spiritually. Especially spiritually.

I haven't prayed so much in my life. My faith has never been this strong before. Maybe because out here I've got nothing but God. If I didn't have faith, I'd be dead by now. I know Jesus is the only reason I've survived this long. He's the only reason Erik has survived for this long.

I have half a mind to march over and remind Erik of everything God's done for him when I walk out of the sanctuary and find him sitting in a corner with Arianna. The two of them are leaning toward each other, smiles on their unmasked faces, eyes crinkled, cheeks dimpled. He's in a hoodie. Arianna is still wearing his flannel. It's too big on her. She's tall for a woman but Erik is 6'3 and heavy like a lumberjack. His shirts would be big on anyone.

I can't stop myself from staring at the shirt. Wondering if it smells like him. Or if Arianna has worn it so long that it smells like her now. Heartbreak tries to worm its way into my chest, but I flush it out with anger.

I get it. Erik's an adult, like I said, but I didn't go through hell and highwaters for him to trample on this journey like it means nothing to him. I got dragged across the state for him as much as for my family.

My feet move before I can think to stop myself. I'm stomping across the hall with a fire burning in my belly and my hands balled into fists when something tugs me to a halt. That same Still Voice that spoke to me about forgiving Jeremiah. It resounds in my heart like a peaceful song.

Salvation must be his choice.

Of course…

God's very first gift to humanity, besides life itself, was freewill. The ability to love God for yourself. The power to choose life or death.

Erik has been given plenty of chances and opportunities to choose for himself—even before the explosions. His wife, Angelena, was a Christian woman who dragged him to church with her as often as she could. I've shared my own story and testimony. I've given him scriptures. Even Arya has helped share the Gospel with me, praying with me, discussing the Bible, explaining the secret message here in the church. Together, we've been an example to Erik. Proof of God's love and comfort in this dark world. Our survival itself is proof of His hands around us like a shield.

And yet… Erik chooses to be distracted by a pretty smile.

My shoulders sag. I can't make Erik believe. Not any more than I can make him stay away from Arianna. But I want him to. That much, I can admit. I don't even have to wonder why. The truth is in my burning cheeks and aching chest. I don't know when things changed between us, but the shift became obvious the moment we let Arya and Arianna into our little

247

world. A place that'd had a population of two for far too long.

Whatever new feelings that've developed became painfully obvious two days ago when Erik walked away from me wearing that defeated expression. A look that said he hadn't lost his life or his will, he'd lost *me*.

To Arya of all people.

As if summoned by my thoughts, Arya appears by my side. I jump at the sound of his voice. "You good, Mama?"

He's been calling me that lately. I know enough Spanish to recognize it as a term of endearment, not an insult to my age. Arya knows I'm older than him, but he doesn't seem to care. It hasn't stopped him from trying to spend as much time with me as possible, and it hasn't stopped him from giving me his dangerous smirks whenever he speaks to me.

He's wearing one of his crooked grins now as he lifts his mask and steps into my personal space. I can smell his scent up close, dirt and—somehow—cedarwood. The only trees out here are dead, so I've no idea how Arya manages to smell so manly. Maybe he found some aftershave or cologne during his looting excursion.

Speaking of which...

I glance down at the bag in his hand and quickly steer the conversation away from myself. I'm not sure how Arya will react if he figures out I was standing there fuming over his sister and Erik.

"What'd you bring back?"

Arya holds up his sack with a grin. "Found this gem in an abandoned school," he beams, showing me a fidget spinner.

I deflate. I'd been hoping for food, but I guess this is cool too.

"Glad you found something to pass the time."

Arya frowns. "I'm never bored around you, if that's what

you're suggesting."

I resist the urge to roll my eyes and start down the hall in the opposite direction of Erik and Arianna.

Arya follows me.

"We can split the beans," he offers, digging into his bag to reveal a can of baked beans.

"I'm good," I grunt.

"I don't mind sharing."

"They give me wind."

Arya laughs over my shoulder but when I don't laugh back, I feel his hand gently grip my arm. I stop walking and let him turn me to face him. There's a look on his face that's filled with emotions I don't want to deal with right now.

Why can't we just focus on the apocalypse??

I sigh, thinking of my mother—who may or may not be dead—she used to always tell me there was no such thing as a good story without a good romance. *Well, I guess we've reached the romantic part of this journey.* I roll my eyes again and face Arya dead on.

"What's wrong, Mama?" he asks in his thick Spanish accent.

I shake my head. I do not want to deal with this right now, but it isn't going to just drift away on its own.

"I don't really know what's wrong," I admit.

Arya sighs and motions for me to sit with him. We threw together a pile of cushions from the pews in the sanctuary the other day, so we'd have places to sit around and relax while we kept watch over the lobby. Arya takes a seat on a plastic covered pillow, and I sit beside him, ignoring the crinkling of the tarp.

He immediately reaches for my hand. "You know you can always talk to me."

249

"That's the thing," I pull away, "I'm not sure it's good for us to talk. Like this."

Judging from the look on Arya's face, I know he understands exactly what I'm trying to say. He might be younger than me, but he isn't stupid.

The corners of his mouth turn downwards, and I feel a small pain swell in my chest. I'm not good at letting people down. It hurts me just as much as it hurts them.

"I'm sorry," I say softly.

To his credit, Arya simply nods and brushes his hand through his thick hair. "I thought it was worth a shot. You know?"

"It was worth a shot."

He smiles at me. "Can I know what happened? I mean, I thought we were getting along well."

"We were." I swallow.

He raises his eyebrows in response, urging me to go on.

"It's just... I mean..." Without meaning to, I glance down the hall and immediately regret it.

Arya lets out an annoyed little snort. "Please do not tell me it's the old man."

"He's not an old man." I frown.

"He's got *grey* hair." Arya folds his arms over his admittedly firm chest. I caught him changing his clothes yesterday, and I have to be honest, I see the difference between him and Erik. I really do. But ... I just don't care.

"His hair is *salt and pepper*," I correct Arya. "Not entirely grey."

"He's got to be at least fifteen years older than you!"

"Shh!" I warn, glancing down the hall again. I do not want Erik to overhear this conversation. I feel like a schoolgirl chatting about her crush, it's the stupidest feeling in the world.

I promise you.

Arianna is still leaning toward Erik, a bright smile on her face. I don't know her exact age, but I bet it's close to mine. But that's not stopping her. Or Erik. And it hasn't seemed to bother Arya one bit.

My brows knit together. "You don't care about Arianna flirting with Erik," I say. "What difference does it make if I like him too?"

He runs his hand over his face. "So you *do* like him?"

All I can do is look away in response and hope my cheeks aren't burning red. I'm brown as a nut, so they probably aren't red at all, but still. They *feel* red. And that makes everything worse. Arya has a point; Erik *is* older than me. In his early 40s while I'm only 27. But my stance is the same; I don't really care.

Arya leans toward me. "I'm Christian, Mama. Doesn't that count for something?"

"Arya…" I don't know how to say this. "It doesn't matter that you're Christian."

He blinks at me. "Did you miss that scripture about being unequally yoked?"

"That's not what I meant." I laugh nervously. "I meant… Being Christian doesn't make you *the one*. It makes you compatible, but it doesn't mean you're the life partner God has chosen for me."

His faces twists up in something very close to anger. "So, Erik The Atheist is *the one*?"

"He's not an atheist," I say defensively. "He just hasn't gotten things right with God yet. But he will."

I hope.

Now Arya smirks again and I hate the way his voice sounds when he says, "Well it looks like he's getting things right with my sister instead."

I don't have to put up with this…

"Look, I've said what I needed to. I've got to go, alright?" I push to my feet and start down the hall.

Arya calls after me, but his voice is loud enough that it catches Erik's and Arianna's attention down the hall. They both look up at me, but it's Erik's eyes that my gaze drifts toward. We stare at each other for a moment, then I regain my focus and turn toward the sanctuary without another word.

I hear footsteps behind me as I make it to my tent. I'm not surprised that Arya came after me—but as I turn around to yell at him, I realize it's not Arya at all.

"Erik?"

He looks just as bewildered as I do.

"You looked upset. Out there." He points over his shoulder, like I have no idea what 'out there' is.

I nod dumbly. "Sorry. I didn't mean to cause a scene."

"You didn't."

"Well, I caused enough drama to drag you away from Arianna."

He steps closer to me. "Shon, can we talk?"

"I saw her leaving your tent last night," I blurt.

Erik sighs and sets his hands on his hips, looking at me from beneath his heavy brows.

"She's been wearing your shirt since last night," I tell him. "That's *all* she was wearing last night."

He's silent for a moment. As if ashamed, he drops his gaze and says softly, "Are we really gonna do this right now?"

My answer is immediate. "Yes."

Erik looks up, and for a long moment, we stand there staring at each other. I'm begging for answers that I don't want to hear, he's begging me to just let it go and move on. But I can't. I need to hear this.

"Well, go on then," Erik grunts. "Ask what you really want to."

I take a breath, hating the way my voice shakes. "Did you…"

I can't finish the question, but Erik answers anyway.

"Yes." He drops his gaze. "I did."

My heart turns brittle. Tears fill my eyes and Erik sees them before I can turn away. I feel his hand on my back, but he doesn't try to turn me around. He doesn't rub circles. He just stands there with his palm pressed between my shoulder blades.

"I'm so sorry," he says softly. "She offered. I was weak. You'd turned me down… I—I don't know. I *didn't* know how much it would matter."

I gasp and let out a sob. His hand presses more firmly against my back.

"Cupcake—"

"Don't call me that!" I snap, whirling around.

"What do you want me to say then?" Erik asks hotly. "That I'm sorry? I've said that. That I regret it? You know I do." He opens his arms, like he could fit all our problems between them. "What else do you want, RaShonda?"

I want to turn back time and erase this entire conversation. But the past is set in stone, all I can do is move forward now.

"I want to focus on the mission," I say, scrubbing at my cheek, trying to wipe away every tear. "I didn't go on this journey for love. I set out to find my family. That's it."

Erik takes a step back, his face shifting into calm understanding. "Alright, then."

"If you don't mind…" I glance at the door, silently asking him to leave.

He obliges. "Right. I've got first watch during lunch,

anyway. I guess I'll see you around."

"I guess so," I say. And then I watch him turn and walk away. I have no idea how I feel about it, but I know this is the way it's got to be.

24

Erik

Sleeping with Arianna was a bad idea. Don't even ask me why I did it because I have no answer except that she was there and willing and I was hurt and desperate. It didn't mean anything. It wasn't even very good, if I'm being honest. Just two naked people touching each other. No love involved. No passion.

All the love and passion in my life ended when my wife died.

I've had a woman or two since her death. But the encounters left me so miserable and guilty afterward that I'd declared myself a eunuch. Then things got complicated with Shon and for a brief moment, I thought I could feel those things again.

Another bad idea.

Shon didn't just turn me down, she *shut* down. Reminded me that we weren't here for love and then sent me away. What could I do but give her what she wanted?

Besides, Shon is right. We aren't here for love. I'm positive you didn't start this story to hear about my *feelings*. You're here for the barren fields, so I promise that's all you're gonna get from me from now on.

I can't afford to focus on Shon anyway. Not when we're just hours away from Twelve Springs Campgrounds. If I'm focused on Shon, who will watch our backs? Who will make sure we're on the right path? Who will keep us all safe?

I've got to get back to doing my job.

The four of us cover the next three days in silent misery. Arya is abnormally quiet and sullen from getting rejected by Shon who is quiet and sullen from the mistake I made with Arianna who is quiet and sullen from being ignored by me.

I'm depressed because I'm alive. That's the conclusion I've come to.

Depressed or not, I've got a job to complete. So I dig my heels in and march with fervor until I see something from the corner of my eye. We're well into the Georgian outback, marching through what used to be marsh area six years ago. Now, it's dried up and grey. Like everything else. The trees that used to grow here are shriveled, nothing but hollow tombs standing upright. The grass is long gone, the bushes have turned to dust. This is the dead forest, and it gives me chills.

I stop walking when I notice unnatural movement. Oddly, the wind has been blowing in this area, so every now and then a dusty branch will roll by or a pile of brittle leaves. But the movement I see isn't a plant or a rock at all. To be honest, I'm not sure what it is.

Arya walks into my back and grunts, "What's going on, old man?"

"Watch it," I snap.

He says something in Spanish that I know he'll never say in English, but I ignore it and speak in a low voice. "Movement, one o'clock."

Everyone stiffens, heads whipping up to scan the area. Shon reaches for her hunting knife which makes me smile behind my gasmask. Even though we aren't really speaking anymore, she's still focused. Good girl.

"What sort of movement?" Arianna asks, taking the initiative to sweep our six. She looks behind us with her muscular shoulders tensed and her arms up with her hunting knife raised, ready to attack or defend.

The best thing about the Grey is that it's barren. The land is mostly flat except for abandoned buildings. We should be able to see Faceless or drifters long before they get to us. But we're in the dead forest now, dangerously close to a campground that could be the end of us.

The trees in this area are dried up, but they haven't toppled over or turned to dust. They're just dead. Some have rotted from the radiation, but some have sprouted neon daisies and offer bursts of vivid color in the cloud of grey stretched before us. There are enough of these dead and infected trees to block our vision, so when I think I see something, it's gone before I can pinpoint exactly what it is.

At least I still remember where it came from.

I point in the general direction. "Over there. Don't know what it was, but it was definitely something."

"That *something* could be anything," Arya says angrily.

I grunt.

"Should we check it out?" Arianna asks.

It takes me a moment to realize everyone is looking at me. I'd been leading Shon around for so long, taking charge because she has no idea how to read a compass or navigate

257

celestially. But, for some reason, I thought taking Arya and Arianna with us would give me a break. I thought I wouldn't be the one making all the tough decisions anymore.

Now I've got three kids blinking up at me with expectant looks on their faces.

Sure, they aren't exactly *kids*—and I've gotten to know one of those kids in a very *adult* way—but as I look down at them now, I see them for what they truly are. Still so young. With so much potential. We've come so far now, if I fail here, I don't know if I'll ever forgive myself.

I take a breath and sneak a glance at Shon, she's waiting like the rest of them, except her face looks more confident. Like she knows I can handle this. Like she believes in me.

My nerves jump up a hundred notches.

"Let's check it out," I say with a nod.

"You sure?" Arya's got that punk expression on his stupid face again. The same one he had on when he panicked and ran wild through the city, forcing me to leave Shon to chase him down.

I step forward and grab him roughly by the collar. I am not dealing with his antics today. If he runs away again, I'm leaving him.

"Whoever or whatever it is likely saw us just as much as I saw it. They know we're out here. I'd rather find them before they poke their head out and find us. Got it?"

Arya nods but I don't let him go just yet.

"Stay calm. Do as I say. And we'll make it out of this alive, you hear?"

He nods again, but this time I see Arianna and Shon nodding from my peripheral. Great. At least we're all on the same page.

With a shove, I release Arya and turn to the women,

hefting my crowbar. "Ready?"

Without words, we fall into our usual formation, sweeping every direction, carefully checking around dead trees and gingerly walking through the fields of neon daisies. They grow in clusters around infected trees and plants, ethereal in their beauty but deadly in every possible way.

When we're less than ten meters from the tree I saw movement, I glance down at the daisies and feel sweat trickle down my spine. One by one, the glowing flowers begin to bend toward the dead tree ahead. Reaching out toward the nearest and largest source of radiation.

It's an effort to keep my voice calm as I say in the loudest whisper I can muster, "*Stop!*"

Everyone halts.

I feel their eyes on me. I feel the questions swirling in their heads, creating a storm of worry as I stare down at the daises, willing them to straighten. Begging them to stand up again and pretend everything is all right.

They never move, in fact, more of them shift toward the tree. I hear Arianna gasp to my left, and when I glance up, I'm not surprised to find her studying the daisies too.

"What's going on?" Arya says too loudly.

"Hush!" I reprimand him, but he bites back, "Make me, old man."

"Guys, look at the daisies." Arianna points, cutting me off before I can snarl at her brother.

"What's that mean?" Arya asks.

A low growl in the distance is his answer.

The daisies shift again, drawing my attention. I follow their motion to the dead tree ahead. A shadow steps out first, then a beast appears behind it. I can tell from the snarl that pours from its mouth that it's a dog, but nothing about its appearance makes me *believe* it's a dog.

First of all, it's huge. Paws the size of mitts, and a head that belongs on a wolf. It is hairless and its eyes glow the same eerie neon blue as the daisies and the Faceless. The skin that covers its muscular frame is leathery and taut, stretched over a body that looks fit enough to fight a lion. I would wonder how it got so large and strong, but it's pumped full of radiation and has plenty of people—and Faceless—to feed on.

This is not a cute pup like my Ozzy. Ozzy was a survivor. She'd lost her hair, her tail, and one of her eyes, but she didn't grow three times the size of a normal dog and she didn't turn into a deadly beast who hated anything that made eye contact with it.

This thing in front of me isn't even a dog anymore. When its lips peel back for it to growl at us, I see two rows of teeth in its bottom jaw. That's when fear truly sets in. This is no longer an animal. This is a killer. A predator in its finest condition. And it's not alone.

More growls fill the air. I glance around to see other dogs crawling from behind dead trees, even rising from the tall daisies that come up to our knees. The other dogs are hairless with neon eyes. But they're also normal-sized—much smaller than the one in front of us, which explains why the daisies only bent toward this one. It's their alpha, pumped with so much radiation. But the smaller ones are still deadly.

There are dozens of dogs out here. And they have one goal in mind.

If they were Faceless, I would feel more confident. I would believe that we could run or fight. But these things—these *beasts*—are on a different level. These are monsters that send Faceless running.

I squeeze my eyes shut. *God, please—*

260

The alpha barks loud enough to shatter my eardrums. All four of us drop to our knees with our hands clamped over our ears. I can barely think, let alone focus on the beasts closing in on us.

Somehow, Shon manages to overcome her pain. She pops to her feet as a dog sprints right at us, and takes off running. They meet with a clash, claws swiping at the knife in Shon's hand. She holds on tight, shifting her head away when the dog bites at her throat, and brings her blade up to pierce its leathery underbelly. The mutt howls as it falls to the ground. I get a two-second flashback of Ozzy in the same position. Lying motionless in the basement of that school, blood spilling from her body. When reality returns, I see the mad dog dead at Shon's feet. The other dogs move in slowly, sizing us up.

Shon looks over her shoulder at the three of us, her face twisted in anger, blood dripping from her left ear. "Get up!" she orders. "Fight!"

Her words ignite a fire inside of me, it spills onto the field and catches flame in Arianna and Arya too. The three of us find our feet and raise our weapons. I have no idea if we will survive this, but we will not go down without a fight.

"Use our scouting formation!" Shon shouts. "Arya, flank right. Erik, flank left. Arianna, watch our six!"

I'm stunned by Shon's demeanor and control. She takes charge of the situation with a sense of leadership I haven't seen in her before. We're all too shaken to do anything but follow orders, taking up our positions and glaring at the dogs that want to kill us.

I can hear Arya panting even from my stance a few feet away. If there is a weak link here, it's him. Even the dogs can sense it. They run at him, two of them together, and attack at the same time. One leaps into the air while the other keeps sprinting forward.

Shon is in front, but she reacts faster than any of us, pivoting and yelling, "Go low!"

Thankfully, Arya understands her command and hunches over to swipe at the dog sprinting through the daisies. Shon throws her knife at the one in the air. Her aim is true; the blade sinks right into its eye, and it falls backwards into the grass, right beside the body of its comrade who goes down to Arya's brass knuckles. He brings down his fist four times right on the dog's head after it tackles him in the flowers. His arm is scratched up, but he's fine, nonetheless.

This is the opening we needed.

The other dogs get spooked and start to back away from us. We're three for three at this point, and Shon is responsible for two of those kills. That's why the alpha targets her.

When the other mutts start backing off, the alpha lets out an angry howl and charges forward. The other dogs snarl at us, their confidence boosted by their leader. Shon doesn't see the alpha charging; she's too busy helping Arya to his feet.

I move without thinking.

My crowbar comes down on the alpha's spine. I swing as it runs by, but the strike is enough to get its attention. It stops almost on a dime and releases a growl so deep, I swear I feel it in my bones.

There's only one thing I can do—I turn and run.

The alpha chases after me, and it's all I can do to stay ahead of it. My legs move like I'm on fire, my breaths come out in desperate gulps as I suck for oxygen through my mask. I can feel the wind pushing against my back as the alpha runs, moving so fast it kicks up dirt in its wake. The sound of its claws scraping against the dead earth sends horror skirting up my spine and I pump my arms to run even faster. But it's not enough.

The beast swipes at me, cutting open my jacket, my hoodie, and the flannel I have on underneath. Mercifully, the cut doesn't break the skin, but I'm thrown to the ground from the force of the blow.

In that moment, I know God is real. Undeniably, irrefutably, unquestionably real.

As I fall, my body moves on its own, refusing to die. I shift so that I'm facing the alpha, and I raise my arms like a coward. But the crowbar is still in my hands—it goes up too, the sharp end pointed right at the mighty beast.

The dog is moving too fast. As I close my eyes in fear, I hear its painful shriek as it impales itself on the iron rod. Its paws kick up as it flails madly. I barely manage to dodge its toxic claws, but it's so heavy that I'm nearly buried beneath it as it writhes in the throes of death. Its life does not leave it peacefully. I feel the air squeezed out of me as the dog howls once more, defecates itself, and then topples onto my chest.

I'm pinned beneath deadweight. Hundreds of pounds of pure muscle threaten to suffocate me, but with a cry of anger, I shove it away and gasp for breath beneath my mask. There is no time to celebrate this shocking victory. All I can do is thank God in my heart before I get up and start running back to my group.

They're not doing much better than me. Somehow, Arianna, Shon, and Arya have managed to huddle together, back-to-back, and are taking turns hacking at the dogs who throw themselves at their meager defenses. It's working for now, but I'm not sure how much longer they can last.

Arianna is bleeding from her leg, she's leaning against Arya just to stay upright. Arya isn't even wearing his mask anymore; I can see the panic in his eyes as he punches at a dog and manages to shove it away. The sleeve covering his right arm is soaked red, there are three large gashes going down his exposed bicep.

Shon's state is just as bad. Both her hands are bloody, like she had it in one of the dogs' mouths. Her knife is up and ready to attack, but I can see her hands shaking even from my distance.

As I approach, the dogs shift their attention. They can smell the blood of their leader smeared across my stained clothes. They can smell the stench of its emptied bowels that covers my legs and shoes. Instead of cowering and scurrying off like most pack animals, the dogs let out a howl as one and rush in at the same time.

"No!" I scream, lunging forward, trying hard to protect my friends.

The crowbar is still in my hands. I use it to knock one dog off its feet and sweep the legs from beneath a second one as I run. My heart hammers against my ribcage, my ribs ache with every pounding step in my desperate sprint.

A dog leaps through the air, I'm so focused on my friends, I almost don't see it until it's right in front of me. But, again, my body moves on its own, filled with a vigor that I cannot explain except to say that I know it is God.

We have made it through so many situations, impossible fights that we should have lost, things cannot end here. *Please!* I cry to God, a God I haven't prayed to or believed in for far too long, a God I'm embarrassed to even call on after ignoring for years, but a God I know is merciful enough to answer.

Arianna goes down and Arya steps in to protect her. Shon watches his back as he drags his sister away, right toward me. I meet them in the daisy field and start pulling Arianna by the collar of her shirt, but she fights me the entire time.

264

"Don't leave him!" she screams, kicking at the air.

I understand her fears. Arya charges back into the fray to help Shon and the sight leaves me short of breath. I have no idea how the two of them will make it out of this. They are surrounded by vicious radioactive dogs and must hack and slice their way to freedom. Meanwhile, dogs begin to snip and snarl at me as I ignore Arianna's cries and drag her as far away from the battle as I can.

I give a few of them a good whack over the head with my crowbar, it's enough to make them wary of me, so I keep moving. When we're a good distance, I lean Arianna against a boulder and kneel to look her in the eye. "Stay here, keep your knife ready!" I shout; then I turn and run back for the second time.

Shon is holding on to Arya, he made it back to her, but he was punished for his aid. He's limping badly, clutching his leg and slowing them down but Shon refuses to let him go. Dogs surround them, getting ready for the kill. I hear a whining noise that shocks me when I realize it's bubbled up from my own throat.

I am sobbing, choking on my grief as I watch the wild mutts close in. "No!" I scream and my plea is echoed by Arianna behind me. She's screaming louder than I am, but her words are drowned out by the horrible barking that storms around us.

A dog runs forward, it slows as Shon slashes at the air with the knife in her free hand. She's closer now, close enough that I can hear her panicky cries as she half drags Arya along with her. He's doing the best he can, limping and urging Shon to keep her feet, to keep moving forward. When he looks up, I see the true terror in his eyes. I see how badly he wants to live, and I feel a spark of fire surge through me.

"Run!" I shout, swinging my crowbar at a dog that tries to bite me. I'm sure I break its jaw, but I don't care to find out. I'm more than satisfied with the sickening *crunch* that fills the air and the way it falls and doesn't get back up.

My legs are like jelly when I finally make it to Shon and Arya. She shoves him at me and immediately holds up her hunting knife. "Go!" she shouts, but I'm not leaving her behind.

"We'll move together!" I shout back, it earns me a glare but I can tell she's thankful for the help. Arya, on the other hand, is not.

He slaps at my shoulder and starts yelling for me to move. Like before, the kid starts to panic as the dogs move in. There are a lot less of them now, a lot have been killed, others have run off after realizing we're as desperate to live as they are desperate to eat. The ones left are here for sport, snipping at our heels and yelping excitedly like this is all a game to them. A game I am not interested in playing.

As Arya tries to hurry, I brace him against my side and swing the crowbar like a wild man. A dog goes down from a blow to its ribs, another backs off after I whack it directly on the top of its head. I actually start to feel good. I feel confident we're going to make it now—until I hear Shon scream behind me.

There's a dog attached to her ankle, it's jaws clenched shut around the bone. Another is snapping at her as she stabs at the one on her foot. Without thinking, I let go of Arya and turn back.

Both the kid and his sister shriek. I know I've just abandoned him. I know that he's just as scared and injured as Shon. I know his sister is depending on me to get him to safety, but I'm not leaving Shon behind. I'm not letting her die to

266

these stupid dogs.

To no one's surprise, Arya keeps running when I let him go, limping madly towards his sister. A dog chases him down. I manage to close my eyes as he's tackled to the ground, a desperate cry slipping from my lips.

"God, no—"

Screams erupt around me, I'm not sure if they come from Arianna, Shon, or myself, but I'm suddenly by Shon's side, moving without thinking, hands shaking as I beat the dogs away from her and scoop her up in my arms. I run like the ground is crumbling beneath my feet, beating the earth with my boots until I make it to Arianna. It's hard to sprint by Arya as he rolls in the dirt with two dogs, but my hands are full. I can't save them both—not right now at least.

I literally throw Shon on top of Arianna and turn back for the kid, but she grabs my sleeve and stops me in my tracks. "You'll die!" Shon yells.

I glance back at Arya. The sight is gruesome. I can tell from all the blood that it's too late. I can tell from the way he weakly swings his arm—bent at an odd angle—that my chances of saving him are low, but I can't leave him. Not in front of his own sister.

I grip the crowbar. "Get her out of here, cupcake," I say sternly.

She starts shaking her head, but I grab her shoulder roughly. "Get her out of here!" I yell. "You know the way to Twelve Springs. I'll hold them off. Now go!" I shove her backwards and she trips into Arianna, her eyes wide with fear.

"I won't!" she shouts, but I shove her again.

"Yes, you will!" I glare at her through my mask. "You aren't here for love, remember?"

That seems to snap her to her senses. Shon gives me a slow,

solemn nod, then she stoops to pull a hysterical Arianna to her feet. The woman is blubbering madly, her attention focused solely on her brother. I don't try to say goodbye to either woman, I just turn and run toward the kid who needs my help, hoping God is still on my side.

25

Shon

Arianna is hysterical the entire time we run together. It's more accurate to say that I've dragged her half a mile through the dead forest than run with her. She's crying so hard she can barely see past her tears, plus her leg is hurt pretty bad—not to mention the condition I'm in. But, unlike Arianna, I'm not overwhelmed with grief. I'm filled with raw fear and adrenaline, despite the scene I walked away from, despite watching Erik run back into the fray armed with a crowbar and wishful thinking.

I swallow my own emotions as I drag Ari along, mindlessly mumbling words of comfort I'm sure she doesn't even hear.

"It'll be alright. We're almost there. I'm sure Erik made it in time."

That couldn't be further from the truth. I knew before Erik even turned around that Arya was lost, and I could see that truth written on his face too. But I could also see the determination, the stubborn will to keep going. Not to leave

269

anyone behind.

I can't blame him. As much as I want to.

The last time Erik was responsible for anyone, he was hurt and left for dead while his wife and best friend were dragged away by people who would use them as sex slaves for months. He'd been awake as his wife had screamed for him. He'd had his eyes wide open when they'd pressed a gun to his son's temple. He'd lost everything. And I knew from the look in his eye that he refused to lose it again.

All I can do now is hope that his resolve was enough. Hope that somehow, against all odds, Erik made it to Arya in time. Saved his life. And got himself out of there too.

"God, please," I sob, tripping over a small rock. I fall hard with Arianna leaning against me. We tumble to the ground and my knee whacks against a stone so sharply I feel the pain in my teeth.

My jaw clenches shut as I hiss at the injury, clutching the torn hem of my jeans. "This can't be happening!" I shout in frustration.

Arianna sits on her butt and hugs her knees. She looks nothing like the strong woman I remember from the last week or so. Her arms are still muscular, her face is still hedged by a meanness that makes me hesitate to speak. But the look in her eye is different. She isn't determined anymore. She isn't even angry. She's just there. Alive. And nothing else.

"Arianna," I say slowly, "we've got to keep going. We're not far from Twelve Springs."

She doesn't answer.

"Ari—"

"We left them," she sobs. "We left them."

"Erik went back—"

"What difference could he make!" she snaps.

270

"What difference could we?"

We stare at each other, trying to ignore the harsh truth that's screaming around us. I didn't want to leave them, not any more than Arianna did. But I didn't have a choice. Arianna's leg is busted, and I don't even have a weapon anymore. If I had gone back with Erik, I would have died screaming. Just like Arya.

"Erik told us to keep going. So that's what I'm going to do. We can still make it to Twelve Springs—"

"There is no Twelve Springs!" Arianna screams.

I wince at her words but choose to ignore them. I can't afford to think about Erik and the what-ifs. I need to focus on what's right in front of me, or Arianna and I may not survive at all.

I shove myself to my feet and glance around, turning every which way. My sense of direction is awful. This entire time I've been travelling with Erik, I've let him take the lead because I'm sure I'd only lead us in circles.

"Alright," I mutter to myself. "We can't be that far." I glance down at Arianna who's rocking back and forth on her butt now. "If we hurry, we can find Twelve Springs and maybe convince them to send help back."

Arianna stops rocking to glare up at me. Her face is streaked with bitter tears, her voice cracks as it fills the air in a dark whisper, "There. Is. No. Twelve. Springs. What part of that don't you understand?"

"The only thing I don't understand is why you're so sure this place doesn't exist."

"Look around you!" She opens her arms wide. "There's nothing out here! We've been walking aimlessly."

"That's not true."

"It is!" She gets to her feet to get into my face. I'm not

271

offended by the sudden proximity, I'm just happy she's up and moving. Hopefully, I can get her to start walking again.

"I thought teaming up would finally bring Arya to his senses, but you all played right into his madness! Chasing after churches. Believing God has some magical, mask-free place for Christians. You're all insane! And now your insanity got my brother killed!"

"That's not true!" I yell back. My voice is loud enough to shock Arianna, she stumbles back a step as she blinks at me in bewilderment.

I take a deep, calming breath. "Arya was right to believe. And so were you. You stayed at the church with your mother and your family in Mexico. You witnessed God's protection firsthand. You know for a fact that God is real and that He protects His people. You know Twelve Springs is real too."

Arianna loosens her jaw to speak. "If God protects His people, then why did I just watch my brother die?"

I don't have an answer. I have no idea why Arya died so violently. I have no idea why the world is in shambles. But it is. And arguing about the grief we face won't change that. We can choose to believe or we can abandon God. Those are the only two options.

I've chosen to believe. Because the alternative is that there is no hope. This is as good as it gets. I won't accept that.

"I don't know why Arya died," I admit. "I'm sorry that he did."

"Your apology won't bring him back," Arianna sneers.

"Neither will your hatred."

She glares at me. I don't really blame her. I know this isn't what she wants to hear right now, but it's got to be said.

"I don't have all the answers," I say in a softer tone. "But I know that's the purpose of faith. Choosing to believe despite your confusion. Choosing to trust God even when all the evidence is stacked against you."

She scoffs, shaking her head like I've just said the stupidest thing she's ever heard. "The evidence is that my brother is dead. And God did nothing to save him."

"That doesn't mean He isn't real anymore. Our pain does not negate His existence. Whether Arya lives or dies, God is still on the Throne. And as long as He's on the Throne, His expectations remain the same."

"He expects us to just get over our pain?"

"He expects us to believe in spite of it."

An uncomfortable silence settles over us. I have no idea if I've finally gotten through to her, but I honestly don't care. Like with Erik, it isn't my job to make Arianna accept salvation and love Jesus. It's my job to tell the Truth. Now that it's been told, I've got to keep moving.

"Look," I sigh, "I really don't care if you believe in God or not. It makes no difference to me. But can you at least choose to believe in me? Believe that I'm not insane. Believe that there is a reason I would chase after Twelve Springs."

Arianna just stares at me, a million cogs churning behind her hazel eyes.

I take a cautious step toward her. "You have two choices, Ari. Stay here and die or believe that there is a safe place out there waiting for us."

I meant what I said earlier. I don't care what Arianna believes. So when I've finished my statement, I turn on my heel and start a slow limp into the forest, praying all the way.

Please guide me, Holy Spirit. I have no idea where to go, but You do. In Jesus' Name—before I can finish the prayer, I hear movement behind me and I can't help but smile. I doubt she just became a convert, but the fact that Arianna's chosen to follow me is

273

far better than the alternative.

We walk for about fifteen minutes before the stiff silence between us is broken. A long howl resounds through the dead forest, freezing me in place. I feel a blanket of fear roll over me. It's so thick, I break out in a sweat, panting for breath as I turn to look back at Ari.

She's just as panicked as I am, but her panic sends her into action. She limps toward me, clutching her thigh as she grunts in pain. "Move!" she orders, shoving me back around.

I do as she says, picking up my pace to the sound of pounding feet.

There are a million thoughts shooting through my head right now. How close are they? Did the dogs kill Erik and Arya and then hunt us down? Are they coming for us or just warning us to stay out of their territory?

There's no way to tell. There's no other option except to run like mad.

We move as fast as we can, despite our injuries, crushing daisies as we go. Those demonic flowers are the only things alive in this grey wasteland. They're everywhere in this part of the forest. Popping up out of the ground all around us, climbing up trees and bursting from their branches in clusters of neon blue. As beautiful as they are, I hate the sight of them. I hate the way they bend toward the beasts I hear chasing us down. I hate the way they cover everything in beauty, hiding the death and destruction beneath their roots.

I want to close my eyes as I sprint. I want to somehow outrun the barren fields. It's got to end somewhere. There's got to be a rainbow somewhere in this bleak storm.

Jesus, I pray inside, dragging Arianna along. We're hardly moving faster than a brisk walk with how badly we're limping now. But we don't stop moving, and I don't stop praying, even though the howls are getting closer. Even though the sound of paws grows nearer every second.

"Help us, God!" I scream, shoving past a massive tree covered in daisies.

And just like that... the sight before me is a miracle. Massive gates tower over me, just twenty yards ahead. The space between the dead forest and the camping grounds is nothing but lush green grass, no daisies in sight. I can hardly believe it.

I step forward and drop to my knees, too exhausted to go on. The grass is soft beneath my bloody fingertips. The wind here smells sweet, even through my gasmask. I reach up and yank it from my face, sucking in a lungful of precious air. Clean air.

Arianna is beside me, lying in the grass like she's making a snow angel. It's been six years since I've seen grass that wasn't poisoned. Six years since I held a tiny blade in my hand. Suddenly, I yearn for that freshly cut lawn smell, even though I hated mowing the backyard when I was a teenager.

I lie on my belly and take a deep breath, filling my lungs with the scent of nature. Untainted, unmarred nature. Just as God created it.

And then terror strikes my heart when I hear another howl.

I jerk upright, staring at the gates before me. They are set in the middle of a large fence that looks like it was hastily put together. I've been to Twelve Springs plenty of times, I don't remember a fence surrounding the campgrounds, then again, I don't remember Faceless roaming about when I was a kid, either.

I don't care how the fence got there. Right now, I just want to get on the other side of it.

I shove myself to my feet and limp toward the gates,

frantically waving my hands over my head. "Help!" I scream. "Help us!"

Arianna is right beside me, shouting and waving her hands too.

"Please!" I cry when I hear the familiar snarl of the dogs behind us. We have seconds before they catch us.

Just when I think I'm going to tragically die outside the haven I spent weeks trying to find, a man appears above the gates, standing on a raised platform. He glances down at us for a fraction of a second before lifting his arms.

He's holding something—I gasp when I realize it's a bow and arrow, but my shock turns to relief when he sets an arrow loose and it goes straight through the eye of a dog right behind me. More people appear on the gates, taking aim with their own bow and arrows. They shoot down the dogs with precision that I envy, my heartrate slows with every beast that dies.

When the last one goes down, I let out a sob of joy, relief, and exhaustion, but the sound is drowned out by the creaking of the gates as they finally begin to open.

26

Shon

I passed out as soon as the gates opened. I have no idea how I got in the bed I've just woken up in. I have no idea where I am.

I sit up very slowly, aching all the way. White bandages are wrapped from my fingers to my elbows on both arms. One of my legs has a bandage wrapped tightly around the ankle, and when I lift my hand to touch my face, my fingers graze a thick wad of gauze.

I blink.

The bed is soft. The room is clean—the air is clean. I suddenly realize I'm not wearing my mask and I gasp. The noise catches the attention of someone sitting in a comfy chair beside the bed. It's a woman—a woman I recognize.

She has the same dark brown skin as me, the same thick, afro hair. It's even pulled back into a single braid that disappears down her back, just like mine. Her eyebrows are heavy and drawn together so she looks like she's scowling but I can see the tears welling in her eyes as she whispers my name.

277

"RaShonda?"

"Mama?" I whisper back.

She erupts from the chair and crushes me in a hug so tight, my eyes water from the pain. It's a pain that I welcome. This reunion is nine years in the making. I wouldn't have it any other way.

"I can't believe it's you!" my mother shrieks.

I rub her back with my bandaged hands, sobbing into her bosom. My mother is not a large lady, she's always been thin as a rail with a pretty face and high cheekbones, but she's somehow filled out over the years. Her face is rounder, and her body feels healthy as I hug her. I have no idea how she's managed to keep herself fed in the barren fields but I'm not going to question it.

Wait...

"Mama..." I pull away and take her hands in my own, squeezing them. "Where am I?"

She smiles warmly. "You don't recognize the place? This is Twelve Springs Campgrounds."

If I weren't so sore, I'd jump for joy.

"I knew it was real," I whisper, tears pouring down my cheeks.

Weeks of travel. Weeks of pain. So much fighting. So much loss...

Memories flood my mind and I have to let go of Mama's hands to clutch the side of my head. The grief I feel is almost too much to bear.

"Shon, what's wrong?" Mama leans closer, panic filling her voice now. "Shon, talk to me."

"I'm sorry," I whisper. "It's been a long journey."

She lets go of a long sigh. "I can imagine. When the guards said they brought in two survivors, I didn't pay the news any

278

attention." She laughs. "No one believes a place like this truly exists. As rare as newcomers are, I thought there was no chance the survivors were anyone I knew."

I look up at her through my tears, urging her to go on.

"When Nurse Wrenley said she recognized you, I thought she was playing a cruel joke on me. I thought there was no way. But I see now…" her voice cracks. "God brought my baby home."

"He's the One Who told me to return home," I say, and then I almost laugh at the look of surprise that takes over her face. My mother is well aware of how weak my relationship with God had been when I'd left years ago. I'm not at all shocked or offended by her disbelief. But out here, in the barren fields, it's either believe or die. I wouldn't be here if it weren't for God, and I'm not ashamed to say that.

From there, I tell my mother the entire story. From the very beginning. How I felt like a failure for getting pregnant at such a young age. How I was embarrassed to call myself a Christian because of the mistakes I'd made. How I left because of all the trouble I'd caused the family. And I tell her about how God spoke to me. How His Still Voice whispered for me to return home, and how I thought I was insane for six years until I finally took that leap of faith. By force, but still…

When I get to the part about how I got here, I feel myself getting choked up and I can't go on. I can't talk about Erik or the last time I saw him.

Mama kisses my forehead. "You made it back to your family. That's all that matters. At least your one friend is safe."

My one friend…

I pull from Mama's embrace. "Arianna, how is she?"

She pats my cheek. "She's fine. Been up for two days now—"

"Two days?" I say, frowning.

Mama nods. "You've been passed out for three, honey."

I toss my covers back, fueled by a surge of adrenaline. "I can't believe it's been that long."

"What are you doing?" Mama asks.

"Did anyone else come to the gates after I showed up?"

Her thick brows pinch together. "No. It was just you and—"

"Did you guys send anyone out to look for others?" I cut her off in a panicked voice. There's a pile of clean clothes folded on the bedside table, I grab them and start shrugging on the long-sleeved shirt and then reach for the pants. "How could you let me stay asleep for that long!" I nearly scream. My raised voice brings unwanted attention. The door to my room swings open and a nurse steps inside.

Wrenley, the woman who recognized me. I recognize her too; she was an usher at Fire Baptized Ministries. She used to slip me candy during long services—I was a chubby girl, I guess I always looked hungry to her. Right now, she's standing in my doorway with a frightened look on her face, eyes darting between myself and Mama, unsure how to approach the situation.

"Were any teams sent out to search the woods for survivors?" I ask Wrenley.

"Um…" she starts to shake her head and I let out a cry of anger.

This can't be happening. We were thirty minutes away. The plan was to get to Twelve Springs and send back help. Even if Arya was lost, there was still hope for Erik. But that was days ago. *Days.*

I'm wearing a pair of sweatpants and a shirt when I march over to Wrenley and order her aside, but she doesn't move.

280

"You've got to rest," she says in her sweet, older lady voice.

"I need to go out there and find my—" I cut myself off. What is Erik to me? "My friend," I finally decide. "He's out there. He was left out there because you people didn't care!"

"Hey now," Mama snaps behind me. I hear her footsteps cross the room and I feel her hand on my shoulder, turning me to face her. "You were passed out. How were we supposed to know there were others?"

"You didn't make the assumption that I might have been travelling in a group?" I almost yell. I would feel guilty for speaking this way to my mother if she didn't have a fire burning in her eyes right now. Mama is not a woman who backs down, especially not from her own child.

She steps into my face, and I can smell the light fragrance of mint on her breath as she says, "You need to watch your tone, young lady."

I step back and hug myself, trying hard not to exhale a sob. I hold my breath to keep from breaking down. *This can't be happening. God, please.*

"We did assume you were in a group," Mama finally says, then she sits on my bed and her shoulders slump. "Your friend, Arianna, told us they had passed on. She said they'd died before you guys even made it here."

My mouth goes dry. My tears are suddenly gone. Every sorrowful emotion I felt simmers into a pool of rage.

"She told you what?" I whisper.

Mama blinks at me, shooting her gaze toward Wrenley for support.

The nurse speaks up, "Arianna said your other companions were dead."

I fly out of the room, shoving past Wrenley so hard, she trips and falls into the hallway, but I don't care. The only thought in my head is finding that witch.

"Where is she!" I yell, storming down the hall. I don't feel a single one of my injuries as I march past open doors that reveal empty rooms. If I cared, I would comment on the cleanliness of the campsite, on how well they managed to keep up the infirmary. I would comment on how great it is to see sunlight and grass outside the windows I pass. I would comment on the children I hear laughing in the courtyard outside. But right now, I don't care about any of that.

"Where is Arianna?" I scream.

Summoned by the noise, Ari steps out of a room just ahead of me. Her face is dark, as miserable as it was the last time I saw her. The day she claims everyone died.

"How could you?" I yell, walking toward her. When I'm close enough, I shove her backwards into her closed door. She doesn't fight me back. "You lost Arya, so I had to lose Erik too?"

Arianna doesn't speak.

My blood begins to boil, but I don't have the time or the energy to take it out on this insufferable woman. I turn back toward my mother and Nurse Wrenley who have both made it down the hall now.

"I need whatever supplies you can spare," I tell them in a rush. I'm marching back down the hall now, I have no idea where I'm going, I'm not even wearing any shoes, but I've got to get out of here. I've got to get back to Erik.

Mama puts her foot down, literally, and steps in front of me. "Absolutely not, RaShonda."

"Mama, please—"

"I just got you back!" she says loudly.

The panic in her voice silences me. It clears all thoughts from my head. As I look at my mother with tears in her eyes

282

and a look of anguish conquering her features, I realize these years haven't been easy for her either. She's been waiting for me. Hoping against everything that not only was I alive, but that I'd find my way back to her someday. That day has finally come, thanks to God Almighty, I've made it home. And now I'm leaving again.

I can't imagine the terror that's gripped her as she reaches for my shoulders and shakes me. "I just got you back," she says again.

"God brought me back—"

"Yes, He did!" she shouts. "And I'm not wasting this blessing by letting you go again!"

"It's not up to you!" I say loudly, tugging myself free of her grasp. She stares at me in disbelief. I know there's no way she will ever understand why I've got to do this, but she can't stop me. I'll sneak out at night. I'll fight my way past the guards if I have to. I'm going to find Erik.

"It's been a long journey," I tell my mother. "But I didn't make it alone. Along the way, I met some amazing people. People who fought beside me. People who were willing to give their lives to make sure I finished the mission—to make sure God's Word did not return to Him void."

Mama bristles at the scripture I know she remembers. She used to quote it to me all the time, reminding me that once God speaks, no one can change or alter His will. His words are set in stone, whether we like them or not. When He told me to return home, He knew I'd get there. There was never a promise for Erik, but I'm taking my own advice right now. I'm choosing to believe God is good. I'm choosing to have faith despite all the evidence telling me that all is lost. That Erik is dead.

"I've got to find him," I whisper.

Mama lets go of a miserable sob. "You haven't even seen

your father yet—"

"Daddy's here?" I ask.

She nods, wiping her tears. "The explosions happened during a church service. Your father happened to be there that day—said God told him to go to church again. I realized later that God gave him those instructions because He wanted our family to be together again, Shon. And we are now. Even Jeremiah is here."

I step back and squeeze my eyes shut. A sob bubbles up my throat but I cut it off before it slips past my lips, clamping a hand over my mouth. I haven't seen my son since he was an infant. Now he's nine years old. And he's alive. He's here waiting too. But I can't see him.

If I set eyes on my son, I will never leave these gates again. Erik doesn't deserve that. He doesn't deserve to be left alone in the Grey like this.

I take a deep breath. "I've got to do this, Mama." I glance over her shoulder at Wrenley. "Can you spare supplies or not?"

Wrenley wrings her hands like she has no idea how to respond.

"Get her the supplies." Mama's words shock me enough that I take a step back. She offers me a weak smile. "You're going to go no matter what. Might as well be prepared."

I hug her tightly, wishing things could be different. "God brought me this far," I say in her ear as she squeezes me. "He'll bring me back again."

When I pull away, Mama reaches up and touches my cheek. She has no words for me, and I can't think of anything to say to her. So I leave her in this overwhelming silence as I turn and walk toward the doors Wrenley left through.

Outside, the world is entirely different. This is no longer the barren fields. It's truly paradise. Green grass surrounds the entire area, acres of radiant plant life, trees, and beautiful flowers stretch out in every direction. I can hear birds chirping, I can see squirrels darting between the bushes in the distance. There are children playing in the grass, a man hanging laundry, a woman at a grill. No one wears a gasmask.

"How is this possible?" I ask in what I think is a whisper but someone answers behind me.

"Your mother told me it is God who keeps this place safe. Just like He did for the members of my church."

I turn around to see Arianna standing in the doorway of the infirmary. Her leg is in a boot, and she walks toward me with an awkward gait, the boot pressing into the rich soil with every step.

"At first I didn't believe her," Ari goes on. "I thought there was no way. There must be some sort of reason or scientific explanation." She shrugs. "The truth is that it's Him. It's always been Him."

"And it always will be," I tell her. Then my gaze hardens. "You told them they were dead."

She looks away. "Isn't it better this way?"

"How could it possibly be better this way?"

"What if they *are* dead?" she asks, snapping her eyes back toward me.

Now I get it.

Arianna's afraid. She truly doesn't know whether Erik's dead or alive. And even though we both saw the state Arya was in before we left, after witnessing the ongoing miracle of Twelve Springs, there's room to hope that he's alive too.

But hope is dangerous. Because the disappointment that follows could be too much to overcome. It's easier for Arianna to pretend they died out there that day than to take her chances and see for herself. She's afraid to hope. Just like she's afraid to let God in again.

But I'm not.

I let go of a breath I didn't know I was holding. "I forgive you, Ari," I say.

She looks so shocked; she doesn't even offer a reply. The words aren't as easy to speak as it might seem, but they come more easily than when I had to forgive Jeremiah. I realize now, once you choose to let God in, it gets easier. Because you don't have to do it alone anymore.

My hand is still clutched tightly over my emotions, especially the negative ones, but with God's help, I've been letting go. I've been learning to hold tightly to the hope that is Jesus instead. And it's so much better than the hate. So much better than the pain. I only wish I could somehow get Arianna to understand. For now, all I can offer is my own forgiveness as I pray the example she sees in me is enough to impact her someday.

"I forgive you for lying," I tell her plainly. "I forgive you for putting Erik and Arya in further danger. But I can't say whether they will forgive you. Because I *will* bring them back. God is going to help me save them. And when they return, you will have to answer for what you've done."

Arianna's eyes fill with anger, but when she opens her mouth the only thing that comes out is a sob. I don't offer her any comfort. I just stand there and watch her suffer in the storm she's brought on to herself.

Mercifully, Nurse Wrenley appears again, jogging over with a backpack, a gasmask, and a pair of boots. She's huffing for breath when she sets the items down in front of me. I waste no time stepping into the shoes, slipping on the mask, and digging into the bag. There's a hunting knife, a can of food, a bottle of water, and a few bandages inside. I smile, thankful for

286

this small gift.

"They'll open the gates when you're ready," Wrenley says.

I nod. "Thank you."

"We can send a team with you—"

I shake my head.

"You don't have to do this alone, RaShonda."

"I'm not alone," I say confidently. I never have been.

27

Shon

Even in that short amount of time, I got used to the clean air of Twelve Springs. Having my mask on now almost sends me into a paralyzing anxiety attack. I shouldn't be surprised... That's what it's like once you get a true taste of God's glory; stepping back into darkness feels foreign and frightening. The Bible describes it as a dog returning to its own vomit.

Obviously, this is a different comparison. I'm not running back into sin, in fact, I'm out here to save someone's life. A life I know has not been forgotten by God.

Lord, I pray as I sprint through the daisy-covered trees, *You lined everything up perfectly. Jesus, You made it possible for me to meet Erik when I needed him most. You gave me someone who would protect me no matter what, and You gave him someone who would stubbornly feed him the Word no matter how many times he rejected it.*

Please don't let him die out here. His life is worth more than a one-way trip.

My foot catches on a small rock and I nearly stumble to

the ground. My hands go out in front of me to grab the rough bark of the dead tree ahead. I feel sharp splinters of wood dig into my palms, and I bite my lip in pain.

I feel insane, running back into the barren fields for a man who'd just admitted to sleeping with another woman days ago. But this isn't about love or romance at all. It's about a life that still has a chance. Erik's been out here in the Grey for four days now. He doesn't have much time left. I can't afford to make this about my feelings. And besides…

The truth is that I don't care about what happened between Erik and Arianna. If we make it back somehow and he decides she's the woman he wants, I will respect that. I won't let myself determine the value of his life by the pain I feel at his betrayal.

"Jesus died for people who hated him. People who'd spat on him as He'd carried His own cross up the hill," I say as I straighten and stare into the distance. "If Jesus can give everything for the people who hurt Him, then I can take a chance for someone who's hurt me too."

But I can't do it alone.

I turn in a circle, trying to decide which direction I should go. I have a vague idea of where I'd left Erik, but there's no way to tell if he'll still be there when I arrive. I have no idea what happened with the dogs once I turned and ran. I have no idea if Erik is dead or alive. But I'll never find out by just standing here.

With courage I didn't know I had, I settle on a direction and take a step forward.

Holy Spirit, guide me. Prayer—**faith**—is all I've got right now. But how many people in the Bible survived on the same thing? The Israelites left Egypt with clothes and gold. They had no food. They had no water. But they had a God Who'd miraculously delivered them and had promised to keep them on their travels.

Jesus had nothing but faith when He walked on water. He had nothing but faith when He raised Lazarus from the dead. He had nothing but faith in God's plans when He walked to His own crucifixion.

The same God who parted the Red Sea and led the Israelites through the wilderness is the same God Who answered Jesus' prayers when He said, *Lazarus, come out!* He is the same God who has miraculously kept Twelve Springs, and He is the same God who saved my life three days ago. I have faith He will save me again, with Erik and even Arya too.

God has never stopped performing miracles. We've just lacked the faith to claim them.

The Bible even says that Jesus Christ could not perform miracles in His own hometown—not because He lacked the power, but because the people lacked faith in His power. I won't make the same mistake they did. I'm choosing to believe that the God I call to for help is ready and eager to give it. I'm choosing to believe that when I say God will make a way, He slides to the edge of His Throne and says with a smile, **Did you hear the faith she just used? Do you see how much My daughter believes in Me?**

And I choose to believe that when I pray, God answers.

My feet move without me telling them to, like my body knows where it's going. I run until I can't breathe, and then I run some more. When it feels like I might faint, I lean against a tree and gulp half the water from my bottle. There's also a homemade granola bar and a heel of bread wrapped in a small sack inside the bag.

I don't remember the last time I had bread. It might have been a few years ago. There were ovens in the airport, but we didn't have power and the gas was disconnected so there was no way to use them. Plus, we were never able to grow wheat very well in the nursery.

But Twelve Springs Campgrounds has brick ovens that run on nothing but wood, and with the area free of toxins, there is plenty to burn. My eyes roll to the back of my head as I take a bite of the bread. I limit myself to eating just half of it, then I wrap everything up and glance around to recuperate.

After the big fight, Arianna and I ran for half a mile before we stopped to have that argument. Then we walked another twenty minutes or so before we heard the dogs and began sprinting the rest of the way.

From the distance I've travelled so far, I shouldn't be more than ten minutes from the spot I left Erik and Arya. So, if Erik's alive, he would be somewhere in the vicinity. But if he's injured ... Would he have decided to hide and wait for help instead? I shiver at the thought of him counting the days for help that might not have ever arrived if God hadn't sent me out here. All I can do is pray that I find him in time.

I start moving again, slowing my pace so I can scan the area while I walk. I've been travelling for weeks now. I've gotten used to noticing things I used to overlook. Broken twigs, footprints, paths that've been covered up. All evidence of activity. Those are the things that become easy to notice once you know to look for them; the hard part is determining whether the evidence was left by humans or Faceless.

Or radioactive dogs, I remind myself. Apparently, those sorts of monsters exist out here too. A threat that is as rare as it is deadly. I never want to see another toxic dog again, but I'll fight off an entire pack if it means saving my friends.

After a few minutes, I step into a clearing and I suck in a slow breath. This is it. This is the field of daisies where all of us nearly died. The neon flowers are stained red, there are even bodies of dead dogs here and there. I'm almost amazed by the carnage. I had no idea how many of them we'd managed to kill. Then I think of Samson who killed a thousand men all by himself with the jawbone of a donkey. If God could empower him with such strength against his enemies, I don't see why He couldn't for us as well.

Clearly … He had.

There is no way any of us should be alive right now. If we hadn't been eaten, we should have succumbed to our injuries. If we survived our injuries, we should be in the first stages of transitioning into a Faceless. All of us were scratched and bitten that day. All of us should have been infected. But Arianna and I are just fine.

Twelve Springs doesn't even have a very fancy medical facility. As far as I can remember, they only gave me bandages and gauze. I shouldn't even be walking around right now. But that's what happens when God is your doctor. Your recovery is not just a miracle, it's an example to others of what our Father can do.

To think I had ignored God for years. To think I had believed myself too far gone to ever truly return.

"I need one more miracle, Jesus," I say behind my gasmask as I follow a trail of blood.

The path began near the boulder I remember Arianna resting against. That was the exact location where Erik and I split ways. The trail of blood goes in the opposite direction of where I'd taken off after telling him goodbye. The only explanation is that a toxic dog limped away, or Erik did. Judging from the lack of pawprints, I'd say this was left by a human.

I follow the trail for almost ten minutes, my heartrate increasing with every step. By the time I make it to a split in the trees, I'm nearly out of breath but not from all the walking. My nerves feel like they're on fire.

I haven't seen a body anywhere. Not even Arya's. If there was going to be one, I thought it would be his. He'd seemed lost to us before Arianna and I had even set off. If Erik had survived, dragging Arya along would have been foolish. He would have slowed him down as dead weight.

Unless he wasn't dead.

The woods before me split into an overrun path, something lost to nature six years ago when the world fell apart. On my right there is another burst of trees covered in neon daisies; to my left is the covered path. That's where the blood trail goes.

I keep walking, following the droplets, even as they fade into nothing but overturned rocks and crushed daises. I have no idea what to expect at the end of this trail, but it doesn't look like I'm going to find much. If Erik is hiding somewhere in these woods, he's hidden himself quite well.

He could be anywhere. Half a mile in any direction. There isn't any more blood on the ground. The daisies are still bent and flattened, as if someone walked through them, but there are other patches of daisies in the same condition. I don't know which way to go.

Despair hits me hard and my knees wobble before dropping me to the ground. I gasp and let go of a miserable sob. "God, please," I whisper behind my mask. My voice sounds muffled through the filter blocking my face. It makes my cries sound eerie, almost haunting. Like a wounded animal.

"Where do I go?" I bend over, digging my fingers into the hard earth. The daisies around my hands are bright against the grey rocks that surround them. I stare at them with anger and sorrow both building inside, but just when I reach my breaking point, I gasp with realization.

These flowers aren't bent or crushed.

They're leaning to the side, stretching out towards the nearest and largest source of radiation. A source like two fully grown men who've been trapped in the Grey for nearly five days.

I glance to my left and right, scanning the daisies around me to make sure I'm not seeing things. Some of them do look like they're crushed, like someone besides me passed through here. But the rest are perfectly fine, leaning away from the sun as they seek out the true source of their nutrients.

This is it. The breakthrough I've needed.

The daisies don't lie. They are the compass that will point me toward my friends—friends who can't be too far from here. The revelation makes me sob again, but this time I'm crying tears of joy as I get to my feet and take off into the woods.

28

Erik

My wife is beautiful as she stands in the distance. She is wearing a long white dress and her dark hair is loose so the afro curls cascade over her bare shoulders, almost down to her round hips. Her dark brown skin is glowing in the evening sun. We are minutes before it sets, the horizon is beautiful, glowing fiery orange instead of bright blue. But for all its beauty, I cannot take my eyes off my wife.

I walk toward her, following the old dirt path that led to our ranch style home before the explosions. As I grow nearer, I see my son emerge from the little white house we used to live in and hop down the porch steps. He stands beside his mother, the color of caramel, and smiles brightly as she leans down to whisper in his ear that I'm home.

My wife points at me and she tosses her head back in laughter as our son takes off running. Zion's always been fast, but he seems to cross the distance between us at lightning speed. Before I can even react, he's in my arms, his little face

295

smooshed against my chest.

I wrap him in my arms and carry him to the front steps of the house. It's not until I've set him down that I realize I'm crying. As I kneel before him, he reaches up and touches my face, eight-year-old hands cup my cheeks and wipe away the wetness that streaks them.

I see the confusion on his face. I see the question in his eyes. But it's my wife who speaks.

"You're home," she says in a gentle voice.

My son still pats my cheeks. I close my eyes and enjoy the feel of his hands on my face. I enjoy the warmth of his palms. I enjoy the way he smells standing so close. I enjoy the sight of my wife, alive and healthy and whole.

As Zion turns toward his mother, I see the side of his head and my heart aches. There is no bullet hole.

"Angie," I whisper, rising to my feet.

She comes to me without me saying anything more. I hug her so tightly I'm shocked she doesn't grunt in pain. If I hold her any closer, she'll be crushed. But I can't let her go. It's been five long years since I lost her. Five years since I saw my boy. And here they are, dressed in white and perfectly healthy. Perfectly happy.

"Heaven is real," Angie tells me, whispering against the red flannel I have on. It was my favorite shirt before the lights. She'd bought it at some discount store even though I told her not to. We'd been tight on money at the time, but Angie didn't care. She dipped into her savings to get me the shirt because she refused to have her husband driving around in grungy clothes. Bless her heart, I wore the shirt until there were holes under both arms.

There aren't any holes in it now as I lift my hands to her face. I feel her smile against my lips as I kiss her mouth. I feel the vibration of her laughter in her throat as I kiss her neck. I feel her hands wrap around me as she pulls away to look into my eyes.

"Heaven is real," she says again.

"Is this Heaven?" I ask, glancing down at Zion whose cheeks are red from watching our little moment of intimacy. He glances away shyly when I catch him staring at us.

Angelena shakes her head. "This is the place where I'm allowed to meet you."

I frown. "I don't understand."

She places a hand over my heart. "It's not time yet, Erik."

"But…" I blink at her. "I'm ready to go home. I don't care about dying."

For a long moment, Angie doesn't speak, she just stares into my eyes like she's reading something. Studying something.

"You can't die yet, Erik," she says.

"You're all I have." My voice cracks. "These last five years haven't been worth living without you and Zion."

"There is another reason for you to live."

I gasp as Shon pops into my head. But not just her, I see Jeremiah too. A kid I've never even met before, his face is so clear in my mind's eye it almost makes me want to weep. He's about the same age as Zion, his skin a few shades darker, like Shon's. And he's smiling and laughing, running through a field of bright green grass.

How is that possible? There is no grass out here in the Grey. The barren fields are *barren*. The only thing that grows is the neon daisies.

"Twelve Springs," I whisper, opening my eyes to see my wife still studying me.

She nods slowly. "It's just as real as Heaven."

"But…" I have no idea how to say this. "If I die, I'll be

with you and Zion. If I stay, I'll be with…"

Another woman and her son.

"I can't do that to you, Angie. I won't."

She breaks my heart with a smile. "I know how much you love me, Erik. But you don't know how much I love you. I love you enough to let you go. To step back so that you can find happiness again."

"I'm happy with *you*," I nearly sob. "I want to go home."

She shakes her head again. "If you leave now, you won't be with me and Zion."

My body tenses. I know what she's saying. I won't make it to Heaven.

I've gone to church plenty of times, I've even had Shon read the Bible to me. I've prayed. I've quoted scriptures. I'll even admit to believing in God, but even a sinner like me knows that's not enough. Believing in God is the first step— even Satan believes in God—it's accepting Jesus Christ as the true Messiah, the Lord of your life, that saves you.

I sigh…

"It's not time yet," Angie says, gently placing a hand on my cheek.

I look into her eyes, almost ashamed.

"I wish I had gotten saved when you were alive."

"It's never too late."

"Yes, it is." I pull away from her. She doesn't know I've been hiding in the Grey for days now, unconscious from my own injuries. She doesn't know that I'm half-dead already and will likely wake up in Hell in a few minutes. I had the chance to give my life to God when I was up walking around, and I didn't. I chose to ignore Shon and her testimony and the Scriptures she read. I chose to believe Twelve Springs was a foolish lie. And now I can't even go home with my wife. I'm going to die alone and filled with toxins.

How cruel…

"I'll never see you again," I say miserably, glancing up at the sunset behind her. Somehow, I just know my time is coming to an end. "I'm almost dead, Angie. By the time the sun sets, I'll be gone. Burning in Hell forever."

"Oh, Erik," she whispers. Then she takes a step back and pulls Zion in front of her so they're both watching me with solemn smiles on their faces.

"Is this goodbye?" I ask.

She nods. "But only for now."

"Angie…" she still doesn't get it. "I … I'm not going to see you again."

A sweet laugh fills the air and I look up in shock, wishing I could tell her nothing about this is funny. But instead, I just stand there and watch, I look at my wife and son and take them in one last time as the light behind them begins to fade.

"I'll always love you," I say softly. "I wish I could've been the man you deserved."

Angie delivers her last words. "You are more than what you have become."

When I peel my papery lids back, I see the sun peeking in through the splintered bark of the tree I've been hiding in. It's dead and hollow, an open coffin ready for a body. Or, in my case, two bodies.

After Shon and Arianna took off, I did manage to fight my way out of that mess. To be honest, the toxic dogs that were left had as much fight left in them as I had in me. But I wasn't fighting for a meal, I was fighting for my life. I had the advantage in that situation, and I grabbed hold of it with a vice grip.

For what it's worth, Arya fought until he couldn't anymore. And I stayed by his side until his screaming stopped. Then I dragged him as far as I could until his whimpering stopped. And that's when I realized what'd happened.

He'd died right there on the ground in front of me. His arm torn to shreds, his chest clawed open. When I stared down at his lifeless body, I saw nothing in his eyes but a blankness so empty it sent a shiver up my spine. I didn't want my eyes to look the same. I didn't want to fade away, not with the knowledge that Shon and Ari had gotten away.

They'd managed to escape. That meant there was a chance they could make it to Twelve Springs and send back help. Even though I didn't believe the place was real. Even though I hadn't even decided if God was real at the time. I needed one of them to exist. If Twelve Springs was real, help was on the way. If God was real, then I had a chance at survival.

If...

I was left with a dead body and a fading sense of hope in my heart. I didn't have a gasmask—it'd gotten torn in the fight. I didn't have supplies. I didn't even have a weapon anymore— I'd abandoned the crowbar as I'd dragged Arya away. I couldn't afford the deadweight.

The only place to hide was inside of a hollow tree. Even though he was dead, I kept Arya's body with me. He was in terrible shape; bites all over him, and he hadn't been wearing a mask when he died. His body was pumped full of radiation, which meant he would give me the cover I needed to hide in plain view—just like Shon and I hid beneath the contaminated sheets when the herd passed through.

Getting Arya's body into the tree wasn't easy. I went in first, and then I tugged his body inside with me, laying him on top of me like a human-shaped blanket. I lay there, inside the trunk of a dead tree, staring at the sky as exhaustion, pain, and despair flooded my mind and body. The first day passed in a haze. I was in and out of consciousness, still bleeding from my wounds. The second day was worse. I didn't pass out and I couldn't get any sleep. I was stuck beneath a smelly body, getting filled with radiation by the hour.

On day three, I wondered how much longer I had left to live. I was severely dehydrated. I was hungry. I was sleep deprived. I was injured.

Day four, I made my peace and finally closed my eyes, drifting into what I thought would be an endless sleep. But then I saw my wife and son, and she gave me that very alarming news. That if I died, I wouldn't make it to Heaven. Then she told me I'd found a new purpose, a new reason to live, and left me with that cryptic message.

I don't feel like wondering what any of this means. Right now, I'm squished inside of a dead tree with Arya's body on top of me, crushing me. If I didn't have any chance of making it out of this alive before, I don't see how I could possibly have a chance now. But as despair works its way over me again, I hear my wife's last words ring through the dead forest.

You are more than what you have become...

I could say she's wrong. She's my wife—she will always think highly of me. And she's in Heaven, she's full of old proverbs and wisdom now. I think that's how it works. But I know the truth. I know that in that moment she saw me for who I could become if I did the one thing Shon's been bugging me about, if I do what Angie bugged me to do before she passed on.

301

I could become the man I was meant to be if I give my life to Christ. And until that happens, I cannot die.

That revelation sparks to life a will to live. It fills me with a passion I hadn't felt before. I wish I could say it is that passion—that fire inside—that gives me strength to get up and find my way home, but the truth is that as I push against Arya's dead body, he rolls off like he weighs little more than a feather.

And then I see Shon standing there, a wide-eyed expression on her face.

She blinks once and then erupts in tears, yanking me from the hollow tree with more strength than I think is possible, and crushing me in a hug.

"You're alive!" she shrieks. "I found you!"

I hug her hard. "How... How did you know where to find me?"

Shon drops to her knees and lifts her mask, she wipes her eyes as she says, "God led the way."

Her words tug a sigh from my lips, and I lean against the tree behind me. I'm so tired, I feel like if I drop to my knees beside Shon, I won't get back up. "God led the way..." I repeat slowly.

"Yes." Shon leans forward, staring at Arya's body. "But we can fight about Him later. Right now, I've got to take care of this."

Fight about Him later... I feel horrible hearing her words. To think that Shon believes the very mention of God would spark an argument between us. Sheesh, what sort of jerk was I when it came to her faith?

Whatever the case, I've changed now. I know I have—

Shon catches my attention as she straightens out Arya's body and touches his cheek. She's staring at his face, at his lifeless eyes and his bruised cheeks and nose. I lean away to

302

give them privacy, though it sends sharp pain straight through my heart.

I'd forgotten all the drama we'd faced before. That seems so insignificant now, but I can't pretend that Shon didn't care about Arya. His death is probably the last thing she needs right now but there's no way for me to protect her from it. So here I am, standing by like a coward while she whispers her goodbye.

I wait a few moments, listening for her to end her last words to him, but Shon keeps talking. Mumbling to herself. I don't want to invade her privacy, but it's been a few minutes now. She cared about Arya but not enough to say goodbye for this long.

I step a little closer and strain to hear... That's when I realize she's not saying goodbye. Shon is praying.

"Shon," I say in a calm voice, "Arya's dead. There's no point in praying for him."

She ignores me, her lips moving quickly. I grunt and shift my weight from one foot to the other, feeling awkward now.

"Shon," I try again, but she still doesn't respond. In fact, she doesn't even acknowledge me. Shon unclasps her hands and shocks me by climbing on top of Arya's dead body. She lays down, lining up her hands with his and placing her face over his, then she closes her eyes and starts praying again.

Now, I feel angry. It's a familiar sort of anger that reminds me of every reason why I never fully believed in Christianity in the first place.

Christians are nuts. Plain and simple.

Twelve Springs being real is one thing. God and Heaven being real is another thing. But this? This is madness. What does Shon even think she can accomplish? Is she honestly praying for a dead man to... to *come back*?

303

"Shon!" I snap, pushing off the tree. I step forward with the last of my strength and grab her roughly by the arm. "Get up!" I nearly snarl.

She yanks her arm away. "What do you think you're doing?"

"What do you think *you're* doing?" I shout. "Arya is dead. Just accept it! He's not coming back. He's…" my voice cracks, and I suddenly see Angie's face before me. "He's gone…" I whisper. "Let him go."

Shon stubbornly shakes her head. "I'm not accepting that, Erik."

"What you're doing is insane—"

"God saved you!" she yells. "Why can't He save Arya too?"

"Because he's already gone!" I yell back, and then I turn away, hating the look in her eyes.

She was right. Mentioning God did spark a fight between us.

"Shon…" I say slowly, but I know my words will fall on deaf ears. Shon has already gone back to praying. She doesn't care at all what I have to say.

That makes me angry.

"This is a joke," I say hotly.

Shon looks up at me, ending her prayer. "What did you say?"

"I said this is a *joke*," I repeat. "You didn't pray like this for Jeremiah. You watched him die and moved on. You didn't pray like this for me when I was surrounded by rabid dogs, you turned and left me out here!"

I don't realize I'm screaming until Shon scoots backwards away from me. She's more shocked than afraid but her shock quickly turns to anger. In one quick motion, Shon yanks off her backpack and tosses it at my feet.

"If you aren't going to believe then leave." She points into the distance. "Twelve Springs is that way."

"Seriously?"

She nods without missing a beat. "You're only hindering me right now anyway."

With that, I grab the backpack and start marching in the opposite direction. I don't have to put up with this delusional woman and her ridiculous faith. I'm just a *hindrance*. I'm in the way of her freaky reunion with Arya.

I walk for a few minutes, fuming in anger, replaying Shon's words in my head. *I'm hindering her.* I kick a rock as anger swells inside of me, but as I tilt my head back, the rage doesn't come out in a scream, it runs from my eyes as tears pour down my cheeks. My wife was wrong about me. I am not anything more than the man I've always been. This is me. A faithless jerk.

I stop walking as the tears become too much. I can't see past the blurriness in my vision, I almost trip as I try to take another step. Weak as I am, I know if I fall, that'll be the end of me. And I doubt Shon will come running to pray me back to life.

I chuckle darkly. That's the stupidest thing I've ever heard—to think that anyone would seriously believe God could bring someone back to life.

I can.

I fall to my knees at the sound of that Voice. It resonates all around me, coming from within and from the outside too. I heard it clearly and I have no doubts Who it belongs to. I'm just too stunned to reply. So He speaks again.

Why do you doubt?

My throat feels dry as I swallow. "You ask for too much,"

I whisper.

I raised My Son from the dead three days after His crucifixion. Through My power, Yeshua raised Lazarus four days after he died. Even the bones of the Prophet Elisha were so anointed that they had enough of My power inside to resurrect another man's body when it was thrown into his grave.

I sit there in the dirt, blinking dumbly, trying to find words to say.

Why is it too much to ask you to believe that I can resurrect your friend? Though I have never needed to, I have proven My power to all beings on this earth. This earth which *I* created. You know I am able, but you refuse to believe.

"Because I don't understand." I sniffle. "Why would You bring Arya back but not my wife? Not my *boy*." I look up at the sky, choking on my tears. "You got *Your* Son back! But I lost mine!"

No, you haven't.

I freeze.

Zion is with Me. Angelena is with Me.

"They're with *You*!" I shout. "You don't know what it's like!"

The wind blows violently, nearly knocking me backwards onto my butt.

Was I not separated from My Son for a time while He was here on earth? Are We, the Trinity, not separate from our Bride right now? The Bride of Christ has yet to return.

The wind blows again, kicking up dust around me.

I know what it means to lose those you love. I lose children every day who die without accepting My Son as their savior. But you, Erik, you have not lost your family

at all. Your separation is not permanent. If you believe, you will see them again.

With those last words, the wind dies down and the dust settles. I'm not stricken with fear or grief anymore, all that is left when God is finished, is a serenity I cannot explain. I am in awe. Shocked that He would seem to scold me yet leave me with such peace that it brings me to tears once again.

I just spoke to God Almighty. A privilege most Believers don't even get, but I—a faithless sinner—was bestowed the honor. He didn't have to explain Himself to me. He owed me nothing. But He gave it anyway, and He even left me with this gift of peace that I cannot even put into words.

I wipe my tears and begin to laugh. Because I'm an utter fool. God is right. I've known all along that He was real. Angelena told me. Shon told me. I witnessed His power and protection for myself on the countless times Shon and I miraculously dodged death. I have no right to be angry at God. And without me even asking, I know He's forgiven me. But I ask anyway. I clear the air.

"I repent," I say in a hoarse voice. "I'm sorry, God. I'm sorry for not believing and rejecting the Truth. I'm sorry I never forgave the men who hurt my family." I take a breath. "I forgive them now… and I accept Your Son as my Lord and Savior. Jesus is the Christ, Son of the Living God."

I stand and brush the dirt off my knees, overwhelmed and dizzy with elation. I just spoke to God. I can't believe it.

I suck in a gasp. I've got to tell Shon! She probably hates my guts for the way I left, but she'll be happy once I tell her everything that happened. She'll be overjoyed that I just got saved. That I finally believe.

Before I can talk myself out of it, I turn on my heel and start back toward the hollow tree where I'd left her. But I don't even make it halfway before I stop in my tracks.

There, ahead of me, Shon is walking with a smile on her face. And she's not alone.

29

Erik

When I wake up, I hear birds chirping outside my window. It's been this way for three weeks now and I still haven't gotten used to it. I don't think I ever will.

I swing my legs over the edge of the bed and groan as I sink to the floor and turn around to say my prayers. That's another thing I haven't gotten used to yet. Having a relationship with God. There is no denying the existence of God anymore. I'm over that phase. But I must admit, I've only learned a little about God in the recent weeks I've been here at Twelve Springs.

There's been no time. Since we limped through the front gates of the campgrounds, we have been swarmed by people who've wanted to see the Miraculous Three. That's what they've been calling us, and I honestly don't blame them.

Shon is the one who boldly applied her faith, Arya is the one who was raised from the dead, and I was there to witness it all. I wouldn't have believed this story otherwise. But the

309

people here do. They've asked us all to retell our testimonies so many times, I could write a book about it. Actually, the scribe here has asked me to share my story with her on weekends; she keeps a written record of everything, documenting the tales of Twelve Springs the way historians documented the World Wars and the way the Disciples documented the life of Christ. She's a sweet woman named Amana, wise and intelligent like a librarian.

When I'm not with Amana, I'm with Pastor Anne-Marie, the Head Pastor from Fire Baptized Ministries. She's the one who packed up the church and made their great exodus. Under her leadership, an entire congregation of 793 members relocated to Twelve Springs. They called themselves Israelites and dubbed the chapel here the Promised Land Church.

It's an incredible story that I've been hearing in bits and pieces over my study sessions with Pastor Anne-Marie. She's a wonderful woman, and she's helped me a lot these past few weeks, but she's also kept me busy. Everyone here has been keeping me busy—there's hardly any time to breathe.

Arya and Arianna have been inseparable since their reunion. She practically moved into his room at the infirmary when he was recovering, but that didn't last long. When God brought Arya back to life, He healed every last one of his injuries. There wasn't a scratch on him, and no signs of contamination. They kept him in the infirmary for two days to make sure he was well fed and hydrated, mostly because they hadn't cleared a cabin for him to stay in yet, but no one complained.

I, on the other hand, had to stay in the infirmary for an entire week. I was severely dehydrated, starving, wounded, and should have been transitioning into a Faceless. But God was with me.

There aren't any real doctors in Twelve Springs. And their medical equipment is minimal at best. But I've fully recovered. I remember Pastor Anne-Marie, Shon's mother, Nurse Wrenley, and a Deacon from the church standing around me praying every evening before bed. That was my treatment, and after seeing Arya come back to life, I had no doubts that prayer was all I needed.

Thank You so much… I pray to God, thinking of how much pain I'd been in before. Thinking of how I should be dead right now or mindlessly hunting for human flesh as a wild man. But here I am. Healthy and whole. *Thank You, Jesus.*

I open my eyes and push to my feet. There's a cane in the corner of the room that I used to walk when I was first released from the hospital, but I don't need it at all anymore. I walk to the desk where my clothes are folded neatly and change into a blue flannel and a pair of jeans, then I step into my boots and walk out of my small cabin. The men's bathrooms are a short walk from my place, normally I'd run there in a hurry, barely holding my bladder. But today is a quiet morning.

Other than the singing birds and the noisy crickets, there isn't much else out right now. But it's just after sunrise, everyone will be up soon. Twelve Springs still doesn't have power, but they seem fine functioning without it. Pastor Anne-Marie told me they've been praying for a way to get the radios up and working again. That'll make it much easier to find survivors and tell the world about this place.

Even though I've just gotten here, I'm not ready for that to happen yet. There is something about the serenity here that feels like it's more than just the people and their kindness toward each other. It isn't just a place that is protected by God, it's a place that God has kept for Himself. Like these people really are His chosen ones, just like the Israelites.

One day, Twelve Springs will expand, but I'm enjoying the secrecy for now. I enjoy the fresh air as I walk toward the bathrooms. I enjoy the open space that surrounds all the cabins. I love to see the children playing in the woods, running freely the way they used to before the explosions. I love seeing the scouting teams on jogs through the trees, running without gasmasks, sucking down gulps of crisp clean air. And I enjoy how much everyone—every single person here—loves God. Twelve Springs would be nothing without Jesus, they've made that clear.

There are church services three times a week, plus an extra service every Sunday. There's a huge barbecue every Sunday evening, and on the first Sunday of the month, the barbecue is a potluck dinner. Every family brings their first fruits as an offering to the church, and they eat together. Over two-thousand people. I've heard it's incredible—but I haven't been here long enough to witness it for myself.

This coming Sunday will be my first time. I don't have anything to bring… I was hoping I could get permission to go out to the pond and try fishing. I'm not bad at making baked tilapia. Or I could fry up some catfish if they've got that. I'm not picky.

Apparently, Shon's mother—Mama C—makes incredible biscuits and homemade jam which she brings to every potluck. I'm certainly looking forward to that. I'm also looking forward to seeing Shon.

I try not to think about her as I gather a bucket and fill it with water from the barrel in the corner. It's changed every few hours for us to use for showering. I could take the time to heat the water but I'm trying to stay ahead of the morning crowd, so I sponge myself down at the sink and then shiver as I pour the cold water over my head.

Once I'm dressed again, I step outside into the sun. Sure enough, there are people leaving their cabins now, going about their morning routines. I wave to Nurse Wrenley as she crosses the courtyard toward the infirmary; a husband and wife had their first child two nights ago. The entire camp has been talking about it. The parents named the kid Arya—still amazed at his miraculous resurrection.

I laugh as I think about the poor child. He has no idea who he's named after. Then again, Arya isn't so bad, and there are worse people to be named after. Like Jeremiah…

Without meaning to, I glance in the direction of Shon's cabin and shuffle my feet, shifting off my usual path. I don't know why I'm heading over there now, but my conscience doesn't try to stop me.

I saw Jeremiah Jr. after I was released from the infirmary. He's exactly the same as when he appeared in my vision. A happy kid of nine-years-old who snorts when he laughs and always seems to run everywhere he goes—the kid is full of energy.

I haven't gotten the chance to introduce myself. Whenever I've seen him, it's been at a distance. And Shon's never offered to have me meet him. Honestly, Shon hasn't really been around for me to officially meet anyone in her family. It's not because of Arya, ahem, I'm kind of embarrassed to admit that it's sort of my fault.

I've been here for three weeks, and I've seen Shon twice.

The first week, I was in the infirmary, confined to my bed. The second week, Shon was spending time with her family. They'd been apart for nearly a decade. Her son hadn't seen her since he was an infant. I decided to give her space and spend my time with Arya, Arianna, and Pastor Anne-Marie.

Now, it's week three, and I'm out of excuses. Other than

the two times Shon visited me in the infirmary, we haven't had any contact. I wasn't entirely warm toward her when she visited me, and she was distant too. Neither of us could look the other in the eye, afraid of what we'd see when our gazes met.

I owe her so many apologies for how I gave her grief over believing in God. I owe her an apology for feeling so jealous over what she had with Arya. I owe her an apology for ever touching Arianna. But I've yet to say anything to her.

Until now…

I take a huge breath as I approach Shon's door. From what I've heard, she lives with her mother, father, and son. Like one big happy family. I hope showing up at her front door first thing in the morning isn't rude. But I'm here now.

I knock at the door and then step back. A few seconds of silence pass, and I debate knocking again, but just as I raise my fist, the door is tugged open, and I almost knock on Shon's forehead.

She takes a quick step back and blinks at me in surprise. "Erik?"

I lift my shoulders sheepishly. "Hey."

"What are you doing here?"

I step back, cramming my hands into my pockets. "I don't know."

We stare at each other. The storm of our emotions rages between us, saying everything we haven't been able to say in the last three weeks. Shon looks beautiful in her flowery dress with her thick hair puffed out around her like a 70s disco dancer. I've never seen her hair out before; she always had it braided up.

I stare at her mane of curls as I try to think of something to say.

"I've missed you," I blurt.

314

Her eyes snap to mine, but before she can speak, a little person darts past her and down the cabin steps. "Is that you, Uncle Rya!" he exclaims before he stops on a dime and stares up at me in embarrassment. "Oh… I thought you were someone else."

"Uncle Rya?" I lift an eyebrow at Shon.

"Arya's been coming by," she admits.

I nod slowly, palming the back of my neck. "I see."

"Jeremiah," Shon calls, reaching for her son, but he doesn't turn away from me. He's staring with his head tilted back, making me feel taller than I really am.

"Do you know when Uncle Rya is coming by? We're supposed to go fishing together today."

"*Jeremy*," Shon says more insistently.

"I should go." I turn away, feeling like an idiot. Here I was, filled with guilt over avoiding Shon, when Arya's been here all along. Taking her kid fishing.

Shon calls out to me. "Erik, wait!"

I stop, but I don't turn around, not until I hear footsteps behind me. When I face Shon, she's looking at me with an expression I can't name. Her eyes are filled with emotions I can't place.

"Arya was supposed to take Jeremiah fishing, but he cancelled." She shrugs. "He's got plans with a girl—one of the *many* girls who invite him out for breakfast."

I deflate. Now I feel like an idiot for an entirely different reason. My emotions are all over the place. I have no idea how to feel about anything, so I decide to make things clear and be upfront for the first time.

"Can we talk?" I ask Shon.

She immediately nods and calls out to Jeremiah without ever breaking eye contact, "Jeremy, go inside."

"Can't I stay and wait for Uncle Rya?"

"I told you, he's not coming today."

Even from here, I can see the crocodile tears forming in the kid's eyes. The sight tugs at my heart, reeling in memories of the days I went fishing with Zion. He wasn't very good and never caught anything, but we still had a lot of fun.

"I can take him," I say without thinking.

Shon stares at me. "What?"

Jeremiah cheers behind her. "I'll go grab my stuff!"

"Jeremy!" she calls, but he's already back inside. When the door slams shut, she slowly turns to face me again. "You don't have to do this."

"I want to," I say, stepping closer to her.

"He's very energetic. I'm afraid of him rocking the boat and falling in." She laughs, looking so mature right now I'm not even sure I'm staring at the same woman.

I remember when Shon couldn't walk a mile without me by her side for fear of getting lost. I remember when she was afraid to kill any Faceless because she thought they could be cured. I remember when she cried in my arms over the horrors she faced at the hands of her ex-boyfriend.

She's still that woman, but she's stronger now. She's got to be. Jeremiah is her son; he's depending on her. Even though we live in this oasis—this Promised Land—a mother will always have her own concerns. I can see them clearly written in the creases of her brow.

"I don't even know if he can swim," Shon says exasperatedly. "I haven't asked. It's only been a few weeks," her voice cracks.

"It's alright, Shon," I say softly, then I reach for her, shyly at first, but when she welcomes my arms that wrap around her, I hold her close and say, "I'll take care of him."

"I've barely done that myself."

"You just got him back. It's a process."

Shon pulls away and looks up at me. "Erik—"

"I can help you," I say before she can speak again.

"You … You finished your job."

I sigh at her words, understanding the distance that'd been between us. It wasn't Arya, it wasn't my overdue apologies. It was fear. Fear that I would leave this place and return home and never see Shon again.

"My job will never be over," I say quietly. "I'll always be here to protect you, and to take care of you. And your boy." I pause. "If you'll have me."

She blinks, and tears fill her large brown eyes. I want to hear her say the words but she's too emotional right now, so I settle for the slow nod she gives me as I pull her close again.

"I love you, Shon," I whisper into her fluffy hair.

She's a blubbering mess, but she finally manages to say it back. "I love you too."

As I hold her in my arms, I can't help but think of my wife and my own son. I think of the strength she had to let me go and let me find happiness again. I won't run away from this. I won't push Shon away to live in the anger and the sorrow I'd been drowning in before. I won't push Jeremiah away to replay the painful memories of Zion over and over again.

I will never forget my first family, but I won't ignore the joy I've been given in finding another. Actually, I've found more than that. I have God now too—I got Him first. And now, because of Him, I have a woman who loves me and a boy who is pleased to go on fishing trips with me.

To think I've found all this in the Grey is almost too much to believe. I started this journey brokenhearted and struggling to find a reason to live. Now I have a list of reasons, and each

317

one was discovered in a place where life was lost, peace seemed impossible to grasp, and the world appeared dead. Truly, God gives beauty for ashes.

The Barren Fields are not barren at all. There is much to find out here, if you know where to look.

Epilogue

Three Years Later

Worry starts to set in as I stare at the courtyard. It's been more than three hours. They should've been back by now. I start pacing on the front lawn, barefoot, my housecoat sweeping out behind me. The robe was a gift from Nurse Wrenley, she's pretty handy with a needle and thread. She's also made me tons of baby clothes which I have stashed in the nursery that will be put to use in exactly four weeks.

I reach up and touch my massive belly. I thought I'd be the cute sort of pregnant with an adorable baby bump. I'm so swollen I actually lean backwards when I stand, otherwise I'll be hunched over like an old hag. My feet are too fat for shoes, and I don't even want to think of how chubby my cheeks look. Erik says I'm prettier with the extra weight—even says he can't wait to make another baby. That always makes me snort.

But right now, I'm not laughing, I'm shaking my head as I waddle back and forth. Erik should've been back by now—

Just as the thought crosses my mind, I see two figures appear in the distance and my anxiety washes away. Erik is

319

walking with two fishing poles over his shoulder, Jeremiah is right beside him, holding up their catch. Three fish that are so big, I wonder where my twelve-year-old son got the strength to carry them all this way. Let alone wave them over his head as he grins at me.

Jeremy and Erik have been going fishing twice a week together since I let Erik into my heart that day three years ago. It's their personal routine, *bonding time*, as they both like to call it. The few times I hinted about tagging along, Jeremiah frowned and said, *No girls allowed*. Erik and I burst into laughter.

I want to laugh now as the two of them walk up the trail to our cabin. They look like the best of friends, the perfect father-son pair. I'm so proud of both of them. Erik has kept his promise. He takes care of us in every way he can, and Jeremiah made it a point to get along with him right from the start. The kid is so forgiving, I could weep. He's never once blamed me for abandoning him and he's never looked at Erik as anything but the loving father that he is.

As they walk up to me, Erik pulls me in to plant a kiss right on my lips. Jeremiah makes a gagging noise and takes the fishing poles from him. "I'll store these in the back, Dad."

The word pops from his mouth with such ease, I hardly notice it anymore. In Jeremiah's eyes, Erik *is* his dad. It doesn't matter the difference in their skin color, Erik's the only man he's ever known in his life. I haven't told him anything about his real father. And I never will. As far as I'm concerned, Jeremiah will never even know his father's name. In my eyes, his dad's name is Erik.

"You look beautiful," Erik murmurs against my lips.

I giggle like an idiot. "And you smell like fish."

Erik snorts as he pulls away, the corners of his eyes crinkling. His hair is thicker now, and longer too—almost to his shoulders. He's even got a beard now which makes him look like a lumberjack. He's such an old man.

Our age gap hasn't bothered anyone except my father, bless his heart. But even that old grunt has softened over the years. Erik's fried catfish might have played a role in that. My mother loved Erik from day one, he's the only one she's shared her biscuit recipe with. Not even me. That's why Erik insisted on having them over for lunch this afternoon.

There's going to be a big celebration later.

It turns out, Minty *did* find her way to Rebirth Colony. It took a year of pleading and trading supplies before the Rebirth Colony Council trusted her information. In that time, they set up trade routes with Minty's drifters and established a relationship that has lasted until now. With their trade agreement in place, Rebirth Colony slowly got back on its feet, and as a reward for their aid, Minty was given complete access to their military-grade lab equipment.

In the back of an airport, it wasn't much, but it was all Minty needed. She was right all along. Radiation isn't the only thing in our air. There are other toxins present, gases I've never even heard of, but nothing that surprises Minty. She says there isn't a cure to reverse someone who's already transitioned. But she can develop an antidote to prevent anyone else from turning into a Faceless if they're bitten in the future.

The people of Twelve Springs don't need an antidote. No Believer does, if they've got faith. But I know that not everyone has the same level of faith. Not everyone can believe as easily as I do. It took Arya coming back from the dead for Erik and Arianna to get it together—even though Arianna had lived in a God-protected church before.

I don't judge her for losing faith. I don't judge the members of her church for walking away either. Even the Israelites abandoned God at times. All that matters is that Arianna is back on the right path. Her faith has been restored and she's found a new place protected by God.

In my letters, I've tried explaining to Minty that we don't need any antidote out here, but she isn't a woman of faith. She just doesn't get it. I'm proud of her achievements anyway, and I pray the antidote is a blessing for those who need it.

The world is finally taking a step in the right direction. We're putting ourselves back together, piece by piece. I still don't know what caused the explosions, I suppose I never will. But I've come to realize that wasn't the point of this story. Everything I've experienced was one big demonstration of God's love and protection. God's way of honoring His promises. God's way of separating His people from everyone else.

I smile, hoping that one day the people of Rebirth Colony, the rest of the entire world, will learn of God's love and power too.

The last letter we received from Rebirth Colony was a month ago, the line of communication is still pretty slow since the letters are delivered by hand. That's right, we've established a trade route too. Minty's drifters aren't slow travelers moving from place to place anymore. They're a group of traders and guards who call themselves Runners. Fifteen brave men and women made the very first trip from Rebirth Colony to Twelve Springs two years ago.

They were met with a warm welcome. Penelope showed up, along with Mike and Taylor, which made Erik cry tears of joy when he saw them again. I cried when I saw Everett! It'd always been his theory that more people were out there somehow surviving in the barren fields.

When a group of scouts from Twelve Springs showed up

at Rebirth Colony telling them stories of the campgrounds, he was the only one to believe them. It was at his insistence that the RCC formed the Runners Alliance with Minty's group. Everett was the first one to join, and not just because he wanted to see the outside world, he also wanted to see his older sister again.

I thought he wouldn't let me go when he first hugged me in the Twelve Springs courtyard. He stayed for two weeks, after making trade arrangements and gathering recruits to go back to Rebirth Colony with him. He had a long trip home, but he didn't mind the travel. There were five kids waiting for him back home, plus his lovely little wife—who was pregnant *again*! Apparently, their last pregnancy had been twins. No one had known until the day they were born.

The Runners Alliance makes trips once a month. We have two groups who leave at different times. It takes 30 days to get to Rebirth Colony and 30 days to get back. Whenever a group leaves, one family volunteers to host a big dinner for them. This month, Erik and I volunteered. We couldn't raise our hands fast enough when Pastor Anne-Marie asked for a dinner host. This trip is special to us because it's being led by Arya.

He was just promoted to Captain of the Runners. He isn't a scaredy cat like he used to be—this will be his seventh trip straight, in fact. He's never lost a man, and he's always brought back the best goodies. Even Arianna is impressed, though she prays for him daily as Pastor Anne-Marie's disciple.

I think Arya is obsessed with the Runners, it's like he can't stop travelling. Erik thinks he's just obsessed with a new girl. Apparently, there's a lady he met at Rebirth Colony. She works in their radio station on the comms team, a nineteen-year-old beauty named Raven. I don't know how their long-distance relationship will work out in the future, but I'm happy for them, nonetheless. Speaking from experience, any man who will cross the state for you in a post-apocalyptic world is worth keeping around. Trust me.

The man of my dreams grins at me when I step into the kitchen to find him leaning over the counter, watching Jeremiah slowly descale the fish.

"How's he doing?" I ask, walking to a wooden chair.

Erik's grin stretches even wider. "He's a natural."

"I was taught by the best." Jeremy winks.

"I can chop the veggies," I say, but both of them shake their heads.

"I can do it," Erik volunteers.

"No, really—"

"Sweetheart," he gives me a stern look, and I know what he's going to say next. "You've got to stay off your feet."

I sigh. "I feel so useless sitting around all day."

"You'll be plenty busy once our daughter is born." Erik smiles.

"What makes you think it's a girl?"

"I've already got two boys. I want a baby girl now."

I can't stop myself from smiling. Erik's considered Jeremiah his own son from day one, but he's also never forgotten about Zion. He talks about him more often now, and sometimes he mentions his first wife. He told me about the vision he had before he gave his life to Christ. I'd cried when he said she had wanted him to be happy. He'd cried too.

That was the day we'd gotten married, two years ago. It was a small ceremony with Pastor Anne-Marie, my family, Arya, Arianna, Nurse Wrenley, and Amana—the camp scribe. Afterward, Erik fried catfish for everyone—like a true southern gentleman—and we stuffed ourselves with Mama's freshly baked biscuits.

324

"What should we name her?" I ask, my hand subconsciously going to my belly.

Erik gazes at me but doesn't speak.

"I wouldn't mind the name Angelena," I offer.

He surprises me by shaking his head. "I … I appreciate the gesture, but I think it would be too weird."

I nod. "What about your mother? What was her name?"

He sighs. "You know, my family wasn't that great. We can name her after one of your family members instead."

I feel bad, but I don't press him for details. He doesn't look like he's ready to talk about it and I'm not sure I'm ready to hear it just yet. We're so happy here, but in many ways, we're still healing from everything we faced before. There are nights I wake in a cold sweat, grabbing my own throat because I feel Jeremiah's thick fingers wrapped around them. There are days I hear dogs howling in my nightmares.

Erik has been there each time I've needed him, and I've been there whenever he's needed me. But we both know it's God Who comforts us. It was God who brought us together and it will be God who keeps us together. Safe. Happy. Whole.

I smile as I watch Erik and Jeremiah work side by side. "I've got a name," I say happily.

Erik looks up, but its Jeremy who says, "Tell us what I'm gonna call my baby sis."

"Miracle," I say, and I know from the looks on their faces that her name needs no explanation.

"That's beautiful," Erik tells me.

Jeremiah nods. "I like it."

"We can announce the name at the luncheon," I say, and both of them nod. "Do you think everyone will understand why I chose that name?"

Jeremiah frowns. "Of course they will! Everything about

Twelve Springs is a miracle from God. There's no way we should have clean air. There's no way you or Dad or Arya or Arianna should even be alive." He pauses, setting down his fileting knife. "I shouldn't be alive either." When his chin quivers, Erik moves to pat him on the shoulder.

I hadn't realized my son and my parents had faced hardship while I was away. The journey from Fire Baptized Ministries to Twelve Springs hadn't been a walk in the park for them. God had protected them. But they'd seen so much along the way, it left Jeremy with nightmares that I still struggle to understand today.

The reason they left in the first place is still a blur. There was an attack from wanderers, thugs I imagine who weren't much different from Jeremiah Sr. The fight was bad, the church was forced out. It wasn't until survivors showed up at the campgrounds that anyone had learned about the fire. I was just glad to find out none of the bodies we found inside belonged to members of the church.

"It's alright," Erik whispers as Jeremiah sniffles.

"I'm so sorry," I say softly, but Jeremy shakes his head and wipes his eyes with his flannel sleeve.

"No. Don't be sorry, Mom. I'm happy for everything I've seen in this world."

I blink at him.

"Pastor Anne-Marie taught me to see God in all things, even the valley of the shadow of death." He lifts his head a little higher. "Just because the world is ugly, doesn't mean God is absent."

We sit in silence for a while until Erik clears his throat. "My God, he sounds just like you," he says with a lighthearted smile.

I can't help but laugh, thinking of all the times I'd preached to Erik during our travels. "Well, we learned under the same pastor. What do you expect?"

He grins. "Nothing less."

"Can I pick Miracle's middle name?" Jeremiah asks suddenly.

I shoot a glance at Erik who just widens his eyes like he has no idea how to respond.

"What were you thinking?" I ask slowly.

Jeremiah smiles shyly. "Joy."

The three of us blink at each other, not really knowing what to say.

I speak first. "I—I honestly like it."

"I do too," Erik admits, then he says, "Miracle Joy," and grins so wide it's a wonder he hasn't decapitated himself. But I'm smiling too, and so is Jeremiah. We all look like happy fools.

Miracle Joy. It isn't a name fit for the barren fields at all, and that's exactly why I like it.

The End.

Thank you for reading this novel!

More books by Valicity Elaine & TRC Publishing!

Christian Fantasy
Cross Academy series
The End of the World series
The Scribe

Christian Science Fiction
I AM MAN series

Christian Romance
The Living Water
Withered Rose Trilogy
Fractured Diamond
The Woof Pack Trilogy
Singlehood

Christian Children's Fiction
Too Young

ACKNOWLEDGEMENTS

Jesus is the Christ, Son of the Living God.
I am thankful to God for giving me the idea for this novel. Thank You Lord for blessing me to complete Your assignment!

Thank you, the reader, who made it this far. You are awesome. I hope you take the time to read some of my other work. It's been quite a journey, hasn't it? Let's go on another.

Follow me on Amazon to get updates on new releases, pre-orders, and reduced prices on my books. Also, follow me on TikTok! I love meeting readers and discussing new ideas. See you there!

The Rebel Christian Publishing

We are an independent Christian publishing company focused on fantasy, science fiction, and romantic reads. Visit therebelchristian.com to check out our books or click the titles below!

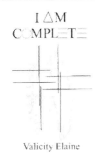

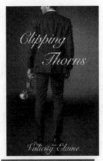

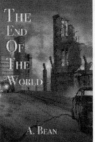

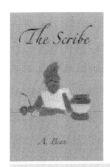

Made in the USA
Las Vegas, NV
19 December 2024

14844601R00196